BY UNKNOWN MEANS

Michael Callaway Thriller Series
Book 1

DOUG GIACOBBE

ISBN: 978-1-943789-66-5

Taylor and Seale Publishing, LLC
Daytona Beach, Fl.
taylorandseale.com
386-760-8987

Dedication

To Gayle and Katie, with love

Acknowledgments

There are many people who helped and advised in the creation of this book.

I want to thank my friend and mentor, *New York Times* Best Selling Author Joan Johnston, for all of the excellent guidance that she has provided me in writing this book. I also want to thank Professor Don Roman for his input on how things work <u>under</u> water, and my *brother*, Colonel Jerry Yanello, USMC (retired) for his help with the military terminology. Thanks to Uncle Pat Hegarty who helped me with information about what makes things go *boom*. And thanks to Officer Tim Callahan, Miramar Police Department for the great seasickness remedy.

My greatest thanks go to my wife Gayle and my daughter Katie for their amazing patience and the help they provided me in making this book happen.

Chapter 1

"Don't get any of that puke on my nice, clean boat, gentlemen."

Special Agent Michael Callaway of the United States Customs Service watched the angry sea while at the same time keeping a wary eye on the two Drug Enforcement agents who were temporarily assigned to his unit.

Callaway and his partner Jorge Hidalgo had been running the Customs Service contraband interdiction boat Blue Thunder III for two years and had racked up an enviable number of drug boat interceptions on the high seas off Florida and the Bahamas.

Their knowledge of the local and Bahamian waters, and their understanding of the criminals they sought, earned them one of the best capture records in the Customs Service. The Post-Office-Blue thirty-nine foot catamaran-hulled craft was built for only one purpose: to intercept boats carrying contraband narcotics to the continental United States. Tonight Jorge was at the controls, running Thunder at idle speed, trying to keep their guests from the DEA as dry as possible on what was literally a dark and stormy night. The two DEA guys were not sea farers by any means. They'd appeared to be very tough when they climbed aboard the boat from the pier behind the Customs office along the Miami River, but that had only lasted until they cleared the outer buoy of the Port of Miami and hit seven-foot swells. With the rough, storm-tossed seas, intermittent rain and lightning, the loud rumble and smoke from the two 540-cubic-inch Mercury engines, DEA agents David Howe and his supervisor Alberto Cruz were instantly and powerfully overcome with seasickness. Callaway was surprised that Howe was sick, since he was a former Navy SEAL. He was less than sympathetic when it came to Cruz, who he'd locked horns with in the past.

"Keep your eyes on the horizon," he yelled over the din of the engines.

The agents alternated between hanging over the side to vomit and staring at the lights of Miami Beach, some seven miles distant, which was the only horizon available. It didn't work. Both men cursed the Dramamine they'd taken to no avail.

"Why aren't those pills working, damn it!" Cruz shouted in despair from his vomit encrusted mouth. "How do you guys keep from getting sick?"

Callaway, who never missed an opportunity to be a smart-ass, answered his green-tinged compatriot in a sympathetic tone. "We use an old sea-sickness cure that my dad learned about in the Navy," he answered. "Right before we come out here, we drink a nice warm glass of pork chop grease. It settles the stomach right down."

Cruz looked at Callaway with wide open eyes for a split second before his head went over the side of the boat, and the rest of the *arroz con pollo* that he'd eaten for dinner flowed into the sea.

"You're the one who wanted to come out here," Callaway said, as the radio crackled.

"Night Eyes to Blue Thunder Three," came over the headsets Callaway, Hidalgo and the two DEA agents were wearing. The pilot of the U.S. Customs Blackhawk helicopter, call sign "Night Eyes," was three-thousand feet above them, attempting to find their quarry for the evening—an in-bound boat loaded with cocaine that the DEA had developed information on. DEA Agent in Charge Cruz was tight-lipped about the method his agency used to develop the information that had them out on such a rotten night. He would only disclose that the intelligence was the result of a long, painful, and costly investigation. After five long months of work, and an equal number of dead informants courtesy of the drug smugglers, the DEA was not going to just hand the information over to Customs and let them make the bust. They demanded to be in on the bust, too. All four agents were interested in the boat the smugglers were using this cool January night. Instead of some stripped-down racing boat, or a ratty old freight ship, the smugglers opted to go first class. The bad guys decided to use a Cary 50, which was a sort of go-fast yacht, to bring in the dope. The Cary was fifty feet in length, with a beam fourteen and a half feet wide. Powered by two 425-horsepower, 7.4-liter-Mercruiser engines, the 28,000 pound boat could reach speeds of seventy knots while kicking up a three story rooster-tail wake behind it. It would be a great catch. The trick was to find this prize, and get it stopped *in one piece* before it reached its off-loading point, which, according to Cruz's intel, was somewhere up the Miami River.

The helicopter pilot was using every electronic toy he had aboard his craft to find their elusive target. The pilot and crew had already been back and forth to their base twice for fuel this rainy night, while the three Blue Thunder boat crews assigned to this district had been out searching the entire area. The rough weather, wind, rain, and choppy seas, along with the lightning, all played hell with the fancy instruments on the helicopter.

Callaway yelled into his voice-activated microphone, "Thunder 3 to Night Eyes, will you please find that bogey so we can get this thing out of idle!"

The pilot responded that he was trying.

Callaway radioed back, "I'm getting really bored down here. If we don't find something to chase pretty soon, I'm gonna break out the fishing rods and do some trolling!"

A different voice shot back over his headset, "The hell you are!"

Callaway recognized the sickening voice of Special Agent in Charge Richard "Dick" Todd of the Miami Customs Enforcement office, former Army Major—assigned to public relations through most of his military career—suck-up to the local media, and general all-around pain.

Todd's idea of a good bust was anything that would make him look like a hero on the eleven o'clock news. His demeanor toward his agents was always arrogant and condescending. The combination of his attitude, his first name, and his former Army rank caused Callaway to dub him "Major Dick."

Todd had alerted the media that something big was going to happen, and, of course, the news people responded by throwing camera crews on every helicopter and boat they could put into the air and sea. Callaway knew that Todd was sensible enough not to give them specifics of the intended bust, but figured Todd had visions of standing on the deck of the fifty foot Cary, beaming at the cameras, while his agents dutifully unloaded thousands of pounds of cocaine from the cabin.

"I don't want any shooting out here tonight," Todd boomed over the radio. "I want to make that especially clear to you, Agent Callaway."

Special Agent Howe, who was new to the area, looked at Callaway after hearing this exchange. "Damn, Callaway. Your boss sounds like a real tight-ass!" he said with a heavy Tennessee drawl.

Glumly, Callaway shook his head and responded, "He's so up-tight that if you shoved a piece of coal up his ass it would turn into a diamond."

Todd was still whining over the radio when the Night Eyes pilot broke in with, "I think I've got him! I've got visual on a fast-mover heading northwest about two miles from Thunder Three."

Hidalgo immediately hung a hard right turn to intercept the smuggler, while Callaway readied the remote-controlled searchlight on the bow. The DEA guys even perked up considerably knowing they would be going into action soon.

"Thunder Three, the bogey is closing on you *very* fast," the pilot advised.

His radar and visual contact was only intermittent from all of the lightning in the area. *Thunder* was cruising blind as her radar was broken. The four federal agents strained their eyes in an effort to find their quarry in the rain and darkness.

Agent Cruz looked off the starboard side of the boat and suddenly screamed something unintelligible in Spanish.

Hidalgo reacted instinctively to the alarm in the agent's voice and put the boat into a hard left turn. As the Customs boat heeled over on its left side, the Cary blasted by the stern, missing it by less than ten feet. As the Cary passed, Callaway saw three men glaring down at him from the cockpit of the taller boat. One of them was inserting a magazine into what appeared to be a sub-machine gun. Hidalgo continued to hold *Thunder* in a hard left turn and then deftly straightened her out behind the fleeing drug boat.

6

Callaway shouted a warning about the gun and switched on the blue light mounted on the forward deck in front of the cockpit. Jorge threw the throttles wide open and the Customs boat began to gain on the Cary. On smooth water, the catamaran would have a difficult time keeping pace with the V-hulled boat, but the rough seas they were running through tended to even things out a bit. Since they were under *strict* orders from Agent-in-Charge Todd not to shoot at the drug boat, all they could do was try to close the distance on the fleeing smugglers and, for the time being, hope that the crew would stop and give up, or that the boat would run out of fuel.

As *Thunder III* closed within one-hundred yards of the Cary, Callaway detected the muzzle flash of the sub-machine gun being fired from the bridge of the boat. The gunman was using *Thunder's* flashing blue light as an aiming point for his weapon. They were beyond the effective range as far as the accuracy of the nine millimeter bullets aimed their way, but Callaway knew that an *unlucky* round could find a target in any of them. He tried his best to keep the beam of the searchlight directly in the shooter's eyes to blind him. Hidalgo swerved to avoid the gunfire as Callaway advised of the situation on the radio.

"Thunder Three, we're gonna back off some, the bad guys are shooting at us."

Todd shouted back, "Stay close, dammit, I don't want him dumping his load into the ocean!"

Callaway could picture how pissed off Major Dick would be if he didn't have a mountain of cocaine to pose next to. *Thunder* continued to zigzag behind the fleeing boat, when suddenly the agents heard the tapping noise of bullets splintered through the fiberglass. The bow and front deck of the Customs boat was suddenly a mass of bullet holes, surrounded by spider-web-like cracks.

Agent Cruz screamed, and clutching his side, fell to the deck. One of the rounds fired from the Cary had passed through the cockpit of the Customs boat and struck him in the side, grazing along a rib. His raid jacket was instantly soaked with blood from the gash left by the bullet.

Callaway and Howe grabbed a first aid kit and tended to the wounded agent, holding gauze bandages on the wound to slow the bleeding. Hidalgo began yelling over the radio.

"Thunder Three, we have an agent shot! I'm gonna break off the chase."

"If he's not hurt too bad, you will continue your pursuit," Todd replied tentatively. He sounded almost as if he were pleading with the agents to stay in the chase.

Cruz, upon hearing this on his headset, looked up at Hidalgo and gave him the thumbs up signal to continue, as his partner held pressure on the wound. The bullet didn't appear to have hit anything vital. His hot, Cuban temper was now evident by the fact he wanted a piece of the person who shot him. "Get that *pendejo!*" he yelled, staring at Callaway.

Callaway smiled at the wounded agent as he pulled an M-14 rifle from a scabbard mounted inside the cabin door. *We will continue, but by my rules*, he thought.

Hidalgo swung the boat in closer to the Cary. Callaway aimed the old battle rifle at the cockpit with the sole intent of disabling the gunman who had shot Cruz. It was difficult to line up the sights with both boats lurching about in rough seas, and his first shot missed. Callaway concentrated on the muzzle flash of the smuggler's gun and fired again, this time hitting the gunman in the abdomen. He went down, but the throttle man on the Cary picked up the machine gun and began firing again.

By now, inside the helicopter, Todd had seen the muzzle flashes coming from *Blue Thunder*. He screamed at Callaway over the radio to cease fire. Callaway ripped off his headset and threw it on the deck. He lined up the sights and fired just as the bows of the catamaran crashed down on an errant wave. The round went low, striking the transom of the Cary, ripping through it as if it were made of paper.

The heavy 7.62 X 51 bullet, made for the military to pierce light armor, shed its copper jacket and lead sheath in the thickness of the transom, but the steel core of the round continued into the engine compartment. There it tore through the soft brass float bowl of one of the four massive, Holly Dominator carburetors feeding super high octane gas to the engines. It also ripped apart a braided steel fuel line behind it. The round continued on, smashing through a high-voltage coil mounted on the forward bulkhead and punching a neat .30 caliber hole through the back

9

of one of the boat's two five-hundred-gallon fuel tanks. The fuel from that tank, as well as fuel being sprayed about the compartment by the wounded carburetor and fuel line, was ignited by sparks from the damaged coil.

The Cary started to slow down.

"I guess they decided to quit," Jorge shouted.

His words were lost as the night was lit up by a tremendous flash in front of the Customs boat. The rear half of the Cary disintegrated in a huge ball of flame. The front half of the boat, pushed forward at incredible speed by the blast, nose dived beneath the waves, never to be seen again. Parts of the rear section of the doomed craft flew high into the air, causing the Night Eyes helicopter, that had swooped down low during the chase, to take evasive action to dodge flaming debris. That same debris fell all around *Blue Thunder III*.

"Hard right!" Callaway yelled.

Hidalgo put the Customs boat in a turn to avoid one of the Cary's engines. The blazing hunk of cast iron came screaming out of the sky like a flaming meteor. The engine was still loudly running on the fuel that remained in its carburetors as it splashed into the Atlantic close to the Customs boat with a loud hiss.

Then there was nothing—nothing but flaming wreckage. No cocaine, no prized boat to confiscate, no prisoners, and no glory for Special Agent in Charge Richard Todd.

Hidalgo stared at Callaway, a mortified expression on his face. Callaway put his headset back on in time to hear the helicopter pilot advise that the Coast Guard was sending a rescue chopper for Agent Cruz, who was curled up in pain on the cockpit floor. *Thunder III* was ordered to search the area for survivors and any contraband and then return to the Customs base in Miami. There the agents would face the wrath of Major Dick.

Chapter 2

The sun was just peeking over the eastern horizon when *Thunder III* cruised the channel into the Miami Harbor after a very rough night. The Coast Guard had dispatched a helicopter to the area of the incident at sea to airlift Cruz and Howe to the Trauma Unit at Jackson Memorial Hospital. Cruz would be in good hands there. Callaway stared at the dried blood on the cockpit floor of the Customs boat. No one had ever been injured aboard his boat before, and he agonized over what went wrong in the darkness of that morning in January of 1991.

Friggin' Todd, was all that he kept thinking.

Major Dick had put many of his agents in harm's way in the past and for all the wrong reasons. His quest for glory caused him to make decisions that put agents in needless danger. Callaway had been keeping a log of Todd's on-the-job stupidity since the man became the Agent in Charge of the Miami office of the U.S. Customs Service. The file had grown thick over time.

"Friggin' Todd!" he said aloud this time.

Jorge looked at him and shook his head, "You know we're gonna get fired over this," he said, fixing his gaze on the channel markers ahead.

Still staring at the bloody deck, Callaway answered, "Okay, I went over the big line when I shot at the drug boat, but we wouldn't have been in a situation where a man got hurt if that dickhead hadn't put us there following so close. I'll be fired, for sure, but you might skate with some time off without pay." Callaway stared at the pastel colors of the South Beach hotels as the sun rose higher in the sky. "Maybe I can go back to my job with the Parks Service," he continued, referring to his first federal law enforcement job. At forty-two years old, he didn't want to start looking for a job in some new field. His brown hair had begun to grey a bit from the stress of chasing smugglers, but he had kept his six-foot tall frame in good shape over the years. He had enjoyed his past employment with the Parks Service, where he began his career catching drug smugglers in the Everglades. On the other hand, he didn't know if he could go back to explaining the different types of Everglades flora and fauna, and the difference between an alligator and a salt-water crocodile, to some tourist after so many high-speed chases at sea.

Laughing, Hidalgo answered, "This is what you were made to do, Callaway. Once you chase someone out here on the ocean, you won't be happy doing anything else."

Callaway and his partner had first met when they chased down a smuggler boat in Everglades National Park. Jorge was a deputy with the Monroe County Sheriff's Office at the time. The chase made headlines when a gun battle erupted between the smuggler and the two law enforcement officers.

The smuggler lost.

His death brought home a very big point to Callaway and Hidalgo as the bad guy was found to be a local police officer who had been quadrupling his salary by occasionally hauling in small loads of drugs. When informed of the identity of this "fallen angel," Callaway's only comment had been, "No great loss."

"I'm not going down without a fight," Callaway said. "I mean, Todd has screwed up so many times, and he always manages to talk his way out of trouble. Maybe I can do the same thing."

Todd was the ultimate bull artist when it came to the press. Callaway always said that he could put a good spin on a 747 full of church missionaries crashing into Lake Okeechobee.

Both men stopped talking when a grey ship approached them from the harbor.

"What kind of ship is that?" Jorge asked as he slowed *Thunder III* to the mandatory-channel-idle speed.

"By the paint, it is obviously one from our fine Navy, but it's a weird looking son-of-a-bitch," Callaway said, pulling out the binoculars for a closer look. The ship was about one-hundred twenty feet long, with massive retractable ski-foils attached to her bow and sides. As they got closer, the agents could see a forward gun turret housing a three-inch cannon. Staring through the glasses, Callaway could make out the stern-mounted launchers that carried eight Harpoon anti-ship missiles. *This baby has some formidable armament for such a little ship*, he thought. "It's gotta be one

14

of those hydrofoils that we heard they've been running out of Key West. The Navy sent them down there to do long-range drug interdiction because they couldn't figure out what else to do with them," Callaway said, watching the Navy vessel approach. The ship passed close to *Thunder's* port side and Callaway read the name embossed on the side of the bridge, "Pegasus," he murmured. "The winged horse." He was rather proud of himself for having stayed awake through some of his mythology class back in college.

"She's got wings all right," Hidalgo said, "and I bet she can really fly."

Callaway looked through the open side windows of the bridge as it passed close abeam. It was evident that the man staring back at him from the taller ship was her captain since he wore a black ball cap bearing two gold bars over his bright red hair. When the two men made eye contact, Callaway instinctively threw the captain a salute, a habit he'd developed from his father's full-time career in the U.S. Navy. The red-headed Navy skipper, recognizing that the craft next to his was a United States Customs Service patrol boat, stood and returned the salute. His grin faded when he saw the bullet holes marking the front deck and cockpit, and the dried blood on the floor of the blue boat.

Callaway and Hidalgo continued up the ship channel and into Miami harbor. The place was crawling with cruise ships and freighters. "I wonder how many of these cargo ships came in to Miami with a little more than what was on their

15

official manifest," Callaway said. Callaway just couldn't understand how successful the smugglers had been. Lately it seemed that a lot of dope was coming in aboard some of the smaller freight ships arriving from the Caribbean islands. As much as they were tracked by the Customs Service, DEA, Coast Guard, and even the U.S. Navy, it was a mystery as to how the drugs, mainly high-quality cocaine, were getting aboard the ships.

Callaway's shore-based brother and sister agents were even more perplexed over the fact that some of the ships were found with the contraband *after* thorough searches by the Coast Guard at sea. It seemed that somewhere between Andros Island and Miami, the cocaine would magically appear onboard the freighters.

After tying up the boat at the U.S. Customs Office Service dock, the two men continued watching freighters and pleasure boats cruising slowly by.

"You know that any one of these in-bound boats could be carrying stuff right past us," Callaway said. "I mean we bust our asses out there every night, and all we do is put a scratch in the dope supply that keeps coming in."

Hidalgo was less philosophical about their current dilemma. "Yeah, and now old Todd will have enough rope to hang us by our balls," he said. "What you did out there was righteous, Callaway. So the fuckers got blown up. Who gives a shit? If they want to haul that crap in here and poison kids, then they deserve to have the crabs eating their livers!"

16

Callaway laughed at his partner's comments. Jorge was never one to hold back when he was pissed off.

"All right, so we tell him just what happened out there. Maybe he'll get it. Maybe we can get Cruz to back us up," Jorge said.

"And maybe I'll hit the damned lottery and I won't have to worry about it," Callaway replied. Their laughter over that comment was cut short by a radio message from Special Agent in Charge Todd, who seemed surprisingly happy.

"Gentlemen, I will be spending my day dealing with the press regarding the mess you caused last night. Not exactly the way I wanted to spend my Sunday, but it must be done. I will see you both in my office at noon Monday. Mr. Hidalgo, I wouldn't buy anything expensive today. You're going to need the money. Mr. Callaway, well, your life is about to change in a drastic and negative way."

Chapter 3

Commander David Eldridge was finding it exceptionally difficult to smile on this trip out of Miami harbor. The sight of the blue U.S. Customs boat, all shot up in the line of duty, didn't help his mood one bit. The captain of the Navy hydrofoil U.S.S. Pegasus was taking his little boat out on her last cruise. When this tour ended, the tough little craft's next destination would be the "mothball fleet" to be kept in storage for a few years. After that, it would be a final trip to the Bremerton Navy Yard near Seattle, to suffer an unceremonious death by cutting torch. Her four sister ships, all based in Key West, were destined for the same fate.

On her final mission, she had not been looking for enemy ships to attack. Those days were gone since the Soviet Navy pretty much evaporated with the demise of its government and the cold war. Instead of tailing fleets of enemy warships and slamming them with her deadly *Harpoon* ship-to-ship missiles, the task for which she was originally designed, *Pegasus* had been cruising around the Bahamas looking for drug smugglers. Eldridge's thoughts kept getting hung up on the *looking* part. Because of the Posse Commutates Act, the Navy ship could not stop vessels suspected of smuggling drugs unless a member of the U.S. Coast Guard, or some other U.S. federal law enforcement agency, was on board. She could only use her sophisticated SPS-63 Surface Radar System to detect ships that might be smuggling. By law, then, she could only fire her guns if she was fired upon, or in defense of another vessel under attack. The little hydrofoil had made headlines for the few captures she'd made, but they were pretty uneventful busts. No druggie was about to fight it out with a U.S. Navy vessel equipped with a three-inch cannon on her front deck, but most of the smugglers were too stupid to even recognize the missile tubes on the stern.

Eldridge was an action junkie and cruising around the Bahamas just looking didn't satisfy his craving. Having come out of Annapolis in the mid-seventies, he'd trained to be a "tin-can" skipper; the Navy's vernacular for the captain of a destroyer. He remembered working his way up the chain of command until he'd accomplished his goal. He felt pretty mighty, cruising around the Atlantic dogging Soviet submarines and showing the American flag to the numerous surface ships of the Soviet Navy. His plum assignment came to a screeching halt due to two slight character flaws — his habit of drinking too much while on shore and letting that little vice unleash his hair-trigger temper. While in port in the Bahamas three years prior, he had gotten into a bit of a brawl with a gentleman from the Cuban government. The report the Navy received from the Bahamian police was not complementary at all, stating that the captain had punched the communist representative from Castro's island in the stomach so hard the man's rear-end broke through a sheetrock wall, leaving his unconscious body hanging by his ass. The fact that the drunken Cuban had just verbally pissed on the United States for the benefit of the Navy men in the room and then tried to get in Eldridge's face when his pronouncements were challenged by the captain, did not calm the State Department's reaction one bit.

With some bitterness, Eldridge remembered being removed from his dream job of destroyer skipper, busted down a rank from captain to lieutenant commander, and placed on desk duty in Washington D.C. He went from king of his world to coffee-boy for some admiral. He tried to fight the "sentence" that he received, stating that the Cuban was obviously insane for picking a fight with him, since Eldridge stood six-foot-three with huge arms and the Cuban was a good eight inches shorter. He played the game, being a good boy and biting his tongue on many occasions in an effort to get command again. It took him three and a half years to do it, but he finally was given *Pegasus*. By that time, however, the Cold War was over. His stroll down memory lane was interrupted on the bridge by his executive officer, Lieutenant

Brian Parks. The hydrofoil was just clearing the harbor when Parks began bothering his C.O. about the shot-up Customs boat they'd just passed.

"Looks like they got beat up pretty bad last night, huh, skipper?" Parks asked.

Eldridge did not like his X.O. at all. Parks was from what Eldridge termed the "new Navy," and, on top of that, he was a bit of a pacifist. This was not an endearing quality to his boss, who was itching to get back into action. "At least they got to do something other than just cruise around the Caribbean looking at seagulls," Eldridge answered. "It's just a crying shame that a warship like this one has never seen any action," the skipper mumbled, still looking out the window back toward the Customs boat.

"Oh hell, skipper," Parker argued lamely, "nobody's going to pick a fight with us out here. Those drug runners would have to be flat-out crazy to pick a fight with a U.S. Navy ship." Parks casually leaned against the fire control console, as if trying to look confident in front of his boss. "We can't go shooting up drug boats out here, unless, of course, they fire on us first," he continued. "I mean, it's not like we're at war, or anything, right?"

Eldridge's efforts to tune out his executive officer were not working. The more the man spoke, the madder Eldridge became. His face was burning a hotter red than his close-cut hair when he'd finally had enough. "Mr. Parks!" he interrupted. "Set a course for Nassau and get *Pegasus* in the air!"

Parks finally shut up and passed the order to the helmsman. The engine room crew shut down the plodding diesel engines while simultaneously firing up the General Electric jet turbine. The crew then lowered the retractable hydrofoil skis as the ship picked up speed. *Pegasus* quickly rose ten feet above the waves and accelerated away from her wounded Customs Service sister.

Perhaps, my friends, Commander Eldridge thought, giving one last glance back at Callaway and Hidalgo, *we will see some action on this trip, too.*

Chapter 4

Callaway and Hidalgo went to the empty U.S. Customs Service office to fill out after-action reports regarding the incident with the Cary. Hidalgo slid his report into the in-box on the outer wall of Todd's office. He noticed that Callaway was making an extra copy of his report before placing the original in Todd's box. "Why do you make copies of everything, man? You writing a book?" Jorge asked.

Callaway smiled at his partner. "I've been keeping copies of everything we do, just in case I have to prove to anyone what an asshole old Todd is," he answered. He stood looking at the paper and chuckled. "I guess I may have to do that sooner than I'd thought I would. Like maybe tomorrow. It probably won't save my job, since I kinda disregarded a direct order not to fire on that boat, but maybe I can use it as a bargaining chip. I wish I was rich, cause then I could just quit, *and* fuck Todd over at the same time."

Hidalgo moved his closed right fist up and down in the air. "You're jerking off into the wind if you think that will happen, bro," he said.

Callaway and Hidalgo finished their work and walked outside to the parking lot. The sun was up, but dark patches of rain clouds obscured most of the view.

"Dude, why don't you let me drive you home?" Hidalgo asked, as he pointed toward his shiny red Mustang rag-top. He said this because he knew what a piece of junk his partner's car was.

Hidalgo knew that Michael Callaway's previous ride was a gorgeous 1990 Camaro Z-28, a car he had lusted after since puberty. Upon joining the Customs Service and enjoying the benefit of extra money, known as "premium overtime," he was finally able to buy his dream car. He was also able to furnish a very nice apartment with decent furniture and live a good life. Then he met Anna. She was from Brazil. She was a bartender in one of the numerous tiki bars that littered the Florida Keys after the Jimmy Buffet song "Margaritaville" became a big hit. Between her sweet smile and her store-bought breasts, she was way more than Callaway could handle. They dated for about two months, usually hanging out with Jorge and his "babe of the month," and then took off for Vegas to get married.

It amazed Hidalgo how a woman could change so quickly. She burned through Callaway's bank account like William Tecumseh Sherman burned through Atlanta during the Civil War. Callaway had to work more overtime just to keep up with the charge cards, and since he was away so often, she began developing other interests, but found out the hard way that cops are a very tight group. Callaway began hearing rumors of Anna running around in the company of other men. He left work early one night, and caught her in the rack with another guy. Though he threw the guy out of his house without his clothes, he had the presence of mind not to shoot him. The divorce wasn't pretty. Because of Florida's wonderful laws, she took him for most of everything he had. Callaway wanted desperately to be rid her. His attorney, the best one he could afford, talked his client into giving her a lump settlement, instead of monthly alimony, but the deal cleaned him out since he still had to take care of the credit card debt. Gone was his beautiful Camaro, along with the nice apartment and furniture.

Hidalgo helped Callaway move into a one-bedroom apartment in downtown Miami, with furniture his Mom had given him right before she died. Callaway ended up buying a 1978 Chevrolet Monte Carlo from a guy who cleaned the Customs Office at night. The car had rust holes in the roof and floorboards that let water and bugs in at their leisure. The car had a range limit of only about ten minutes because of all the crud that had accumulated in the gas tank. It would run for that much time, until the fuel line clogged up, and then just quit. It would usually take about an hour before the sediment in the fuel line would run back into the tank, so it could start again. When it stopped, Callaway would just coast it to the nearest curb, and leave it with his business card on the dash so the Miami police wouldn't tow the car. Whenever this occurred, he always thought, *Sometimes it's good to be a cop.* Today wasn't one of those days. Jorge offered again to drive

25

Callaway home, but he decided to take his chances in the Monte.

"It's Sunday morning Jorge, how much traffic could there be?" Callaway asked his partner. He shook his partner's hand, knowing that they would probably never work together again. Callaway climbed into his car and sat in a puddle of water. More water began dripping down the back of his neck from the sodden headliner.

"Great," he muttered. "I didn't want my ass to be the only thing that got wet this morning." He fired up the wheezing engine and took off for home, leaving a cloud of smoke behind him. About two blocks from his apartment he came upon a car crash. Two Miami P.D. traffic officers were trying to untangle a four-car pile-up that totally blocked the road. Miami Fire-Rescue tended to crash victims, while the cops administered a roadside sobriety test to the gentleman who probably caused the wreck. Unfortunately, this slowed traffic just enough to exceed his car's limited range, and the motor choked to a stop, smoke billowing from the tailpipe. Callaway cursed the car and his ex-wife, in that order and put the transmission in neutral, coasted to the curb, jumped out, and ran the last two blocks to his apartment. As he reached the front porch, he slipped on the slick tile. Callaway landed flat on his back in a puddle that also contained his Sunday *Miami Herald*. He lay there, staring at the ceiling of his front porch wondering what horrible thing would happen next. Grabbing his soggy paper, he painfully stood up, unlocked the door, and went in. He immediately stripped to

26

his shorts and dropped his wet clothes next to the big, comfortable recliner that used to belong to his old man. He made himself comfortable and turned on the television.

The local Christian television service, which was about the only early Sunday off-air morning fare, was just ending. The TV announcer advised that a re-broadcast of the local news, recorded at eleven o'clock the previous evening, would be coming up next, preceded by the previous night's Florida Lottery drawing. In a sleepy daze, Callaway reached down to his crumpled pants on the floor and pulled his waterproof wallet from the back pocket. He opened one of the zip-lock flaps inside and took out the lottery ticket he'd purchased three days prior. Callaway made it a point to play the Florida Lotto whenever he could afford a couple of bucks for a ticket. The news started with the normal introductions, then cut to a repeat of the lottery drawing. The announcer stated that this week's prize was $83 million. This healthy sum had been reached because no one had hit the jackpot for the past three weeks. The money rolled over, and aided by a ticket buying frenzy, grew to this huge amount. Callaway glanced at the three sets of numbers that he'd purchased, committed them to his photographic memory, and then leaned his head against the headrest of the comfortable old recliner to doze. In his semiconscious state, he still heard the winning numbers called off as the little ping-pong balls blew up into the Lotto machine's chute. He was just about asleep when he froze, stiff as a board.

Did he hear those numbers right? Did the announcer say the exact numbers that matched the bottom set on the card that he still clutched in his hand? He snapped the card up and tried to read the numbers in the dim light: 11-19-22-23-40 and 49.

Those were the numbers right? he thought, suddenly awake. Or was he just dreaming his way out of the predicament he had gotten himself into the evening before? He heard the news anchor come on and advise that there was only one winner of the huge jackpot, and that the ticket was purchased in downtown Miami. Thinking it over, Callaway decided that he must have been dreaming. He lay back and began to fall asleep. Suddenly his eyes snapped open. He grabbed his department cell phone and called information.

Who cares if there's a charge, I'm getting fired tomorrow, he thought.

"Give me the number for *Channel Six News*, please," he asked the operator. Callaway dialed the number and a man answered. He stammered, half embarrassed by what he was asking. "Can you tell me the winning lotto numbers that you just announced?" he asked.

The man told him the numbers, and, sure as hell, they matched the last set that Callaway had purchased. Callaway sat there silent, while the man on the phone laughed. "Well, did you win, buddy?" he joked, condescendingly.

Callaway whispered, "Yeah," as he hung up the phone. He could still hear the man's frantic voice on the other end shouting, "Wait! What's your name, I want to do a story on you!"

Chapter 5

Try as he might, Michael Callaway couldn't sleep very well on that rainy Sunday morning. His thoughts ran between how he would spend the money from his Lotto win, to, *I probably got the numbers wrong and I didn't win a thing.* Still, there it was, confirmed on page two of his Sunday *Miami Herald.* The numbers matched the last set on his card. He decided to do things as methodically as he could, given how nervous he was. He would have to work out every detail perfectly to carry out the plan he was concocting. He called a cousin in New York, who was a pretty good tax accountant, and told her the news. She choked on her pancakes when she realized he wasn't joking. She gave Callaway all kinds of good advice on how to accept the money while paying the least amount of taxes. He realized he would still be paying a sizable chunk of cash to Uncle Sam, a chunk that would ultimately have six zeros behind it.

"Maybe they'll use it to buy the Customs Service some decent boats," he told her.

Callaway went to an ATM and withdrew all $500 of his checking account. He thought for a second about the penalty he would receive for cleaning out his account. "To hell with Sun Trust's stupid penalty...I'm frickin rich," he said, smiling. He called a friend who chartered airplanes and booked a small twin-engine prop airplane to take him to Tallahassee that night. He wrote the man a check from his now empty account for the flight. It would take a while to cover the five-hundred twenty miles between Miami and the state capital.

Before he left, he stopped back at the Miami Customs Service Office and faxed all thirty pages of dirt that he had accumulated on Special Agent in Charge Todd to the Commissioner of the Customs Service, in Washington D.C. He marked the opening page "Confidential / Eyes Only," and sent it directly to the fax machine in the Commissioner's office. He knew that the big boss wouldn't see the document until the next day. If his timing was right, it could make for a pretty exciting meeting with Todd. He congratulated himself once more for saving all those reports and debriefings for a rainy day. The incident with the Cary on the high seas, and the fact that he was about to be unemployed and very wealthy on the very same day, sent a veritable hurricane swirling through his mind. When he arrived in Tallahassee late on Sunday night, he reserved a direct, and very expensive, flight back home to Miami on a Delta jet. If the plane took off on schedule, at 9:00 a.m., he might just make it on time. He knew he would be cutting it close, but he wanted to be in Todd's office at noon to witness his occupational execution. He booked a room at the local Motel 6 on Tennessee Street, near the capitol building. He asked the front desk attendant for a morning wake-up call at 5:30, and quickly fell asleep out of sheer exhaustion. On that next January morning, Michael

Michael dressed in his one decent suit and stepped out of his hotel room to find that it was only thirty-seven degrees; apparently, a cold front had rolled through in the early morning hours.

"I can't believe that this is still part of Florida," he mumbled as he walked to a nearby bus stop, shivering. He rode a city bus to the address he had found for the building where lottery headquarters was located, arriving at 7:00 am. He had to stand outside in the cold waiting for the office to open. The Lotto office finally opened at 8:00 a.m. Callaway's lips were practically blue from the cold as he nervously walked into the lobby. A terrible thought kept swirling through his mind that no matter how many times he verified the number, something would go wrong. Something would happen to prevent him from becoming a millionaire eighty-three times over. He figured that the news people were wrong when they announced that there was only one winner, since they had gotten so many things wrong about his exploits with the Customs Service in the past. He figured, at the very least, others had picked the winning numbers and he would have to split the prize with dozens of people. *No big deal,* he told himself. *Even if they split it twenty ways, it still equals rich.*

The FSU coed who appeared to be half asleep at her reception job saw Callaway wandering around in the lobby, and asked, "You need some help, mister?"

He was sweating something fierce now, the cold that had previously gripped him gone. "I think I won the jackpot, yesterday," he answered, almost in a whisper, like he had something to hide as he held the ticket out to her.

She looked at the numbers on the ticket and compared them to the numbers on a printed sheet on her desk. The dumbfounded young woman looked at him wide-eyed now, "Holy ..., you're the one!" she stammered, as if in awe. She grabbed the telephone and dialed four numbers. "He's here!" she screamed. "Yes, the winner of the eighty-three mil, he's in the lobby! No, I'm not conning you, come out and see for yourself!"

Callaway took a step back, startled by her reaction. He thought about what she said. *He's here*. He, as in singular, he, as in only one! Callaway's stomach churned from what he just heard, and from not eating since the previous evening.

Two men dressed in suits ran into the lobby and introduced themselves as they shook his hand. They examined the lotto ticket that Callaway gripped in his hand and smiled. "Sir," one of them said. "You have the only winning ticket from Saturday night's lottery drawing. I sincerely wish that I could trade places with you because you have just won eighty- three million dollars!"

Callaway tried to breathe, but he just couldn't seem to fill his lungs. He felt like he had just been slugged in the gut by a very big fist. He finally stumbled backward, almost passing out, while maintaining a death-grip on the Lotto ticket. *This is where I wake up from this dream, still driving a junk car and still in deep shit with my boss*, he thought. He slowly sat down on the floor. One of the Lotto employees brought him a cup of water.

"Are you okay, Mr...?" he asked.

"Callaway, Mike Callaway," he answered in a raspy voice.

"Mr. Callaway, please step into this room so we can discuss your winnings," one of the suits advised him.

Callaway looked at all of the Lotto people milling around him. *It must suck to be a $20,000 a year state employee and have to hand out huge wads of cash almost every week,* he thought as he walked into a small auditorium. A door on the other side opened and an older man walked into the auditorium accompanied by a man with a camera.

"Mr. Callaway, my name is Russell Mix," the older man said. I'm the guy who runs this operation."

Callaway took the man's outstretched hand and shook it, grinning like he was drunk.

"We're going to take some pictures of us giving you this big cardboard check for the total of eighty-three million dollars. Of course we'll really be depositing the first of twenty yearly payments of $4.1 million into the account of your choice." Mix said the amount with his smooth Tallahassee drawl, like it was absolutely no big deal. Callaway was stunned when he heard the amount.

"Four point what?" he gulped. "Jesus, that's a lot of money."

The cameraman focused and took several pictures of Callaway and Mix shaking hands.

34

Callaway thought that he must look as though he'd just walked through a thunderstorm since he was soaked with perspiration. He advised a clerk of his account number, so the wire transfer of the money could take place.

"I guess I'll see you if I ever win the Lotto again, Mr. Mix," Callaway said with a silly grin.

"Mr. Callaway," the man with the camera said. "I'm John Porter with the *Tallahassee Tribune*. So, what are you going to do with all of that cash?"

"Go home," Callaway answered sheepishly. The stress of the last twenty-four hours was taking its toll on his mind and body. Callaway glanced at his watch and realized he had only twenty-five minutes to make his flight back to Miami. If his plan for dealing with Todd was going to work, he would have to hustle.

As he walked past the reception desk, the FSU student who'd greeted him stretched out her hand to congratulate him. As he shook her hand, he felt a small piece of paper between their palms. He read what she had written as he walked out of the building: "Marry me."

Chapter 6

Out on the street, Callaway was lucky to find a taxi, given the fact that the legislature was in session. He advised the diver to get him to the airport quick. The driver, used to dealing with state representatives trying to beat it out of the capital when a legislative session ended, knew just which back roads to take. He deposited Callaway in front of the Delta terminal just fifteen minutes before the plane was scheduled to depart.

Callaway plopped into his assigned seat as the flight attendant closed the door, and the plane powered up to taxi. His intent was to grab some sleep on the one-hour trip to Miami, but the fine looking young lady in the seat next to him was enough to keep him very awake. She was thin but well built, with long chestnut-color hair down to her waist. Callaway felt weird making conversation with the young woman. He knew he must look rumpled from all of the running around he'd been doing, but she gave him an inviting smile.

"Hi, I'm Mike," he blurted out. *Smooth opening line, dumbass!* he thought. He fidgeted in his seat.

She laughed and said, "Brenda," with an outstretched hand.

They talked and laughed as they flew south. Callaway thought about how this was his first good conversation with a female since "dear" Anna had raked him over the coals in divorce court. He stopped short of buying Brenda a drink because he only had $17.83 left from the cash he'd withdrawn. The previous sum total of his savings. *Previous,* he thought, as he felt the folded receipt for the $4.1 million in his pocket.

"So what do you do, Mike?" she asked.

Callaway had to think before he answered. In about an hour and a half he'd be unemployed. Again he felt the receipt in his pocket and smiled. "Um, I'm kinda between occupations right now," he answered as he contemplated whether the new profession he wanted to take up, that of *sea-going bum*, could actually be classified as work. Callaway asked Brenda for her telephone number before they landed in Miami. He was intrigued by the girl after she told him she was an instructor at a community college. He became more intrigued when she told him that her favorite part of the job was seducing her students! He made a note next to her number to call her quick since she seemed pretty interested, and figuring she would end up in jail pretty soon.

After taking a cab ride to his apartment, he picked up two items, hopped into the Monte Carlo, and nursed the ratty car to the Miami Customs office. Special Agent Michael Callaway walked into Major Dick's outer office carrying a notebook under one arm and a single piece of paper in his opposite hand. Jorge Hidalgo was seated against the wall in the outer office looking positively glum, then positively baffled at Callaway's wide smile.

"Relax *amigo*, things are gonna be fine," Callaway said with a wink.

The buzzer on Todd's secretary Donna Kendal's phone sounded, and she picked up the receiver.

"Yes, sir, they're both here," she responded. She looked at both men with sadness in her eyes. "He'll see you both. Good luck," she said.

Callaway held the door to allow Jorge in first, but then walked past him and stood in front of his tormentor's desk. Todd sat in his big leather chair with a smug grin on his face. As he began to speak, Callaway slapped the piece of paper and the notebook on the desk, hard. "Before you say a fucking word, I want you to see what I brought you," he said sternly. "First of all, this is my official resignation from the United States Customs Service. Effective immediately." He gestured toward the single page. He then pointed to the notebook on the desk, and began thumbing through the numerous pages. He made sure the book was turned so Todd could see the pictures and writing inside. "This documents every stupid-assed thing you have done since becoming the agent-in-charge down here in Miami. Everything you did to put agents in unnecessary danger just so you'd get some headlines. There are names, dates, and witnesses to you being the worst boss in the entire U.S. Customs Service!" Todd fidgeted in his chair as he glanced at some of the documents. He began to sweat profusely. Since Callaway resigned, he no longer had his job to hold over his head like a hammer. Callaway grinned at his former boss.

"Want to guess who else is reading this stuff as we speak, you prick?"

As if on cue, Todd's secretary buzzed in.

"I told you I didn't want to be disturbed!" Todd snapped.

"Sir, it's the commissioner on the phone for you," his secretary responded. "He sounds very upset."

Todd was visibly trembling as he reached for the telephone. Callaway smiled and walked out of his office looking like he had just screwed his high school prom queen. He did what he needed to do, not out of revenge, he told himself, but to try to make things safer for Jorge and all the other good people in the Customs Service. *Oh, bull... You did it for revenge, too!* he thought. As he passed Todd's usually straight-faced secretary, he noticed that she, too, was smiling. She even gave him a wink before he walked through the door to the hallway. Jorge came running out the door behind him.

"Mike, Jesus Christ that was beautiful. Why did you quit, man? You had Todd by the balls. Do you have another job lined up somewhere?" he asked, sounding giddy as a child.

Callaway grinned again. "I hit it Jorge. I hit the damned Lotto!" he said it loud enough for people in Key Largo to hear. "I've been wanting to tell someone since I found out, but I was afraid to. Like it would go away if I did."

Jorge looked at his friend as if he'd grown a second head. "Mike, maybe you should sit down," he told him. "I think you're having a stroke or something."

Callaway laughed and answered, "No man for real, I won $83 million dollars." He pulled the first year's receipt from his pocket and handed it to his friend. Looking like he'd been struck by lightning, Hidalgo started to laugh. "This is a joke, right man?" he asked.

"No amigo, this is the real deal," Callaway answered. "That's why I quit, and that's why I sent the book I've been keeping on Todd to the commissioner in D.C."

Jorge was in shock, his eyes wide open as he stared at all the zeros on the receipt. "You won *all* of this money?" he asked.

"Well, that, and the same amount every year for nineteen more years." Callaway responded.

Jorge looked up at Callaway with his big brown eyes. "Marry me, man," he said as he grabbed Callaway in a bear hug, laughing like crazy. "I am so freaking happy for you, Mike! What's the first thing you're gonna buy with the money?"

Callaway had just opened the door to his rusting heap of a car, when he looked at Jorge, and looked back at the car. "Well the first thing I'm going to do is buy a new car and junk this clunker I've been driving," he answered with a grin. He stared out at the Miami River, behind the Customs Office and rubbed the stubble of beard on his face before he continued. "Then I think I'm going to buy something I've been wanting for a long time. As a matter of fact, why don't you take some of that vacation time the agency owes you? I don't think you'll have any problem getting Major Dick to approve it. At this stage of the game he'll probably give you the okay for time off and kiss your ass at the same time. Meet me at the 15th Street Marina in Fort Lauderdale the day after tomorrow."

"What are we doing the day after tomorrow?" Hidalgo asked.

"I don't know yet, but bring enough clothes for a week, and, oh yeah, bring your passport." Callaway sat in the ripped driver's seat and brought the coughing, wheezing engine to life. He shouted out the window.

"You always said I should make an artificial reef out of this piece of crap car," he said. "Maybe it's time I took your advice."

Hidalgo yelled at Callaway as his friend pulled a piece of paper from his pocket and read the name and number on it. "What are you doing tonight, man?" Jorge asked.

Callaway smiled at him as he pulled away.

"Brenda!" was all he said.

Chapter 7

On Wednesday morning, Special Agent Jorge Hidalgo walked onto the dock at the 15th Street Marina in downtown Fort Lauderdale. He carried a duffle bag full of clothes, his passport, and a whole lot of concern over what his old partner was up to. Midway up the dock, Hidalgo spotted Mike Callaway sitting with his feet over the side of the dock. He had the guts of a fishing reel laid out next to him. Callaway was installing some of his homemade leather drag washers in an obviously brand new Diawa spinning reel. Hidalgo saw Callaway reach over the dock into a boat that was tied in front of him and pull a screwdriver out of a toolbox.

So that was the other thing he was going to buy, after a new car? he thought.

The brand new, shiny white Hewes Bonefisher was a sleek sixteen feet long with a one-hundred-thirty horsepower Yamaha outboard on the stern. She had all the usual flats boat accoutrements, like a poling platform suspended over the outboard on aluminum legs and a push pole to go with it. Another man sat inside the boat with the cowling off the engine. Hidalgo surmised it was last minute tune-up for the new motor.

Why do I need a passport and clothes to go out on a sixteen-foot boat? Even Callaway isn't nuts enough to go to anywhere out of the country in a boat this small. Well, maybe Bimini, he might be nuts enough for that, he thought. "So where we going in that thing, Bermuda?" he joked as Callaway looked up at him.

"No," Callaway responded. "We're going to Nassau—on that," as he pointed over his shoulder with his thumb. Next to Callaway and the Hewes sat an old wooden-hulled shrimp boat. The wonderful old boat was seventy feet long and older than either of the men who were contemplating going to sea on her this day. Callaway grabbed an electric switch on the deck of the Hewes and pushed a button. Two plastic-coated steel cables rose up out of the water, pulled along pulleys on davits on the stern of the old wooden boat. The cables tightened to the bow and stern lifting rings on the Hewes, and gently lifted the smaller boat out of the water, hanging it neatly on the stern of the wooden-hulled shrimper. The guy working on the motor gave Callaway a strange and perturbed look as the Hewes lifted off with him in it, and then thumped against the stern of the larger boat. It was obvious that this was not the first time Callaway had demonstrated the lift to someone today with the man aboard. The big boat had seen better days by the looks of its exterior, but Callaway assured his pessimistic friend that she was completely sea worthy.

"Her engine and interior were just replaced," he said proudly. "The old owner went broke before he could fix up the outside, though, so I picked her up for a pretty good price."

Hidalgo just shook his head as he took in the ragged-looking exterior of the boat. "With all of that money, why didn't you buy a new Sea Ray, or even a Cary, like the one you blew up the other night?" he asked. "Something with a little speed, and for God's sake, a little class?"

Callaway just smiled as he put the assembled reels in his tackle box. "Those boats are really nice, yes, but they don't have the kind of class this one has," he answered. He continued to talk as the two walked the length of the hull. "She may be ugly, but she'll take you to hell and back without getting you wet, and she's slow enough to let you really enjoy the scenery. Besides, if I want to go fast, I just drop the Hewes into the water and I can haul ass all I want."

As they reached the bow, Jorge read the name that had been hastily painted on the bow gunwale. "*Orinoco Flow?*" he wondered aloud. "What's up with that?"

"It's a song by that Irish singer," he replied. "The one that keeps saying, "Sail Away, Sail Away," over and over. That's just what I plan on doing. And, fortunately for me," he continued, "the original owner never got around to naming it, so I won't have to worry about incurring Neptune's wrath by changing the name."

Callaway escorted his friend aboard the shrimp boat. Hidalgo was amazed at how fresh the interior of the boat really was. The previous owner had hired a decorator to fix the boat up. The artist managed to blend style and function into the old timer, giving her lots of storage space and a good nautical feel. Unfortunately, he also took some liberties with the color scheme and fabrics, using lots of bright burgundy crushed velour that looked right out of the 1970s. He also ran the previous owner into debt before the poor schmuck could enjoy the boat. Callaway showed Jorge the two staterooms, which were quite comfortable and well appointed. While the living room was a bit loud and gaudy, the trawler could be the poster child for the old adage, "Never judge a book by its cover," as the ragged exterior gave no indication of what was inside.

Jorge was opening all of the cabinets when he came to a long one that was about two feet tall. "What's this for?" he asked. He opened it and he found a small arsenal inside. The cabinet was full of weapons that Callaway had accrued through his life. It contained everything, from an old Marin .22 rifle to an AR-15, and a scope-sighted Remington bolt-action sniper rifle in .300 Winchester Magnum caliber. In between were an odd assortment of pistols and a pump action shotgun.

"The last owner had that cabinet put in for his wife's china, but I use it for something different," he replied. "I like to have all my bases covered when I'm at sea, 'cause you never know who you might run into. Besides," he said smiling, "I eat off paper plates most of the time."

The mechanic who'd been working on the Hewes outboard climbed over the transom of the larger boat and entered the cabin. "You're all set to go, Callaway," he said. He carried his tools and what looked like a large Freon tank with him.

Callaway handed the man some folded cash, and Jorge couldn't help but notice that the bill on the outside was a hundred. "What was that guy charging with the tank, the air conditioning on your flats boat?" he asked rather sarcastically. The cockpit of the Hewes was totally open.

"Actually, he was installing a nitrous tank on the outboard," Callaway answered with an evil grin. Jorge was always amazed by Callaway's need for speed. The nitrous oxide gas in the tank would be fogged into the outboard's carbureted intake at the flick of an electric switch that was mounted on the console. Instantly, it would give the engine another one hundred or so horsepower, for about forty-five seconds at full throttle or at least until the gas ran out or the engine blew up.

"The guy was here to install an oxygen tank, and ended up selling me a nitrous system," Callaway said, as he checked the big boat's instruments before start up.

Looking puzzled, Jorge asked, "What's the oxygen for, your famous "cop's cure" for a bad hangover?" Jorge recalled the many mornings after squad parties, watching ten deputies huffing on the oxygen bottles in the trunks of their patrol cars, flooding their blood with pure oxygen to try to clear the booze out of their systems.

Callaway smiled at his friend. "The oxygen tank is for the livewell on the Hewes," he answered. "It keeps bait alive and a lot fresher. It's one of those tricks of the trade things, and you have no stinking idea what I'm talking about, do you?" he asked, laughing.

Jorge shook his head. Callaway always ragged on him for being the only Cuban in the world who didn't know much about fishing. Callaway stopped laughing when a bright yellow taxi pulled up to the dock. His smile turned into an angry frown that Jorge had only seen when they had been around some of the worst criminals in town.

"What's wrong, man?" Jorge asked. He turned toward the window while instinctively putting his hand on the gun under his shirt. Jorge stared at the person in the rear seat of the cab and froze as if he was staring at the Creature from the Black Lagoon. "Anna," was all that he could say. He saw Callaway's ex-wife emerging from the cab. She was very noticeable to everyone on the dock in her red and white print sundress. Her store-bought breasts almost bounced out of the low-cut front of the garment as she stumbled up the gangplank in high heels. Callaway met her at the door to the cabin, opening it, but not letting her past. "What do you want?" he asked in a low voice.

"Come on, Callaway, let me in. We need to talk," she said in her sexy voice. He reluctantly opened the door and let her in.

"Jorge, *como estas*, handsome?" she asked, flashing her big brown eyes at Callaway's old partner. Jorge nodded, trying not to laugh.

Callaway was not feeling so jolly about the impromptu arrival of the woman who took him for all that he'd previously owned. "What do you want?" he almost screamed at her.

"Oh, baby, you and I need to talk alone," she answered. "Do you mind, Jorge?"

Jorge looked at Callaway and shrugged his shoulders, telling him, "I'll be up on the bridge if you need me, man." He stepped out of the cabin, leaving the door open, and climbed the ladder to the bridge.

Anna sat on the couch and patted the seat next to her. Callaway kept his distance, sitting on a chair across the room. "I've been doing a lot of thinking lately, baby, and most of it has been about you," she purred. "The fact of the matter is, I miss you, Callaway, and I'd like to give our marriage another try." She parted her knees, revealing that she wasn't wearing any panties. Callaway couldn't help but stare for a brief moment. Then he remembered that he wasn't the only one that had visited that island when they were married. He was suddenly struck with why she was there. "Who told you, Anna?" he said, staring at the ceiling.

"Told me what, baby?" she asked, smiling.

"About me and the money, that's what," he responded, narrowing his eyes. She was always a terrible liar. Her face flushed red.

"Well, one of your old buddies from Customs came in my bar the other night and mentioned that you had come into some money, but that's not why I'm here," she responded. "Honest, Callaway, I'm in love with you again!" Callaway rolled his eyes. He couldn't believe his greedy, gold-digging, bitch of an ex-wife could think he was that stupid. "How did you know where to find me?" he asked in a calm voice.

She assumed that sexy look again. "Well, that guy from Customs, he was nice enough to call your old office and get your forwarding address," she answered. "He said it was for the bait shop at this pier."

Yeah, and what did you gave him to get that little tidbit of information? he wondered. She needed to go. Now. He stood up and opened the door to the starboard deck. "You know what, Anna, maybe you're right," he said. "But I need to think about it awhile. Tell you what, Jorge and I are going for a quick ride up the waterway, just to test this old wreck out. Why don't you wait on the dock, and when we get back, we'll go out to dinner and talk some more. Maybe we'll have something to celebrate."

She was not pleased. She frowned and stood up with her hands on her hips. "Well, why can't I go with you, baby? You know, Jorge can drive, and you and I can test out the bed in the cabin. This thing does have a bed, doesn't it?" she said licking her lips.

"Oh yeah, it has a nice bed. But I wouldn't want to take you out unless I know the boat is completely safe. You're not a very good swimmer," he replied, flashing his sincerest smile.

She shivered slightly. Callaway knew of Anna's fear of boats and deep water. He walked her out the door and down the gangplank. He gave her a hug, feeling her hard breasts against his chest. "We'll be back in twenty minutes. Twenty-five tops," he said. He ran aboard the boat and pulled the gangplank up behind him. He smiled and waved as he ascended to the bridge, turning to wink at Jorge, who read the play perfectly and climbed down the ladder on the other side of the bridge. Callaway fired up the diesel on the shrimp boat, still smiling and waving at her as he did. Jorge untied the lines from the dock and climbed back up to where his partner was working the controls.

Former United States Customs Enforcement Agent Michael Callaway put the rudder hard to port and the engine in reverse, as he gently maneuvered the big boat away from the dock. Both men waved as they slowly pulled away, with absolutely no intention of coming back soon.

Laughing, Jorge asked, "How long do you think before she figures it out?"

Callaway smiled and answered, "Hopefully long enough so we're out of screaming range."

You know I could hear everything you two were saying downstairs," Jorge said with a smile. "You should have screwed her one last time, man."

Callaway looked back, smiling and waving at his ex standing on the dock.

"I just did."

Chapter 8

She turned fairly tight for a vessel with such a large beam. Mike eased her into the Intercoastal Waterway and began heading south under the 17th Street drawbridge, past the huge sailfish mural that the artist Guy Harvey had painted on one of the pilings holding up the draw span. A few hundred yards later, after a sharp turn to port, the *Orinoco Flow* was cruising out of Port Everglades inlet and into the Atlantic Ocean. The ocean and the tropics were amazingly calm for this time of the year. People in the area were still real jumpy since Hurricane Andrew had done its atomic bomb imitation on South Florida just one year earlier. Callaway put the boat on a course to the southeast and set the autopilot. He dialed in a stop just six miles from shore.

"I know your navigation skills suck Callaway, but why are you stopping us six miles out?" Jorge inquired.

Callaway just smiled. "Unfinished business," he answered. At about four miles from the inlet, the water changed from light green to dark blue — an indication that they were entering the Gulf Stream. As they approached the location Callaway had dialed into the GPS, Jorge pointed out a self-propelled barge up ahead. The barge had a small crane and an object covered with a tarp on the forward deck. Callaway maneuvered up alongside the barge and yelled to Jorge to throw the spring line to the old man running the rusty old flat top. After the two vessels were tied together, Callaway walked out of the cabin carrying the pump shotgun. He didn't miss the look of alarm on Jorge's face. "What the fuck are you doin', man!" Jorge blurted out. His Spanish accent always became more noticeable when he got excited.

Callaway began loading the Remington pump with double-ought buckshot rounds. "Settling an old score," he answered with the same mischievous grin he'd displayed when Jorge asked why they were coming here in the first place. For one very long, horrifying moment, Hidalgo envisioned that the tarp would be raised and a kidnapped Major Dick would be in a cage under it, waiting for Callaway to turn him into shark food. Before Jorge could say anything else, the old man removed the tarp revealing Callaway's old Monte Carlo sitting on the deck lashed to a wooden pallet. The old man started up the crane, lifting the car into the air, and then he swung it out over the water. Hidalgo started to get the picture. "Mike, I was kidding about making your old car into an artificial reef, man," he said as the car swayed back and forth in the breeze. "Besides, if you get caught dumping this thing out here, they'll lock you up for screwing up the environment."

Callaway pulled a piece of paper from his pants pocket and handed it to his friend while keeping his eyes on the swaying vehicle. Hidalgo scanned the very official looking document bearing the seal of the Department of Natural Resources

Artificial Reef Program. The certificate gave authority for one Michael Callaway to sink one 1978 Chevrolet automobile at this particular spot in the ocean to create Broward County, Florida's newest artificial reef.

"She's been cleaned out of all gasoline, oil and lubricants, as well as anything else that's not environmentally friendly," Callaway replied to his amazed friend.

"How did you get this certificate so quick? It usually takes months to get a reef site certified," Jorge stammered in disbelief.

"There's a little known codicil to the laws regarding the reef program," Callaway answered as he racked a round into the chamber of the Remington. "It says that money talks and bullshit walks."

"Just how much money did you have to give away to pull this trick off?" Hidalgo mused aloud.

Callaway indicated that it was a lot, as he took aim at the thick rope suspending the car in mid-air. "This is for all the times you left me stranded, wet, and pissed off, you rotten piece of crap," he said calmly. Then he pulled the trigger. The nine lead pellets tore through the rope, shredding it to the point of breaking, and dropping the car into the sea where it slowly began to sink.

"May fish have sex on your cheap vinyl seats," he said. "God knows, I never got to."

After giving the old man, still chuckling over the newest artificial reef, a healthy tip, Callaway started up the shrimp boat and turned her southeast toward the island of New Providence, more

53

commonly known as Nassau. The old boat moved at a slow, comfortable pace through the beginning of the Bahamas chain of islands. Along the way, Callaway and Hidalgo put lines over the side to troll ballyhoo in an attempt to catch something fresh for dinner. About thirty miles northeast of New Providence and just south of the island of Eleuthera, Callaway and Hidalgo caught sight of a flat black-colored Midnight Express. It belonged to someone very well known to them. The craft was part of the private Navy of drug lord Anton Drake.

Drake, an expatriate Englishman and a former Commander in the Royal Navy, owned the small islands that Customs and DEA agents had nicknamed Golgotha, after the Biblical "Place of the Skull" where Christ died. The islands were so named based on rumors that one of them had a hidden cave full of the skulls and bones of some of Drake's enemies. Drake's huge house faced them on the leeward side of the larger island, with his private marina close by. Drake fancied himself to be the modern reincarnation of the English Crown sponsored privateer of the same last name. But while Sir Francis Drake plundered gold and silver-laden Spanish galleons back in the sixteenth century, Anton Drake, after being unceremoniously and dishonorably discharged from Her Majesty's Navy for conduct unbecoming an officer, plundered America's youth by smuggling high-grade cocaine into the country.

He supplied a good portion of the coke flooding into the U.S. *Cary I,* the boat that Callaway had accidentally blown up, was allegedly

54

owned by one of Drake's associates. That boat had probably picked up its load from a passing freighter Drake had supplied with the drugs. The problem, for anyone trying to tie Drake to smuggling, was that no one could figure out how he moved the stuff off his islands. All of the reports written about Mr. Drake's alleged involvement in the cocaine smuggling business all ended with the same phrase: "Suspect is suspected of transporting drugs from his islands *by unknown means*."

Like many of the people in his line of work, Drake had another business to cover his more lucrative and sinister undertakings. His legitimate business was the operation of tourist submarines. The undersea vessels took paying customers hundreds of feet below the surface to view incredible reefs and tropical fish in the area. Paying customers could look at the underwater scenery through large windows in the hulls and take in all the beauty without having to learn how to scuba dive or even get wet. One of the subs operated in the waters near the island, using the marina near Drake's residence for battery charging, since it ran on electric motors, and for repairs. A large, sea-going dredge ship was anchored a few hundred yards from shore. Callaway surmised that Drake needed the dredge to keep the channel leading away from his islands open so the sub could be towed to the area closer to Nassau where it made its dives.

It was amazing to Callaway that Drake still had any business at all after one of his subs sank past crush depth and exploded along one of the miles-deep trenches in the Bahamian sea. All of the men, woman, and children, along with the crew aboard, were lost. The remains of the sub, mostly twisted hunks of metal and plastic, settled in water that was five thousand feet deep, and were later photographed by a remotely guided submersible. It was not a pretty sight. The shredded remains of some of the passengers were evident. Body parts floated to the surface for almost a week after the catastrophe. The incident was covered by most of the news agencies around the world since the Bahamas are such an international tourist destination. Drake resurrected his business by buying a new and improved submarine, and spending a lot of money on advertising to calm the fear of any tourist who knew of the disaster.

Still, from what they knew, Callaway and Hidalgo thought it was obvious that the submarine was just a cover and a money laundering operation for his drug business, since his tourist business was way down. Callaway fought the urge to mix it up with the guard boat, considering that he was driving a shrimp boat, not *Blue Thunder*. The last time he and Hidalgo had come through this area in a Customs Service boat, they messed with one of Drake's guard boats so much that it led to them receiving a nasty complaint from Drake's lawyer in the states.

In that instance, Jorge, a superb boat pilot, capable of making any boat do tricks that no one else could, chased one of Drake's men all over the area in front of Drake's island. Driving a larger forty-one foot Formula V-hull, Jorge was able to turn inside of the usually more maneuverable Midnight Express several times during that meeting, spraying his wake all over the other boat. It got so bad for the Midnight's driver that he turned and ran for the safety of Golgotha. The encounter was observed by Drake and several of his compatriots on shore, who most likely assumed the boat was property of the United States government. The Commissioner of the U.S. Customs Service handled the complaint by assuring Drake's attorney that what the agents were doing was well within procedure. The commissioner then merely notified Special Agent-in-Charge Richard Todd of the complaint, asking him to explain to his somewhat aggressive agents that they needed to be a little more "diplomatic" when dealing with Anton Drake's people.

The commissioner probably did not care about a scumbag like Anton Drake's feelings being hurt because one of his guard boats got run off by a couple of Customs guys. However, the slight reprimand the commissioner thought was warranted turned into a severe ass chewing for Callaway and Hidalgo by Major Dick. He threatened the agents with suspension and termination if this sort of thing happened again. Callaway and Hidalgo both laughed about the incident later on, since they sincerely thought it was the right thing to do, and it was a hell of a lot of fun, too.

So here they were now, facing the same type of situation. Callaway was overwhelmed by temptation, and he cut into the three-mile property boundary that Drake openly declared around his islands. The guard boat quickly swerved toward Callaway and Hidalgo, tearing through the water across the bow of the *Orinoco Flow*. Callaway did not touch the throttle or change course in any way, just to piss off the pilot of the guard boat. The Midnight Express circled in front of Callaway and then accelerated directly at them. Callaway again did not change course. He figured that unless the pilot of the go-fast boat was a suicidal fool, this game of chicken would end with the druggie veering off to port or starboard. He was right. The pilot of the Midnight did not want to go head to head with a sixty-three thousand pound shrimp boat. Instead, he circled back around, slowing, and coming up next to the *Orinoco Flow*. He then pointed an AK-47 assault rifle at Callaway and Hidalgo, and motioned for them to leave the area by pointing out to sea.

Callaway figured it would be better to continue his vacation to Nassau rather than fight it out on the high seas with the druggie's goons. He turned the *Orinoco Flow* outbound from Drake's Island and slowly moved out to sea. He looked back just in time to see that the Midnight driver had put away the gun and was now holding a camera. He appeared to be snapping pictures of Callaway, Hidalgo, and the shrimp boat, with a camera equipped with a telephoto lens. Callaway shot the Midnight pilot a one-fingered salute, while veering his vessel to port and continuing out of the area. Somehow he knew this incident wasn't over.

About three hours later, Callaway drove the big shrimper into the harbor at New Providence, Nassau. He radioed the harbormaster's office, requesting a slip large enough to handle his boat. He was directed to slip number thirty-three, nestled comfortably among several multi-million dollar yachts. Callaway's boat received some very strange looks from the yacht set aboard their luxurious cruisers as he docked his boat. If those people only knew the net wealth of the captain of the ugly old boat that just docked amongst them they would probably think differently. Callaway and Hidalgo showered, changed into their bar-hopping clothes, and walked into town. They followed the route they'd taken many times when stopping overnight after patrolling the waters between Nassau and Florida. Down Bay Street they went and up a small, unnamed alley to a bar called *Greasy Dick's*.

"Man, it will be nice to drink some beer and not have to go to work in the morning," Jorge said, stretching out his arms.

"Well don't get too wasted, amigo," Callaway responded. "The whole idea is for us to do some fishing down here, as part of my new lifestyle as a sea-going bum. So we're up at dawn tomorrow." Jorge gave him a nasty look as they entered the bar.

This place was a favorite hangout for both saints and sinners. On many occasions, the two Customs agents had sat across the room from some of the most ruthless drug smugglers and killers in the hemisphere. Everything was kept on "businesslike" terms, as they were on what both sides considered somewhat neutral ground. It was a good way for the Customs guys to find out just who was in town. The place, as nasty as it was, had the best selection of beer, and women, on the island, and this was a big draw for both men.

Callaway and Hidalgo walked in and sat at a table against the back wall of the bar as any good cop always does. This allowed them the luxury of the wall covering their backs, while giving them an excellent view of everyone entering or leaving the bar. After ordering a couple of cold beers, they began to talk and people watch, noticing a couple of people they knew on the wrong side of the law. They were starting to make some serious eye contact with two young tourist girls sitting at the bar, when through the front door walked two very large, nasty looking men. One of them was wearing a *Subdives Tours* t-shirt, the name of the Anton Drake's company, and sported the kind of tattoos on his hands that told Callaway and Hidalgo he'd done time in a Cuban prison. The two thugs stopped and scanned the room as if looking for someone in particular. Spotting Callaway, they stopped their search, said something to each other, and the one wearing the t-shirt left the bar. A minute later, the same thug walked back in followed by a group of people. One man emerged from the group and stopped about ten feet from Callaway and Hidalgo's table.

It was Anton Drake.

Drake was famous for occasionally putting in appearances in New Providence and Paradise

Island, where he would gamble and pay off some government officials. It was well known that this drug dealer had several big Bahamian government officials in his employ. He was a medium sized, well-built man of about fifty years. Together with his son Derrick, they were the most feared men in the islands.

"Well, I guess my sources were right," Drake said in a low tone. "Welcome to my part of the world, gentlemen of the United States Customs Service."

Callaway and Hidalgo didn't say a word. Callaway's gaze was instead locked on the woman dressed in very masculine looking clothes and standing next to Drake.

She was wearing a button-down, long-sleeved shirt and pants. Her hair was blond and cut very short. The woman glared at Callaway with a look that could fry ice.

Drake couldn't help but notice the exchange. "I see you have an interest in my lady friend, Mr. Callaway," he said almost laughing. "This is Shea, my bodyguard. Don't waste your time lusting after her, old boy. She has a black belt in karate, and she'll tear your bloody head off if I tell her to." He ran a finger down the lapel of her shirt, brushing her left breast. She didn't react at all, but, instead, continued to stare menacingly at Callaway. "Besides, you're not her type. She's not used to dealing with male equipment."

Callaway thought to himself, *The joke's on you!* He knew that "Shea" was actually an undercover DEA operative named Carrie Marvin.

It was obvious that she was able to get really deep into Drake's organization. A pretty neat trick, since Callaway knew how tight Drake kept his group. She had perfected this skill working the drug cartels in Colombia over the past seven years. She was a deep cover operative who Hidalgo did not know. In fact, Callaway wouldn't have known her, either, if not for their romantic encounter three years earlier. The encounter was short but torrid, and when she left, Callaway was kicking himself for not telling her that he had fallen for her in a big way. He figured, correctly, that between her globetrotting undercover work, and his chasing bad guys across the Caribbean, that they would seldom see each other. One failed marriage was enough for him.

He had not even wanted to try a lasting relationship back then, but seeing her again brought back his old feelings for her. Only now the circumstances were all screwed up. Callaway looked long and hard at the situation. He and Jorge versus Drake, six of his closest thug friends, and one deep-cover DEA agent. This encounter was getting worse by the minute. Callaway knew that if a fight started, it could compromise Carrie's operation—if that *was* the reason she was here, as she would be expected to beat the hell out of Drake's enemies. If she held back, it would look really suspicious. Callaway needed to find a way to disengage without Drake figuring things out.

Then things got even worse. Apparently anticipating trouble, in ones and twos, most everyone cleared out of the bar. While most of the locals left, three of the four men at a table on the other side of the bar stayed and watched the situation intently. The fourth, and largest of the group, a big man with bright red hair cut in a flat-top, sat impassively listening with his back to the fray.

"Mr. Drake," Callaway said dryly "I see the boat from the nut house got here early tonight." Callaway watched Drake's face flush red with anger as he continued to speak. "For your information, I'm no longer with the Customs Service, nor any other law enforcement agency," Callaway continued. "But my friend here still is, and I don't want to screw up his career by fighting with you and your friends tonight."

Hidalgo looked at Callaway in total disbelief. He never thought he would see Mike Callaway back away from a fight—especially a fight with a scumbag like Anton Drake. This would be a great way to even some old scores. He had no way of knowing about the situation involving Carrie.

Drake smiled. "So, I guess that means if my boys, and girl, of course, take you outside and beat the hell out of you, I won't be indicted by your idiotic government for assaulting one of their agents?" he asked, politely.

The red-headed man's head twitched to one side, as if he were straining to hear every word of the confrontation taking place behind him.

"No, what that means, dickhead, is if I kick the crap out of you, I won't have to worry about having an internal affairs investigation on me," Callaway responded.

Drake looke as if he was ready to explode. His hands were balled up in fists at his sides. Callaway continued to pour fuel on the fire. "You know Drake, it's a shame the Royal Navy stopped their old policy of keelhauling sailors who smuggle drugs. Hauling your ugly ass under the belly of a ship would have been a much better way of punishing you than the dishonorable discharge you got."

"Fuck the Royal Navy, and fuck you too, *Saint Michael!*" Drake screamed. "Yes, I've heard all about what a good and honest cop you were," he continued. "Instead of taking our generous 'gifts,' to let our boats pass by, you decided to be a saint. Well there are others in your former organization that are much smarter than you. Just remember, my righteous friend, they make saints out of dead people!" Drake gestured wildly with his hands as he continued to rage. "And besides, as stupid as Her Majesty's Navy may be, they're still a damn sight better than your rotten American Navy! They've been chasing me around for years, and the fools haven't been able to catch me yet!" Drake stopped shouting at the sound of a chair scrapping across the floor in the corner where the four men were seated.

The large red-haired man swiftly stood up and turned to glare at Drake. "You were doing fine till you went there, bucko!" the man shouted. Commander David Eldridge, Captain of the hydrofoil, *USS Pegasus* slammed his eyeglasses on the table with such force that one of the lenses cracked and fell out of the frame.

"And who might you be, sir?" Drake asked in an unusually cautious and gentlemanly tone.

"Commander Eldridge, United States Navy," he shot back, glaring at the Englishmen.

Drake eyed the big man with a combination of curiosity and spite. He seemed to be gauging just how involved Eldridge would get if things came to blows. "Well if you feel so strongly about what I said, perhaps you would like to join in the fun, too, old boy," Drake hissed, exaggerating his heavy English accent. "And by all means, bring your friends, too."

Two of Eldridge's junior officers immediately stood up to fight alongside their captain. Lt. Brian Parks, his executive officer, did not. Eldridge did a half turn and met with an approving glance from the two standing officers. When he saw Parks still sitting and looking sheepishly up at him, he gave him a look that caused the young lieutenant to spring straight up from his chair. As the lieutenant shook, Eldridge whispered into his ear, "You and I are gonna have a long talk later on, son."

Meanwhile, Callaway kept looking at "Shea" and wondering what to do to defuse the bomb that was about to go off in the *Greasy Dick* bar. She continued staring fiercely at him, with no hint that she would help him find a way out. Callaway began to wonder if this was really an act, or if Carrie, too, had been lured over to work for the druggies. So much money was out there for any cop or government agent who wanted to jump onto the cocaine payroll. He knew that if she had defected, she would be tough to deal with in a fight, as she did possess all of the fighting credentials that Drake had boasted of. The question was whom would she use those deadly hands and feet against. Eldridge and his men started walking across the room, and it appeared that the battle was about to begin.

Just then the voice of salvation spoke, in a deep Bahamian-accented voice, "The first man to throw a punch will be soon sitting in my jail."

All of the potential combatants turned to see Inspector Rupert Winston standing in the doorway of the bar. Winston was a tall, older man, with a history as an honest cop in a place where honesty could be scarce. It was widely known that he did not like the drug people, but that he also didn't like United States government agents acting like they owned his nation of many islands. Callaway knew Winston well. The man had told him on numerous occasions that if he had his way, he would arrest Drake and put him under the jail, instead of in it, while at the same time kicking every DEA and Customs agent off his islands and back to the United States. Unfortunately, money, in the form of bribes that kept Drake protected and in business, precluded him from doing the former, and big-brother politics from the country to the north, precluded him from doing the latter.

He continued to speak calmly. "There will be no fight here tonight, gentlemen," he paused. "And lady, too."

He walked to the bar, followed by his personal enforcement unit—ten of the biggest Bahamian Defense Force cops Callaway had ever seen.

Winston had recruited his childhood friends. They were honest and believed in what he was trying to do—which was to break the cycle of drug corruption in his island nation. He was pretty much a one-man crusade when it came to dealing with his government and that had already cost him dearly. His teenage son was killed two years prior by a car-bomb that was surly meant for him.

"Well Inspector, out enjoying the evening air?" Drake asked casually. Everyone knew that Winston was one of a few Bahamian police officials that Drake really feared, since Winston correctly suspected him of being responsible for his son's death. Unfortunately, the inspector was never able to come up with enough evidence to make a homicide charge stick. Drake also knew that if Winston ever did take him to jail, it would probably be his last stop before hell.

"Don't be a smart ass with me, Mr. Drake," the Inspector commanded. "I would suggest that you and your rubbish leave this place and go back to your little islands, before I lose my temper, *mon*." Apparently, Drake knew a losing situation when he saw it. With a nod, his henchmen, and "henchlady," quickly filed out of the bar. Drake threw a quick glance back at Callaway on the way out. "Eyes behind you, Saint Michael. This isn't over." Callaway flipped him the bird while smiling at Carrie. Her expression, still one of pure anger, hadn't changed.

Callaway, Hidalgo, and the Navy men walked over to the inspector. Eldridge was the first to speak. "For Christ's sake, Winston, couldn't you have shown up a few minutes later?" he asked. "I so wanted an excuse to beat the crap out of that little bastard!"

"You of all people should be thanking me for keeping you out of this battle, Commander." Winston responded. "If I recall correctly, the last one you were in cost you your captain's rank."

"It would almost be worth being busted to lieutenant to beat the hell out of that slimy limey," the commander shot back as he motioned to the bartender for another beer. He was so angry he almost drained the bottle with one long gulp. "I've spent the last year trying like mad to figure out how he gets the coke off his island, and I'm completely stumped. And your people haven't exactly been much help, either," he added.

This was an obvious reference to the powerful vein of corruption in the Bahamian government. The inspector looked almost embarrassed at hearing this. Everyone knew that Drake was moving large amounts of cocaine off his private islands. They just couldn't figure out how. The DEA, Customs Service and the U.S. Navy had tried very hard to solve the puzzle with no success.

"Regardless," the inspector whispered, "the best thing for your career, Commander, and your neck, Mr. Callaway, would be to steer as far away from Mr. Drake as possible." He turned to walk away, speaking as he left. "I will get him, one day, I promise you that, gentlemen."

It was about this time that Hidalgo's digital pager started buzzing. "Son of a bitch, doesn't that just figure," he said with a look of total disgust as he read the message. "I come down here on vacation to fish, and on top of that I get to screw with Drake, *off* duty, and now I have to report back to Miami, ASAP." He looked at Callaway and Eldridge and just shook his head. "Something big is obviously coming down, and I have to get to the airport," he moaned. He then asked the bartender where he could get a cab. Shaking hands with his old partner, and new friend from the Navy — conflict, it seems, does help people bond in a hurry — Hidalgo walked out the door.

Callaway ordered another beer for himself, Eldridge, and the commander's men. "My dad lost a stripe for a while when he stood up the Captain's Mast for fighting," he said.

Eldridge looked at him for a moment and smiled. "Callaway," he said "your dad wouldn't be Steve Callaway, the sonar school guy at Key West?" Now it was Callaway's turn to smile. Eldridge laughed and said, "Well I'll be damned. He taught me sonar and anti-submarine warfare right after I came out of the academy. He's the best there is. How's he doing these days?"

"He passed away a few years ago," Callaway answered, staring solemnly down at the bar.

Eldridge looked down at the floor and said, "Oh, I'm sorry to hear that. You know he's got to be laughin' like hell, wherever he is, at the thought of you and me almost buddying up in a fight. He thought I was a real bumblefuck in that school."

"Yeah I'm sure he is," Callaway said quietly. He took a long swig of beer. With Jorge gone, he would be alone on this island. "I don't suppose you'd like to go fishing with me tomorrow, since my old partner had to leave in such a hurry?" Callaway asked.

Eldridge began to laugh. "Man I wish I could," he answered. "It's been a long time since I wet a line, but we have to go on patrol tomorrow to try and put a crimp in Mr. Drake's action again."

"What ship are you driving?" Callaway asked, even though he believed he knew the answer.

"Boat, not ship. I am the proud captain of the hydrofoil *USS Pegasus*," Eldridge answered, rising and standing straight and tall.

Smiling, Callaway admitted, "We passed you at Miami harbor a few days ago, on what turned out to be my last patrol with the Customs Service."

Eldridge stared at the man. "So that was your boat that was all shot full of holes? You had a pretty rough night from what I've heard," Eldridge replied.

Callaway closed his eyes, a shiver running up his spine, envisioning the drug boat exploding like a sea-going atomic bomb, and then told Eldridge what had gone on that night on the water.

"So that's why you're not working for the feds anymore?" Eldridge asked quietly. "They canned you over blowing up a boat with a load of dope on board? Boy, your boss must have been a colossal jerk."

"Colossal is a pretty good description, yeah," Callaway said with a grin.

Not wanting to let the whole world know about his new-found wealth, Callaway smiled and changed the subject. "How do you think Drake is getting the stuff off his islands?" he asked taking another sip of beer.

Eldridge shook his head and then finished his. "That, my new friend, is the million dollar question," he answered. I have the best surveillance gear that our fine taxpayers can buy on my little boat, and I can't figure it out. Every patrol ends up the same way. Drake is smuggling the stuff out..."

"By unknown means?" Callaway interrupted.

"Yeah," the big man responded, sounding bummed out.

Eldridge motioned his men over to him, introducing them to Callaway as he continued. "But, *Pegasus* will try again, one last time, this week," he said sadly.

"Why one last time? Where are you going?" Callaway asked.

"Me?" the commander answered. "I'm being reassigned. *Pegasaurus,* as we like to call her, is going to the Mothball Fleet, having unfortunately, never fired a shot in defense of her country." The commander's voice was filled with sadness. Callaway thought about the confrontation with Drake, and how he told the druggie that he no longer had to worry about his job when dealing with him. The implications of that statement, the fact that he could basically do whatever he wanted - legal or illegal—to mess with Drake, finally sank in. He also desperately needed to find out if Carrie was working Drake, or if she had gone over to the other side. He turned and winked at Commander

Eldridge. "Maybe things will be different for you on this trip, skipper," he said. He parted company with the Navy men, heading out the door with a smile on his face and a thousand ideas in his head on how he could screw with one Mr. Anton Drake.

Chapter 9

Carrie Marvin got into law enforcement as a profession for a different reason than most of her peers. Instead of the normal need to help people, she became a cop out of the sheer prospect of revenge. While home on a break from the nursing program at Northwestern University, she experienced a loss that would haunt her and rule her life forever. Her father Alex, and her fiancé, a man named Tommy Reese, who she'd grown up with in the farm town of La Porte, Indiana, were delivering a tractor to a buyer outside the city of Gary. Gary, Indiana was a dangerous place, where gangs of thugs roamed the streets, and the murder rate was so high that the medical examiner never slept. Drugs were openly dealt on the street. The city was considered the homicide capital of the world in the late 1980's. The grim statistics were not helped by the local police, either. Corruption ran rampant in the very Vice Squad that had been tasked with cleaning up the drug problem, which was the root of most of the other crime that occurred in the city. It would be several years later, in 1991, when every officer in that unit would be indicted for a combination of extortion, drug dealing, and robbing drug dealers during phony drug raids. One officer was even charged with murder.

It was into this hellhole that Alex Marvin and Tommy Reese ventured on a cool Friday morning. They decided to stop and get breakfast at a small diner on the other side of town, closer to the farm country where they felt comfortable. After a good meal of eggs, ham and grits, they paid their bill and were turning to walk out to Alex's truck when three men in ski masks burst in through the front door. They all pulled handguns from under their shirts and announced that they were holding the place up. Alex and Tommy froze when they saw what was happening. Two of the robbers spread out and began taking wallets and jewelry from the patrons, while the third emptied out the cash register and the tip jar. Alex and Tommy gave their wallets up without resistance, hoping to just live to go home when the ordeal was over. One of the gunmen tried to pull the gold wedding ring off the finger of an older woman. Even though she offered no resistance, the ring, which had resided on that finger for fifty-two years, refused to come off. The crook pulled harder and the woman screamed in pain.

Tommy couldn't help but react to her situation. He grabbed a glass pot of steaming hot coffee off a nearby counter and smashed it across the face of the man tormenting the old lady. The glass shattered, tearing into the flesh of his face, while the near boiling liquid scalded it. Another of the gunmen pointed his weapon at Tommy, but Alex Marvin punched the man in the side of his face, knocking him sideways. Both Alex and Tommy ran for their respective robber's guns, when the third crook started shooting. Tommy was hit in the side and back and he fell sideways into the counter before sliding to the floor. Alex ran to his bleeding friend and was promptly shot in the back of the neck. He crumpled to the floor next to Tommy. The untouched gunman and his two injured compatriots ran out of the diner and jumped into a car that they had stolen earlier in the day. They tore out of the parking lot and disappeared before anyone could even get a tag number. The people in the diner did what they could for the two injured men before the paramedics arrived. The rescue guys had seen such wounds too many times and their grim expressions gave away their belief that neither of the men would survive.

Carrie arrived at her parents' house at about 2:00 p.m. Her mother Debbie came out to the driveway and hugged her, happy to see that she had made the trip safely. They were talking and laughing by the car when a marked sheriff's car pulled up onto the swale. The deputy who got out wasn't smiling, and both women knew something was wrong. The first thing that crossed Debbie Marvin's mind was that Alex and Tommy had been in an accident on the road somewhere. She thought of how old and rickety that lowboy trailer was that Alex used to haul heavy stuff. When the deputy told them what had happened, Debbie Marvin screamed and burst into tears. Carrie was in shock, shaking, as she held onto her mother. Both women were in disbelief that their men were dead. The neighbors heard her mother crying and ran out of their houses to see what was wrong. The neighborhood was small and close knit. Many others would cry that afternoon for the loss of two men who were more like family than friends.

The deputy received a call from the sheriff, who advised him to transport both Mrs. Marvin and Miss Marvin to Gary so they could identify the body of Alex Marvin. Five blocks away, a similar scene was taking place at the Reese home, as Tommy's parents prepared to journey to Gary for the same reason. The four of them arrived at the Gary Medical Examiner's office at about the same time, and the tearful scene happened again. The deputy who transported the Reeses knew Tommy and had played ball with him in high school. He cried, too.

The one person who had not shed a tear, though, was Carrie. Her face still wore that same look of shock. The families decided to go into the morgue for the identification together. When the sheets were pulled from the victims' heads, the crying began anew, except for one person. Something had changed in the mind of Carrie Marvin. Something in her psychological makeup just snapped. She felt something that she had never felt before in her life, and that was pure, unadulterated rage. She had plenty of time to think about what she was going to do after the funeral and her return to school. When the next semester came around, she didn't register for biology or anatomy and physiology as the other nursing students did.

Instead she began taking courses in criminal law, rules of evidence and forensics that were the core courses in the School of Criminal Justice. When she spoke to her counselors about her change of major, they did not push too much as to why she was making the change, having heard of the tragedy in her life. They noticed a profound change in Carrie Marvin's attitude. Gone was the sweet country girl who wanted to be a nurse. She was replaced by a hard-shelled, determined person, who no longer let people get too close to her. It was also at this time that she immersed herself in the martial arts. She trained continuously in karate and kick boxing. One of her instructors, a former Navy SEAL and Third Degree Black Belt, joked that she came up so quickly he was surprised she didn't get the bends, referring to how quickly she earned her black belt. He also taught her some deadly moves that only members of elite units like the SEALs would use.

Carrie's mother was deeply concerned at her daughter's new path in life. Carrie wanted to go into law enforcement in the worse way. Northwestern's criminal justice program was considered one of the best in the country, and Carrie could take her pick of which police agency she wanted to go to, but she only had one in mind. Since it was drugs that brought about most of the robberies in the area of Gary, Indiana, it would be the United States Drug Enforcement Administration, or nothing. She applied to the agency, and given her educational background, sailed through the testing process and was hired. She did extremely well at the combined DEA/FBI training academy in Quantico, Virginia, scoring the highest scholastic and physical training scores in the class.

One of the requirements to complete the Recruit Training Course was a grueling, cross-country obstacle course, called the "Yellow Brick Road." It is so named because the first tenth of a mile starts out on a path paved with bricks painted bright yellow. Mere completion of the course earns a recruit not only a passing grade, but also a souvenir yellow brick, with the recruit's class number and graduation date written on it in black marker pen. Carrie attacked the course with such determination that she set a record as the fastest female recruit to ever attend the academy. At a tall and slender five feet eleven inches, she ran like a deer on the course. Her "I'll do whatever I have to, to win," attitude was noticed by her instructors. Psychologically, she had just what the agency was looking for in a deep-cover operative. She had become a loner who knew how to look after herself. This was a quality most of the successful DEA spooks had. She started working in Prince George's County, Maryland, under the tutelage of some of the best undercover agents on earth, and she learned her craft well. After moving to a couple of different field offices, she ended up, after many requests, near home in Gary, Indiana. She worked the area hard, infiltrating several of the local drug gangs and gaining their confidence. This was something she had a particular knack for doing. She put on a tremendous show as a coke addict who couldn't get enough blow. They'd watched her the first time they met as she snorted three long lines of what they thought was cocaine. She'd pulled a clever slight-of-hand switch by dropping the bag of the real stuff on the ground. Then she let a bag containing milk sugar fall out her sleeve and shoved the bag of the real stuff up her sleeve.

The dealers let her in to the organization since she was a regular customer, and she would feed the information on shipments and contacts that she gained to her DEA brethren. Eventually, she ran across a drug runner whose face immediately rang an alarm bell in her mind. His name was Fergus, and one side of his face was covered with horrible looking scars and stitch marks. She'd read the police report a hundred times, about the robber that her late fiancé had smashed across the face with a pot of hot coffee, and that the witnesses all said how the man was bleeding profusely from his facial wounds when he ran from the diner. She befriended the man and eventually got him to talk about his past. One night when they were riding around in his car drinking a bottle of whiskey, she steered the conversation to the subject of the damage on the right side of his face. His bravado got the best of him, and he began bragging about the diner robbery and how his buddy Pinhead had capped the two honkies who messed up his face.

Carrie held the anger that instantly built inside of her. She wanted to shoot this piece of drug-dealing garbage right through the side of the head, but she wanted the trigger man way more than him. "I want to meet Pinhead," she said, cooing like an infatuated school girl. "I get all hot over guys who shoot people." She was giving a superb performance as a strung-out coke head with a fetish for killers. Her scarred up friend was immediately turned on by this, and tried to put a move on her while they were stopped at a light.

"No, dammit, I want you and Pinhead at the same time," she said.

Now her friend was seriously turned on. "He'll be back in town tomorrow. I'll get us together for tomorrow night at around eight o'clock. I'll score some good junk to take to our little party so we can really play," he said, grinning.

A few minutes later, he dropped her off at the apartment complex where the DEA had rented her a place to stay while she was working the gang. She went inside and called her supervisor to set things up. She didn't mention that she had a personal attachment to the bust she was planning the following evening for fear that he would pull her off the case.

The next evening, she sat and waited for the two men to arrive. At 8:05 p.m., a car rolled up to the apartment complex and two men got out. Carrie was ready. The DEA tech guys had placed hidden microphones throughout the apartment that would allow the team of agents in the next room to monitor and audio tape everything that was going on. As soon as they came in, she started the game. She let them in and they went to the bedroom. Fergus closed the door between the front room and the bedroom while Pinhead made himself comfortable.

"Fergus told me you like to shoot people," she said and then faked taking a swig out of a bottle of Jim Beam.

Pinhead stared at her breasts poking out of the top of her shirt. "Yeah, I shot a few," he said as he pulled a baggie full of white powder out of his coat.

"He told me you capped the fucker that messed up his face," she said, trying to set the hook on this fish that she very much wanted to arrest. She told herself to stay focused since the words were so painful to say. She realized at that moment that she was in a potentially deadly situation, yet she felt perfectly calm and relaxed.

Pinhead took off his coat and sat down to do some of the blow. "I shot *two* honkies that day, in a restaurant on the west side of town," he said, pointing his right index finger like a gun. That was all she could take.

"Is it starting to rain?" she asked as she turned to look out the window. This was the code word for the other agents to make the arrest. Five seconds later the front door of the apartment was kicked open and ten agents ran in. They reached the second door and found it was locked. Fergus had done this, unbeknownst to Carrie when he closed the door. He figured if anything bad happened, like ten DEA agents crashing through the front door, the second door would give them just enough time to escape out the window. Pinhead and Fergus tried to run to the window. They stopped dead in their tracks when they saw Carrie standing in front of their escape route pointing a Walther PP/k pistol at them. Fergus froze, but Pinhead, knowing he would be going away forever, went for the revolver he had tucked in the small of his back.

Carrie fired three quick shots, hitting the druggie almost dead center in the chest. He stopped and looked down at three holes in his coat so close together they could be covered with a half-dollar. There was very little blood, as the three .380 caliber, Federal Hydra-shock rounds tore open his heart and stopped it from pumping instantly. He laughed, the cocaine in his system masking the pain. He was dying as he stood there. The gun fell from his hand, and he collapsed in a heap.

In the meantime, the other agents had broken down the second door and reached Fergus, knocking him to the floor. Before they could handcuff him, Carrie suddenly exploded across the room and kicked the man squarely in the face, and she kicked him hard. He fell over with his nose in a new location—on the side of his face. She came at him again, but her supervisor and two other agents grabbed her. They couldn't understand why she was going off like this. The other agents pulled Fergus out of the apartment to save him from being killed.

After a minute or two Carrie calmed down. She told her boss why she had lost control, explaining about the two druggies' involvement in the death of her father and fiancé. Her supervisor looked at the ground and shook his head. "Never, never, never, get emotionally involved in an investigation, Marvin!" he yelled. "It will get you dead real fucking fast."

Carrie learned a valuable lesson that night—a lesson that would end up coming back to haunt her years later, on an island in the Caribbean called Golgotha.

Chapter 10

Callaway walked back to the *Orinoco Flow* alone. Not a bright move, considering that some of Drake's men could be waiting for him around any corner. When he reached the shrimper, he went below deck to the stateroom, splashed some water on his face to relieve the effects of the alcohol, and then pulled out a maritime chart of the local waters, including the area around Drake's islands. He studied the channels running to or near the island, looking particularly at the sea bottom topography surrounding the channels. It was pretty common knowledge that Drake had cocaine processing labs that were pumping out some pretty impressive amounts of product. Those labs were hidden somewhere on his private islands.

The big questions were, how was he getting the raw cocaine *to* the island for processing, and how was he getting the processed cocaine *from* the island, and on to freighter ships passing by in the shipping lanes. The first question could be answered many ways. It would be simple enough for a small boat to load up on raw coca paste exported from Colombia, from any freighter crossing through the area shipping lanes. There was enough boat traffic going to his island to deliver supplies and even water, for the goods to be transported in unmolested. Given the fact that Drake had bribed so many people in the Bahamas over the years, there wasn't much scrutiny of vessels going to Golgotha from another Bahamian island. So much for the first question.

The Customs Service, DEA, U.S. Coast Guard, and the US Navy had spent a considerable amount of time and money in an attempt to answer the second question. They monitored very little in the way of boat traffic from the island that hadn't been accounted for. Usually it was only Drake's guard boats circling the island that made up the surface traffic. These boats never got within twenty miles of the shipping lanes. Air traffic was even less. Only Drake's personnel Beechcraft King Air turbo prop flew off the island, and the aircraft usually flew to the U.S. to pick up supplies. It always traveled to the U.S. without the elder Drake aboard, as he would be picked up immediately by American law enforcement. The aircraft, instead, was used to ferry his son Derrick to tend to their business matters in the states, where he normally lived. Anton Drake had purchased a rather expensive condominium for his son on South Beach, Miami. He did not want his junior edition connected with his business in any way, should the day come that the cops, American or Bahamian, get enough evidence to come for him. The landing strip on the island was too short to accommodate jet aircraft due to some small mountains breaking up the land. In any event, Drake's plane would be shadowed by US Customs aircraft as soon as it was spotted by radar based in the Florida Keys. They had ruled the aircraft out as the means of moving the cocaine to the ships at sea since it was too small to carry any great quantity of the drugs, and because Drake knew that it was being constantly watched. The radar system, known as Operation Blue Lightning was actually suspended high above the island of Cudjoe Key, in the Florida Keys, by two huge, helium-filled balloons. This look-down radar would catch Drake's plane as soon as it left the island, even if the pilot skimmed the ocean.

Callaway sat in an easy chair, rubbing his beer-tired eyes. "The only thing left is the submarine," he mumbled to himself. He knew he was not the first person to consider that as a way of secretly moving the dope off shore. It made perfect sense that Drake could load a submarine up with cocaine and cruise under water out to the shipping lanes to rendezvous with some passing freighters to deliver his deadly cargo. And Callaway would also not be the first person to discount the possibility of the submarine's use to move the dope for a number of very good reasons. First and foremost was the physical distance that the sub would have to travel. It was exactly seventeen miles from Drake's island to the nearest shipping lanes. Drake's tourist-type submarine was not developed for long-range travel or military operations. It was designed to take thirty tourists down to depths of up to one-hundred fifty feet in air-conditioned comfort and show them the beauty under the sea through the many large windows built into the hull. In fact, the maximum depth the sub could descend to without the hull being crushed by water pressure was only two hundred fifty feet. This relatively shallow crush-depth was due to the weakness of the side windows and the large array of front windows that the pilot looked through to steer. With a top speed of only five knots under water, and a rather short duration for the batteries that powered it, there was no way that Drake's submarine could make it to the shipping lanes and back, and be charged up for the next day's tourist excursions in one night.

There was also the question of how the cocaine could be loaded onto the submarine at Drake's island while under the watchful eye of surveillance satellites and DEA aircraft. Additionally, the United States SOSUS Net, an array of listening devices attached at various locations on the ocean floor, with the primary mission of detecting submarines in the area, would probably pick up Drake's sub, since it was mechanically noisy as submarines go, as soon as it moved away from his island. The topography of the bottom leading out to the shipping lanes was not very helpful for concealment, either. The area in question was made up of rolling undersea hills, covered with miles of soft coral reefs. These hills were occasionally separated by fairly wide, extremely deep trenches that dropped almost straight down for miles. The depth over the majority of the distance to the shipping lanes averaged roughly fifty feet. If the submarine was being utilized to transport the dope, it would probably be visible, especially under full moonlight, due to the crystal clear Bahamian waters and the fact that it was painted ice-box white.

Callaway's concentration was suddenly broken by the sound of someone walking softly across the upper deck of the *Orinoco Flow*. Maybe Hidalgo's plans had changed and he'd returned to the boat to sleep. Or could it be one of Drake's people, coming to do him in? The cop in him rang the alarm bell in his head, and he bolted for the gun cabinet, grabbing a .357 magnum revolver. He was correct in his assumption that one of Drake's people had come to pay him a visit, but he was totally astonished when Carrie swung the door to the cabin open and strode in. She stood there looking down the barrel of the gun Callaway pointed at her. He did not know if she was friend or foe at this point. The questions from the bar ran through his head again: Was she under deep cover, or had she turned and become one of Drake's paid killers come to kill him?

"I figured you would react this way," she said, as she kept her hands in the open while keeping her distance from him. She gazed up at him with those big blue eyes, while keeping her face somewhat down.

Callaway didn't speak. He knew from his police training not to say a word. He remembered the old unarmed defense instructor up at FLETC, who used to take perverse pleasure in showing recruits that even the physical act of speaking can distract your mind and make you vulnerable to attack at close range. He used to let a recruit, usually the biggest guy in the class, "arrest" him with a blank firing weapon in his hand. When the instructor stood there glaring at him, the recruit would get nervous, and begin saying stuff like, "Don't move" or "Get on the floor." It would be about that time that the instructor would snatch the gun out of the arresting officer-cadet's hand and then level him with a well-placed kick. What scared the hell out of Callaway was the fact that Carrie could just about kick the old instructor's ass. He backed up a couple of feet to open up his comfort zone. He had it in his mind that if she followed she meant to hurt him, and if she tried, that he would shoot her.

"Callaway," she said softly. "Mike," she said a little louder. "I am under deep cover on Drake." She sat down on the couch. That was a good sign.

"Last year I got introduced to some of Drake's underlings by one of his associates that my unit turned," she continued. "The guy was looking at fifty years, minimum, for several counts of trafficking."

Callaway noticed that Carrie was wearing jogging shorts, a tank top, and dirty running shoes. She still had those incredibly nice, long legs. Her shirt had a couple of pieces of reflective orange tape stuck to it. Not exactly the stealthy type of clothing a professional killer would *normally* wear, but who could tell. He kept the gun aimed at her just the same and let her continue to talk.

"The guy told Drake's people that I was a psychopathic killer. They didn't seem too interested until he told them that I was a total lesbian, too," she said. Her lips curled up in a slight smile. "Apparently, the flip knew that Drake likes lesbians and that these bozos would know that. I thought that our Mr. Drake is a bit of a kinky Englishmen, but it turns out that he had an aunt who was gay, and she was one of the few women in the world he felt he could trust." She looked deep into his eyes and began to speak again, saying that when she met Drake for the first time, she was dressed in a dark, mannish, K.D. Lang suit. But Callaway interrupted her.

"So are you?" he asked, raising his eyelids.

She gave him an astonished look.

"I walk into your floating living room, and you are obviously concerned that I have come here to kill you since you're pointing a gun at me, and your biggest concern is if I'm still straight?" she answered, giving him a perturbed look.

Callaway half grinned. "Hey, I'm a guy. What can I say, we have priorities," he replied, with more than a bit of sarcasm in his voice. She looked at him with tired, stressed-out eyes.

"I told you I have been under, deep, for a year, now," she said. "I know I'm not supposed to be here telling you about this assignment, and I know the safe bet would have been to go back to the island with Drake and leave you alone, but..."

Callaway saw sadness in her eyes, now. "But?" he whispered.

She got up and slowly moved to the bar and picked up the bottle of whiskey on a shelf. Carrie opened the bottle and poured a couple of shots into a glass. She turned, her gaze locking on Callaway's lowered revolver and his finger, still on the trigger, indicating that he continued to be concerned about her motive. She sipped the whiskey and then

90

continued with, "I didn't expect to see you and your friend in that bar tonight. Drake obviously already knew that you were on the island, and that you no longer work for the Customs Service. What's up with that, by the way? And where the hell did you get this floating whorehouse?" she asked. She half-laughed as she scanned the interior of the shrimp boat.

Callaway was not yet in the mood to explain to her his recent good fortune, as he was thinking things through in two ways. One was that she was serious and the woman who he fell in love with had just come back into his life. Or, the other was that he might still end up having to shoot her if she was handing him a fake line and was actually there to kill him. "It's too long a story to tell right now," he finally answered.

"So Mike, do you still think I came here to kill you, tonight?" Carrie asked.

He shrugged his shoulders, still gripping the revolver firmly at his side.

She lay back on the couch and continued, "I mean you were this famously great pistol shot back at FLETEC, right? The first time I saw you at the school you were showing off at the pistol range, making some absolutely incredible shots. So, why would I walk aboard your boat and let you arm yourself if I was looking to kill you? Don't you think I would rather be waiting out in the dark so I could knock you off while you were staggering back here?" she asked.

She made sense. "I'm just curious about one thing," Callaway said as he placed the magnum on an end table close to himself, and far from her, and sat down. "How come Drake let you stay here while he went back to Golgotha?"

She smiled as she got up and walked over to him, bending over to give him a kiss that felt too warm and genuine to have come from someone looking to take his life. "I told him that I had this girlfriend in town, and I needed a little... recreation. That's how I get away to report in to the agency," she answered, smiling.

Now Callaway laughed for a second and then stopped abruptly. "You were kidding, right? About the girlfriend thing, I mean?" he asked, all serious.

She smacked him on the head, and sat down in his lap. They hugged, and then they tumbled to the floor.

Chapter 11

Callaway awoke at 6:00 am to the sound of the shower running in the bathroom. He was not bleeding, and his limbs were still attached, so he guessed Carrie was still on the side of law and order. He did notice, however, that he was bruised and sore in several places from the rather acrobatic sex they'd engaged in. Things had not changed in that respect since the last time the two were together. Making love to her was like doing it with the college girl who captained both the gymnastics and the track teams.

"Guess I better find *my* running shoes," he said with a grin. "I'd better build up my stamina to keep up with her." Then his mood instantly changed. He sat up in bed when a wave of fear overcame him. The woman he was in love with, again, was now in great danger. He knew it was her job, and he knew she had been under, deep, many times in the past, but this was Drake she was dealing with —Drake, who would kill a person in a heartbeat if he suspected that anything wasn't as it should be. He broke into a sweat thinking of what that sadistic bastard would do to Carrie if he found out she was playing him. She was good, and she was tough, but he had a lot of thugs working for him. And he had a lot of eyes and ears gathering information for him. There had been a rumor circulating about a mole that Drake had in the DEA. What if the traitor told him that his lesbian bodyguard was a DEA agent? Callaway was scared for her safety.

She walked out of the bathroom with just a towel wrapped around her hair. She expected him to be looking for more of what he had received for hours before the dawn, but instead she saw the fearful look on his face. Her smile faltered when she took in his expression of fear. She had never seen Callaway afraid before. She realized that he didn't even appear this way last night while he was pointing a gun at her, while he was still expecting to be attacked. "What's wrong?" she asked.

He stared at her for a couple of seconds and then, beckoning her to join him, he slowly began to speak. "I'm in love with you, I've been in love with you, I mean, since we first met," he answered.

She gave him a confused look. "So now you're worried about me being undercover with Drake, right?" she asked.

"Hell yes, I'm worried!" he snapped back at her. He took a deep breath and continued. "We have something special, at least I think we do, and I don't want it to go away like it did last time when you left. Most of all, I sure as hell don't want anything to happen to you."

Carrie was a bit startled by these revelations. She had checked him out through some friends and learned that Mike Callaway had a reputation of being kind of cool toward relationships after his first marriage went bust. This, she felt, was understandable, given the royal screwing his ex-wife, and his own inept lawyer, had given him. "So, what do you expect me to do, walk away from the best deep-cover investigation I've ever been involved in just to be with you?" she said. "Besides, then neither of us would have a job. I mean, I love you too, Mike, but we have to have something to live on, right?"

Callaway was listening to her, but his head snapped up when she got to the love part. "Did you mean it when you said you love me?" he asked, hoping for the right answer.

"Yes, I admit, I did!" she answered. "Last night just confirmed your feelings to me. You didn't have to say a word," she said softly with a smile.

"So quit!" he yelled. Now he had a smile on his face. "I came into some money that will keep us going for a while. How do you think I bought this boat, and the flats boat, too?"

Now she looked concerned. Crossing her arms, she looked down at the floor. "And just where did this money come from?" she asked, sounding as if she were questioning a drug runner or as if she suspected that he might have taken a bribe somewhere along the way in his career. Was the United States government after him? Had she fallen in love with what she was sworn to arrest? Her mind was swirling when he interrupted her.

"I hit the Lotto," he said quickly.

"That's funny, Callaway," she responded, shaking her head. "Now where did you really get the money?"

Callaway opened a cabinet next to the bed and pulled out an article from the *Tallahassee Tribune*.

The headline was about the winner of a large lottery jackpot in the Sunshine State. Carrie began reading the paper and stopped when she got to the name of the winner. "Holy shit!" she yelled as she jumped off the bed, losing the towel in the process.

Callaway was then treated to the sight of this tall, naked woman, jumping up and down in one place, while screaming at the top of her lungs. "Quiet, God damit!" he said. He jumped up to grab her and gave her a big, sloppy kiss. "I think we kept the neighbors awake enough last night with all the noise we made, so let's calm it down a little."

She looked at him like she was about to explode. "Callaway, you won the fucking Lotto. You're freaking rich!" she said.

Callaway gave her a big hug. "*We* are freaking rich." He looked at her all serious, again. "So, quit and we'll sail out of here, never to be heard from again," he said.

She sat down. The seriousness of the subject overcame her jubilation. "I'm so damn close to figuring out how Drake is moving the stuff off the Island, Mike," she replied. "I can't just walk away now. I've put in too much time in on this case to just leave it." She laid her head on his arm, feeling the warmth of his skin. "Besides, too many people have died trying to nail this slimy bastard. I can't just walk away. I mean we even faked me killing a guy so Drake would buy into me."

She explained how an informant had volunteered to be the "victim" after he allegedly ratted out a small-time drug dealer. Some bad guys connected with Carrie's last assignment witnessed the hit as Carrie gunned the man down in an alley. There was lots of noise from the blanks that she fired, and a lot of blood from a capsule that the victim had hidden in his shirt pocket. He slapped his chest after the shots, rupturing the capsule and causing the fake blood to pour all over his shirt. The DEA people knew that the witnesses were associates of Anton Drake, and that they would provide a great character reference for the crazed-lesbian-psycho-killer that Carrie was portraying.

"Well, maybe you can't walk away now, but you can't stay there forever, either," Callaway said, still very concerned. He motioned her toward the navigational chart that included Golgotha. "Eventually he's going to figure out that you're not who you claim to be, Carrie." Callaway knew that for safety reasons, there was usually an end date for an operation like this, whether it was successful or not. "Do you have a 'drop-dead' date for ending this deep-cover op?" he asked.

Carrie stared at the map, running an index finger around the outline of the island. "There is no end date for this op," she replied. "It's too damned important. It ends when I figure out how he's moving the stuff off the island. Or when I think things are getting too dangerous for me to stay there."

Callaway felt that Carrie was both adventurous and a little reckless sometimes. "You're going to stay till you figure it out, aren't you?" Callaway asked anxiously.

She just smiled at him, and answered, "I have an opportunity to shut down one of the biggest cocaine operations in the world, here. If I do, I also get to crush one nasty son-of-a-bitch named Drake. The man has killed a lot of people, Mike—federal agents and cops, too. He needs to go."

Callaway was relentless. "I understand the cause, and the need, baby, but I have a new concern now, and that's you," he said. "If you don't figure out his method, then someone else will." He was talking from his heart, now, not really thinking things through. She understood that, and she was feeling somewhat the same way. She thought, for a minute, about going up on deck, untying the mooring lines, and telling Callaway, "Let's go," without so much as notifying her superiors. It was a very short minute of thinking. "I've got to get back to Golgotha, before he suspects something," she said, as she began putting on her shirt.

The only way to get her to disengage from this operation was to find the answer to the question, Callaway thought. "Let me help," he said, picking up the chart.

Carrie looked at him with one of those "aw, gee" looks, meaning, *Thanks, but no*. "Mike, I can't let you get involved for two very good reasons," she said. "One is that you are no longer a federal cop, and two, I don't want you getting hurt, either."

Now it was his turn to smile. "You know in that bar last night, I told Drake that I didn't have to worry about losing my job anymore if I screwed with him. I thought about it some more, just after you made your exit last night, and I'm thinking about it again, right now. I can do whatever the hell I want with that guy, as long as I don't get caught. Hell, if I had a battleship, I could blow his island off the face of the ocean and probably get away with it."

Carrie shook her head. "You don't have a battleship, Mike," she said. "Although you can probably afford to buy one now with all of that money you won. All you have is this fat-assed shrimp boat, and your little ski-boat thing hanging on the back. What are you gonna do, sneak up on him in the middle of the night, and piss in his corn flakes?"

Clearly, he thought, Carrie didn't know very much about boats, and even less about fishing. "It's a flats boat," he interrupted.

She rolled her eyes. "Regardless!" she replied. "He has his own private army and navy."

Callaway thought for a second, and then countered with: "Yeah, but that 'ski-boat thing' you were talking about is as quiet as a mouse, so I can at least sneak around close in and watch him without being noticed. And if you get jammed up, you can call me, and I'll come and rescue you."

Looking concerned again, she asked, "And what will you do if one of his patrol boats shows up? Hold up a fishing rod and say 'Howdy'? You can't outrun a Midnight Express with that little thing. Besides that, cell phones don't work all the way out there."

Callaway raised his eyebrows, and answered, "You would be amazed at what my little boat can do. The engine isn't exactly stock. Besides, I can out-drive any of those idiots he has working for him."

"No! God dammit!" she said. "I don't want you involved in *my* operation! Go cruise around the Caribbean until I figure it out."

Callaway knew he was fighting a losing battle. He put the chart back down on the table. Conceding, he said, "At least we can talk about what you've learned so far. Maybe we can figure it out if we talk about it," he added, trying not to reveal his real motive. She began to calm down, letting out a deep breath and running her hand down his chest.

Callaway and Hidalgo knew more about the waters of the Bahamas than the Bahamian National Defense Force. Charts and information gathered from ships, aircraft, satellites, and their own exploration of the area gave them an excellent grasp of everything happening on and under the water—everything, that is, except how Drake was moving his drugs. However, both Carrie and Callaway also knew of the inter-agency rivalry that prevented the sharing of information between the DEA and Customs Service. The constant competition between agencies in an attempt to garner the most funding was actually hurting attempts to stem the flow of drugs into the United States. It quickly turned into a session of "You show me yours and I'll show you mine" about information that each agency had uncovered.

Carrie started with, "So what have the good men and women of the Customs Service learned about our Mr. Drake?"

"Well, we know he's a colossal jerk," Callaway answered. "That's a given. And we know he is moving large quantities of processed, high-quality coke into Florida, but we just can't figure out how he is getting it to the ships from his island. We've managed to intercept a few of the freighters and some of the boats coming in, but we have hardly put a scratch in his operation. His island is under a close watch by several agencies, but he keeps getting the stuff through. What have you found out?"

She leaned over the map, pointing to different sites on Drake's island as she answered, "Well I know the processing lab is somewhere by these hills, on the smaller island, but he won't let me anywhere near it. He lets me run on the beach near the building where they keep the tourist sub, but I haven't been able to get close to that, either. Drake likes keeping his people segregated. He doesn't want anyone knowing everything that he does. Some of the menial-task workers, who don't get close to any of the important stuff, leave the island when they finish what they're doing. It's weird, though. Some of the others just seem to disappear."

Callaway scratched the stubble on his face. "He won't let you near the sub?" he asked.

"Nope," she answered as she started lacing up her running shoes.

"That seems kinda strange, don't you think?" he asked, giving her a skeptical look. He playfully alternated between looking at the map and looking down the front of her shirt. "I mean, here he has you there for protection, so he must trust you a little, and yet he won't let you near his tourist business? I can understand keeping you away from the lab, but the sub makes no sense at all."

Now it was her to look skeptical. "The man doesn't trust anyone, even those who are paid to protect him," she replied. "The only one he trusts is his idiot son, Derrick."

Derrick Drake was twenty-two years old and one of the biggest spoiled brats in the Western Hemisphere. The boy had been thrown out of some of the finest private schools in the world because of his violent behavior. He was as much of a psychopath as his daddy, but the younger Drake took things a step further than his father in some instances. Where Anton had no concerns about taking a human life, Derrick liked to go beyond murder by torturing his victims first. He also had a bad habit of kidnapping and raping both women and men, who were always "guests" on their islands. Despite Daddy Anton's affinity for lesbians, as Carrie described it, he did not approve of his son's sexual conduct with men. Sonny boy's habit of raping women was permissible in the old man's book, but Daddy's considerable homophobia turned him off to Derrick's sexual exploits with men. Drake Jr. also had a mean cocaine habit and was not above sampling daddy's goods.

"That little bastard creeps me out whenever he's around," Carrie said while staring at the chart. "But he is his father's front man for the drugs and the general operation off the island, and we can't touch him because he has no criminal past..."

"That he has been arrested for," Callaway interrupted.

"Yeah, that he's been arrested for," Carrie answered. "Anton takes great pains to protect him. And he keeps me away from him, too. Usually he stays in his condo on South Beach to lessen the chance of him getting nailed if Anton gets busted. One of his men told me that Daddy Drake was afraid I would tear Derrick's arms off if he tried anything with me. This, of course is true," she said with a smile.

"We're missing something, here," Callaway groaned. "You must have seen this new sub going in and out to work, right? Is there anything odd about it?"

"No, it's just an updated model of the sub that got wrecked," she answered. "Only I heard one of the crew talking about how it had bigger batteries and much longer range." She drank a glass of water as she prepared to leave. "But I see the thing go out in the morning and come back in the late afternoon," she said. "It sits in that hangar he built, charging its batteries all night. It doesn't go anywhere after dark."

Callaway looked at his surveillance photos, but he didn't see a hangar, only the old submarine parked next to a concrete pier.

"What hangar are you talking about?" he asked as he poured over the pictures and handed them to her.

She looked at the photos and asked when they were taken. When Callaway told her that these were the first batch obtained after Drake moved to the island, she shook her head and laughed. "These were taken when Drake still had the old sub," she replied. "Callaway, I thought you had up-to-date stuff here. What's up with you Customs guys?" she chided. "When the old sub sank, Drake immediately ordered up a new one. I mean, it was real immediate. I heard a couple of his men joking around like he knew ahead of time that the accident was going to occur. And I know he's a psycho and all, and he could care less about the tourists who died, but I really expected him to be pissed off about losing a very expensive piece of equipment. Strangely, he didn't seem upset at all. Anyway, he had people in right away to start building the house for his new submarine. I can't say much about the construction, because he kept everyone except Derrick and the workers away from the pier until it was done. Hmm...Come to think of it, I never saw those workers again, either. He kept the pier out of sight by parking that sea-going dredge of his between it and the residences. Oh, and the two guys that made that comment about the new sub went missing a day later, too."

Callaway looked at a photo of the dredge. It was a huge, self-propelled, sea-going monster. It was the kind of machine that companies used to mine the ocean bottom for minerals or to pump sand from the bottom to replenish an eroded beach. Growing up in the Florida Keys, he had seen this type of machine replacing huge sections of beach that had been washed away by hurricanes. "So what does he do with the dredge?" he inquired.

"He told me that he uses it to keep the channel to his island clear so the submarine doesn't bottom out when they tow it out to work," she answered. "He said that the sub draws a lot of water, and the tide change fills the channel with sand."

Callaway raised his eyebrows and looked at her. "Seems like a bit of overkill," he replied. "Hell, the Navy uses machines like that to clear the path for missile subs that draw ten times more water than that little thing does. They have broken up undersea mountains with the cutters on that kind of dredge, so our subs don't scrape anything expensive going in and out of their bases."

She grabbed a banana from the kitchen counter. "Umf, I need the potassium for my run back to the dock where the boat will pick me up and take me back to Golgotha," she said as she wolfed down the fruit. She noticed the dreamy and excited look on her lover's face as he intently watched her eat the banana.

"Damn, Callaway, did you ever get out of high school?" she asked, laughing. "Oh hell, I guess that's one of the things I love about you." Carrie gave him a hug and a long kiss goodbye before starting for the door. She turned to him as she reached for the handle with a stern look on her face. "Look, I feel like I'm almost ready to break this guy," she said. "Don't fuck things up for me, okay.

He had that lost puppy look on his face, again.

"All right!" she said. "I promise that if things get too hot, I'll get out. I don't want to lose you again, Mike. So, go fishing, or bar hopping, or work on your tan or something. I'll be in touch." With that, she looked around the area to make sure she was not being watched, and ran down the dock. She disappeared down the street, running like a track star.

Callaway stared at the chart one more time when something clicked in his brain. "Maybe I will go 'fishing,' tonight," he muttered, as he climbed back into bed and pulled the covers over his face.

Chapter 12

Callaway was not a believer in chance or luck or any other such folklore. He did believe, however, in second chances. He knew that once in a while you got one, and when you did, you had better not mess it up. Third chances just never happened. Until he hit that big Lotto jackpot, he was constantly reminded of his ex-wife and the not so pleasant *ride* she took him for. He usually recalled the experience every time he opened his wallet and saw nothing but air. Even though the money he paid his ex seemed astronomical when compared to his meager U.S. Customs pay, it was covered by less than one-tenth of one percent of his first year's lottery winnings. And he would receive those Lotto payments over the next twenty years. In that respect, second chance number one was good. The second of the two chances troubled him, though. He knew that he was totally in love with Carrie and had been that way since he met her at FLETEC. He was sure that she was in love with him, too.

The problem was that she was so deeply immersed in her cover and her job that she could not let go. Maybe it was all of the emotional stuff she had floating around in her head after what had happened to her father and her fiancé. Gone was the fun-loving nursing student, forever. She had excelled at her job as a special agent. It seemed that her personality, the one that had taken over after the murders, allowed her to become detached from everyday life, making her an excellent undercover operative. She worked everywhere from the mean streets of Baltimore to the jungles of Colombia. Her only flaw was her damaged psyche that kept her from getting close to anyone. That was until she met Michael Callaway. There was something about him that let her relax. She told him the story one night when they were laying in bed in a hotel a couple of miles away from FLETEC, about a week after they met. Callaway felt bad for her loss, and he could see that it had put a real dent in her emotions. He felt pretty special, though, and got a hint of where he stood with her when she told him that she had never spoken of the incident to anyone on the job, other than her supervisor back in Baltimore. On the night she left to go back to work, she left a note that startled him with a revelation he would never forget. "I want you to know two things, Callaway: One is that I think I've fallen for you, the other is that we will probably never see each other again. Goodbye."

He was impressed at how she'd handled the situations she'd encountered during her career, since anyone who wasn't as mentally and physically strong as she was would probably have died on any of the operations she'd been involved in. She was tough, and at this moment, she was all that Michael Callaway could think about.

Just to distract himself from this obsession, he began preparing for a long, peaceful night of "fishing." He gassed up the Hewes at the local Bahamian marina and filled his portable back-up tank, too. That tank held ten gallons of fuel, and he kept it stored in an area under the seat just in case he had to run far to find fish, or run from Drake's cutthroats tonight. The spare gas tank was what all the old guides in the Keys carried for insurance, as he'd learned from the best in his younger days. He checked the three 12-volt batteries the little boat carried, and all were charged to the maximum. One battery started the boat; and the other two, which were deep-cycle, rechargeable batteries; were used to power the bow-mounted Motorguide electric trolling motor. The almost silent electric motor was perfect for sneaking up on a tarpon when they were rolling near the surface. Tonight, however, it would be good for sneaking up on the local drug kingpin on his private island. Callaway made a routine check of the many storage compartments located in the bow and stern of the flats skiff. Next, he checked through his usual complement of goodies that he always carried with him at sea. Up front were life vests and two anchors. He always carried two, to stick the boat from two different directions in rough weather or a strong current.

Thanks again to the old guides back home, he thought. The trick had kept him and his clients out and fishing, providing their stomachs could take it, on windy days when there were no other boats around. He checked the console compartment and found his first aid kit, an army surplus kit in a waterproof case, containing the usual bandages and gauze and an emergency blanket made out of thick aluminum foil. To this he added a pair of razor sharp snips, capable of cutting the barb off a fish hook should it get imbedded in someone's finger. He put the kit back into the compartment next to a K-Bar Marine Corps fighting knife. On top of that he placed an additional item: A Glock Model 22 pistol in .40 Smith & Wesson caliber. Callaway had worked the pistol over slightly to make it more efficient. He'd changed the trigger bar and spring to give the weapon a crisp four-pound trigger pull. He also installed night-sights containing tritium dots that glow in the dark. A Remington 12-gage pump shotgun took its place in the rear compartment. Callaway never liked to be under-gunned when he was a cop.

Why change now, he thought.

Since he was going fishing, he thought he should bring the right equipment with him. He remembered that the Customs Service had frowned upon him fishing on the job and was delighted by the fact that no such problem would exist on this trip. He retrieved four fishing rods from the *Orinoco Flow*. Three were fairly light with line weights from eight to twenty pound-test. The forth rod was equipped with a large, 6-0 Penn deep-sea open reel with fifty pound-test fishing line. This rig was meant for horsing big grouper out of their holes or tangling with a big shark. The reel was on a short rod and equipped with a long forward grip so he could fight a fish while standing up. The Hewes was a little boat with no room for a fighting chair, making it necessary to fight a big, powerful fish while on your feet. Callaway made another trip to the shrimper and returned with his large, new, well-equipped tackle box and a Penn electric down-rigger. This device was a portable electric-powered crane that fishermen would use to lower bait straight down to a pre-set depth. The down-rigger had five-hundred feet of light steel cable on its large reel. It had a counter that could be set to deploy just enough cable to take the bait to the prescribed depth. The bait and fishing line would then be attached to a release clip. A twenty pound steel ball dangled at the end of the cable.

He also packed a couple of items for another kind of fishing, including a pair of large binoculars adjustable up to sixty power that he stowed in the dry storage compartment. A second item was an old, first-generation night-vision scope that somehow found its way into the trunk of Callaway's car before Customs could sell it as surplus. The device was one that was handed down to federal law enforcement in the 1980's when the military got new and better stuff. It was standard operating procedure for the federal cops, and the Coast Guard, to get all of the old crap that the soldiers got tired of, all to save money. The Generation One scope was large and cumbersome; it presented a very grainy and ugly green view of the darkened world. The up-side of this was that it still worked and it was free. It also was totally waterproof, which was very handy in Callaway's line of work. He brought these toys, along with a

35-mm Nikon camera, to catch a very valuable fish named Drake.

It was a beautiful, starry night with almost no wind when Callaway swung the bow of the Hewes away from the dock toward the open channel leading to the Bahamian Sea. He figured if the wind stayed down and the seas stayed smooth, he could make it to Drake's island, check things out, and be back before daybreak. As he cruised along, watching his GPS and the ocean, Callaway couldn't help but think about Carrie, stuck on that Island with a madman and his gang. His thoughts kept wandering to something else though—the submarine. How else could Drake move his drugs to the shipping lanes without anyone noticing?

It just makes sense, but it doesn't make sense, he thought.

Maybe the new sub was some kind of tricked-out super sub. But Carrie had said the new one was just an updated version of the old one—slow, with short range, and not meant to travel long distances in a short time. He remembered reading about the sinking of Drake's first sub and thinking that tragedy had something to do with Drake's current success. He wished he could talk to someone who was out there that day. Maybe then he could put two and two together. Callaway scanned the horizon and thought his luck was holding, as all he could see were clear skies ahead. Little did he know that before the night was over, both the weather and his luck would change drastically.

Chapter 13

The Franco family was thoroughly enjoying their first trip to the Bahamas on that late June day in 1989. Steve Franco's house remodeling business had flourished in the last year. He'd spent the last twelve months hiring more carpenters and painters, buying trucks and equipment, and driving, endlessly it seemed, from job site to job site, making sure that every house was given the same quality work that he was known for when he was doing the job alone. The area that he served was in Rockland County, New York, about twenty miles from New York City. Discovered by the "yuppie" generation of the early 1980's, the county blossomed with many new suburban housing developments. Just as important for him, however, were the many old houses in desperate need of repair or remodeling. This new generation of young, upwardly-mobile type workers would live in this area up state and commute by car and rail into the city to work. The developers of new homes needed guys like Steve Franco. He was fast, reliable, and did a beautiful job of wood finishing and painting the future residences of the young and soon-to-be wealthy. Steve had promised his wife and two children that as soon as the kids finished school he would take them on a vacation like none they had ever been on before. Steve was a man of his word to his family, just as he was with his clients.

His wife, Bonnie and his children, Nick and Carol, were worn out from the past year. Nick had finished fifth grade and was thinking of nothing but middle school. It was a big jump to a big school in a different neighborhood. He worked hard to finish his honors-level classes and did quite well. Carol was unhappy about finishing third grade, knowing she would not see most of her school friends for three months. She was very shy around most people, but that had gone away when third grade began. She did extremely well in school as far as grades went, but had a small problem keeping quiet in class. She and some of the other girls were constantly talking to each other and getting into trouble with their teacher.

Steve Franco surprised his family by coming home with airline tickets to Nassau in the Bahamas. He'd discussed vacation plans with Bonnie, but wasn't specific about where they would go or where they would stay. He waited until the kids stopped jumping up and down about the plane tickets when he laid the brochure for Atlantis resort on the table in front of them. Now they became quiet as they looked at all of the glossy pictures of the activities at the resort. Bonnie Franco started to cry. For the first time since their honeymoon, she and her husband, and now their kids, would take a real vacation. They kept looking at all the tours available from or near the resort. Steve pulled another six tour brochures out of his coat pocket and gave them to the kids. They looked, and looked, but then stopped cold at one brochure. It was the one with the picture of a shiny white submarine on the cover.

Submarine tour vessels had been operating in the Caribbean area for many years. The vessels were built in Europe and sold all over the world. Their production and sale was not heavily monitored by any government agency as the vessels were not considered usable as any type of military vehicle or weapon of war. The subs were essentially tour buses that could submerge to a maximum safe depth of about two hundred feet. Diving past that depth put the vessel dangerously close to its crush depth, thought to be around three-hundred feet. At that depth the hull would be unable to withstand the pressure of tons of sea water and would burst. The hull itself was designed just like that of a military submarine hull. The pressure hull was nothing more than a thick skinned, hollow tube with closed ends. It was covered with an outer hull, shaped to look like what most people believed a submarine should look like. It was broad at the front, with an exaggerated conning tower in the center of the vessel. The conning tower stood fifteen feet above the deck and made the vessel look more like a submarine; it also made the sub more visible to other boat traffic while it was on the surface. There were safety devices aboard for the passengers and crew, such as flotation vests, and small bottles of oxygen, in the event that the vessel had an emergency. The sub was linked to the surface by a two-way radio that allowed the pilot to speak to the towboat floating above. The towboat was necessary to tow the sub from wherever it was based to the diving area, as the batteries that powered the vessel's electric motors were very small and didn't provide much cruising range. The submarine in this brochure in service near Nassau was operated by *Subdives Tours*, a company wholly owned by Mr. Anton Drake. He'd built a dock with a powerful charging station near his house on one of his two private islands between Nassau and Eleuthera, so the sub could receive its electrical fueling. However, even with a good, overnight charge, the submarine could make only five dives a day and still have sufficient power for the drive motor and air conditioner, mandatory in the warm Bahamian waters, and all the other powered devices on board. A larger battery system could give the sub more range, but that would take up valuable paying-passenger space.

The Franco family arrived at the submarine dock at four o'clock in the afternoon, as they were scheduled for the second-to-last dive of the day, set for four-thirty. They were a little confused when they didn't see the brochure's gleaming white submarine tied to the dock. Instead, they found an old, beat up, fishing boat. Steve Franco spotted one of the men wearing a *Subdives Tours, Submarine 1* shirt and flagged him down.

"Hey pal, uh, where's the submarine?" he asked. "We have tickets for four-thirty."

The man appeared very nervous and gave Steve a strange look.

"This boat will take you out to the sub, *mon*," he answered. He explained how the old boat would take their twenty-two person group for the four-thirty tour, along with the group for the dive at five o'clock out to the submarine.

The Francos were a little green from the typical Bahamian cab ride they'd experienced getting to the dock. They hadn't realized that a ride in a Bahamian taxi was kind of like being slammed around inside a very fast clothes dryer. It was hot as hell inside the taxi, and they were bounced around quite a bit. Bonnie Franco was quick to pull a bottle of motion sickness pills out of the brand new straw purse she'd had purchased at the Straw Market on Bay Street. She broke one pill in half giving both children a piece, and she and her husband each took one pill, as well. She knew the pills took a half hour to have any effect, but she figured it would be better to be safe than sick while on the submarine.

"If the cab ride was that bad, I bet the damned submarine will be murder," she said as she put on her sunglasses. She didn't realize how prophetic that statement would be.

One of the crew members from the fishing boat that would ferry passengers to the sub was working feverishly on the old boat's inboard engine. In the stifling heat below deck, Willard Cameron was pushing things to the limit. Born in the hot and nasty environment of Kingston, Jamaica, he was a pretty tough man. He also had a criminal history a mile long, having spent many long years in some of Jamaica's worst prisons for robbery and gun running.

The temperature outside was hovering at ninety-eight degrees, with the humidity at one hundred percent. That would feel cool to him at the moment, as the place where he toiled was like hell on earth. The sweat poured out of him as he worked, cursing the old Cummins diesel. To make matters worse, he had to keep starting and stopping the engine in order to find and fix the many problems plaguing the power plant. One problem that he was not aware of was that the boat's exhaust system was perforated in many places due to salt water corrosion. He was running the motor for a long time, trying to get it right, when he began to feel lightheaded. He shut the motor off, realizing that he must have been breathing carbon monoxide for quite some time. He figured that the compartment would ventilate out the poisonous gas since the deck hatch was partially open.

He was wrong.

He was bolting down a chrome plate on a service door after re-starting the engine, when he noticed his reflection mirrored in the shiny metal. He was struck by the fact that his lips were bright cherry red. He knew, from working as a boat mechanic for many years that the color of his lips indicated he was suffering carbon monoxide poisoning. He also knew he'd be in deep trouble if he did not get to some fresh air immediately. He'd started up the ladder when the whole engine room began to spin. He tried to yell, but nothing came out. He fell, gasping, to the floor, bumping into a rolling tool chest that was always kept below deck, and felt the crushing weight as the large metal box fell on top of him. He lay there trying to breathe and not die, but he realized he was fighting a losing battle. He suddenly began assessing his life. He had no family and very few friends. He had a kind of epiphany, of sorts, that he had lived a very bad and wasted life, filled with nothing but crime and violence. He believed it was too late to fix his past wrongs or do anything else except die. For the first time in many, many years, Willard Cameron began to pray.

The captain of the boat was on the dock explaining to the passengers that a mechanical problem would delay their ride out to the submarine for a short time. He explained that his best mechanic was working to fix the engine, and that they would be leaving very soon. He told all of his waiting customers, in a rather stern voice, to get aboard the boat. The man was sweating profusely, not from the Bahamian heat, but from the knowledge of the timetable he was on. The crew had always worried about keeping to the *Subdives Tours* brochure schedule. Today, however, the captain suffered a different sort of stress. He knew of Anton Drake's insidious plan to modify his submarine for more lucrative and illegal work. His plan was to "sink" his tour sub, but reserve it for other uses. Drake had spent long hours researching how to make his slow, short-ranged, and underpowered underwater bus into a sleek, speedy shark of the sea. His modifications would give the small sub the ability to haul hundreds of pounds of cocaine to the shipping lanes far from his islands.

Drake knew that if he simply bought another submarine and modified that second, new one, the U.S. federal cops and Bahamian police would be all over him. He needed to be able to buy a replacement submarine for the one that was about to be "destroyed," with the rest of the world believing that he was buying a new sub just to keep his struggling tourist business going. Everyone would "know" that the new sub was just as tourist-slow and short-range as the one that "sank." Drake knew that no one, not even Callaway, could suspect him of sneaking a sub that "no longer existed" back to his island for modifications.

The Francos, along with thirty-eight other passengers booked for both the 4:30 and 5:00 sub tours, were ushered aboard the fishing boat at four o'clock for the ten-minute ride out to the submarine. The captain was feeling better about being on schedule, as he could hear the diesel engine running smoothly. He looked around for Willard Cameron, his mechanic, but the man was nowhere to be found. He figured that he must have gone someplace to cool down after working in that hellhole of an engine room for so long. As a crewman was untying the lines, little Carol Franco sat on the edge of the partially opened hatch leading to the engine room. Being a typical, curious child, she slid the hatch over a bit with her feet and peered down into the engine room. She saw machinery of all types, a spilled toolbox and...feet! Two human feet were sticking out from under the large toolbox. She was wondering if it was a real person, when suddenly one of the feet moved.

"Daddy, somebody's hurt," she said quietly, pointing down into the engine room.

Steve Franco looked down the hatch, his eyes widening. He yelled to the captain. "Hey, you got a man down, here!" He threw the hatch open and flew down the ladder. Franco could smell the engine exhaust fumes in the compartment. He knew all about what fumes could do to a person from the painting part of his business, and he knew the only way to help someone who had been overcome was to quickly get them to fresh air. He pushed the toolbox off Willard Cameron and began dragging him up the ladder. A crewman assisted him in pulling Cameron up on deck. The captain hurriedly ran everyone else off the boat, and yelled for another crewman to bring an oxygen bottle from the front cabin. The crewmen placed the mask on Cameron's face and opened the valve, allowing the life giving O2 to flow into the stricken man's lungs. In a minute, Cameron began to cough and roll around. A crewman helped him walk the gangplank and sat him down on a bench near the dock. As he regained consciousness, he vomited relentlessly. He coughed and shouted in a raspy Jamaican accent. "'Oo found me?" He knew full well that someone had saved his life this day.

"It was the kid, *mon*," yelled one of the other crewmen, pointing at Carol Franco. Cameron looked at her and smiled, still too woozy to get to his feet. Meanwhile, the captain was eager to get the boat loaded and the victims out to the sub. "Everyone for the four-thirty and five o'clock tours must get on board, now!" he yelled. The stress of staying on schedule was getting the better of him.

The Francos began walking toward the boat when strong hands grabbed both Steve and his daughter's arms.

"*Mon*, you don't want to go on this trip," a now standing Willard Cameron wheezed at Steve and his little girl. "Just walk away and go back to your 'otel. Don't go out on that ting today." He looked deep into Steve Franco's eyes. The Jamaican man was crying and standing between Steve's daughter and the boat.

"What's the problem?" Steve asked, thinking the poison's after effects were causing the man to act this way. Cameron knew if he told them that the submarine ride was a death trap, they would go to the police. If that occurred, they would never make it off the island alive, courtesy of Mr. Drake. "It is the fishing boat," he answered. "It is unsafe. You saw what happen to me, mon. I am afraid the boat will blow up." Cameron pointed at the row of taxis waiting at the curb for fares. He pulled forty dollars out of his pocket and tried to give it to Steve. "Please *mon*, go back to your 'otel, now!" the Jamaican shouted. He was overheard by the captain, who yelled at him.

"Cameron, leave those people be," he said, smiling. "Everything is good, sir, come on aboard!"

Steve looked at Cameron's face and got a chill down in his spine. He knew something was very wrong. "Ahh, you know what, Captain, my wife is feeling a little sick," he said as he winked at Bonnie. Both children began moaning about missing the submarine ride, and Steve gave them his forceful father look to shut them up. Growing up in a very Italian family, the kids immediately knew it was time to cease and desist from any further protests about missing the trip. Steve waved at the captain and shouted, "Maybe we'll give it a try tomorrow." As he herded his family to a taxi, Cameron smiled at him. "Get away from this place and don't say nothing to no one, *mon*!"

As they were driving away, Steve looked back and saw Willard Cameron watching him. The man gave a slight wave and began walking toward the boat. The captain was glaring down at him from the bridge.

Steve Franco never realized the two things that Willard Cameron had done that day. He had saved Franco and his family from certain death, and, at the same time, he had assured his own.

Chapter 14

Speeding along on the glassy sea, Callaway recalled the headlines about the sinking. The news reporters flocked to Nassau from all over the world to report the story—how the "mishap" took the lives of twenty-two passengers, along with the captain and crew of the submarine, due to suspected mechanical problems.

No one had figured out what really happened.

Drake's thugs had pulled off a perfect crime, exactly as their boss planned it. After submerging with the twenty-two tourists for the four-thirty tour, the crew of the "stricken" sub donned oxygen masks and then pumped the interior of the sub full of poisonous gas, killing all men, women and children on board. At the same time, divers working for Drake detonated explosives attached to a sixty-foot-long propane tank that had been secured to a ledge along the Bahamas Wall, a ditch in the ocean floor five thousand feet deep. By rupturing the air-filled tank, they sent a huge bubble of air to the surface, simulating the result of a submarine descending past crush-depth, imploding the sub hull and then exploding the sub's engine. The bodies of five of the dead passengers that the crew had clad in life preservers were released, along with pieces of Styrofoam and wood from the sub's interior and airlock. The bodies floated to the surface and were recovered within minutes of the first accident report. The Bahamian Defense Force sealed the area just as Drake had known they would. It was impossible for them to do much of anything else since the Bahamian government had no Navy, other than a couple of patrol craft, and certainly no submarines. The depth of the water precluded investigation of the wreck even by the deepest diving subs of the United States, British or any other countries' navies at that time. The shattered remains of the propane tank, painted white to match the submarine, would sink to the bottom of the trench, later to be photographed by a deep-diving remote controlled submersible vehicle.

The information that the reporters received from the impromptu witnesses, the people scheduled for the tour at five o'clock in the afternoon, was icing on the cake to confirm that an accident had occurred. People on that tour appeared on television news around the world that evening. They were seen crying and being introspective about how close they'd come to dying. There were plenty of "it could have been me" comments. They parroted on cue how they heard the captain of the ferry receive a radio distress call from the captain of the submarine, conveniently broadcast on the boat's loud speaker so the passengers on the ferry could hear him. The captain of the submarine had, in fact, audio taped the message one week prior to the accident. They could hear the fear in the man's voice, which was totally manufactured, as he screamed that the submarine had lost power and was unable to hold neutral buoyancy or ascend to the surface. He then began screaming about the vessel sinking. Then his voice faded out, and the ferry captain advised one of his crewmen, loud enough for some of the passengers to hear, that they must have sunk below the range of the radio.

The passengers told the news people how the ferry captain advised the worried passengers on board about a possible mechanical error aboard the sub, and that they were working to fix it. With almost perfect timing, the large bubble of air, generated by the exploding propane tank, now deep beneath the sea, erupted through the surface, with a loud, angry roar. The passengers on the ferry told of how they saw the churning water, along with materials like wood and Styrofoam floating on the surface. One person, thoroughly convinced by the Oscar-worthy performance, spoke of the captain yelling, "Oh dear God!" as he grabbed the microphone on the boat's radio and began broadcasting a *Mayday* call for help. Drake knew that United States Coast Guard vessels in the area, as well as their base all the way in Miami, would hear the call, courtesy of the extremely powerful radio installed on the ferryboat by order of Anton Drake during the previous week. It was all perfectly orchestrated to look like a tragedy, and it worked.

The news people showed videos of the victims' family members weeping, and, a couple of days later, throwing wreaths and bundled flowers into the water where the submarine had sunk. Drake even managed to engineer the perfect ending for the tragic story when the mechanic who'd worked on the generator believed to have failed and caused the accident, a Jamaican man named Willard Cameron, was later found dead of an apparent suicide. Bahamian authorities advised reporters that Mr. Cameron, feeling distraught over the death of twenty-four people he'd caused, took his own life as a result. It would take some serious investigation to figure the mystery out. And the sleuth would have to break some rules to do it.

* * *

Callaway cruised at forty-five miles per hour. It was a cool night for the Bahamas, especially since there was no breeze. He could tell it was getting near low tide from the scent of decaying coral and vegetation as he zoomed through the islands heading toward Golgotha. He watched his newest technological toy mounted on the dash of the flats boat, a Magellan GPS unit. It was impressive new technology when introduced to the general public. It was also expensive technology that Michael Callaway couldn't even think of buying until the fateful day when he hit the lottery.

Now, Callaway saw the expensive GPS technology as a necessity. But he still caught himself working to rationalize expensive purchases, even though money was certainly no longer a problem. He'd justified the purchase of the *Orinoco Flow* by telling himself that he needed a place to live. He also told himself that it was much more sensible to buy a residence that would allow him to move about in the element where he

127

felt the most comfortable, the sea. He'd told himself he needed the Hewes flats boat for the guided fishing trips he planned to conduct all over Florida and the Bahamas. So the high-tech GPS unit was easily justifiable, too, as it allowed him to dial in and record hotspots where the fish were plentiful. Aside from that, he already knew how to operate the unit, since he had been using an identical device on *Blue Thunder* for the past year.

He watched the triangle on the screen representing his small boat zipping along in the channels between islands both large and small. Callaway marveled at the drastic depth changes shown on the small sonar screen, everything from the flat sandy plains to the high, jagged Bahamian reefs. Having studied the charts prior to leaving the dock, as any good fishing guide would, Callaway knew that he would pass over trenches formed by underwater volcanic eruptions, the same volcanic activity creating the area's hundreds of small islands millions of years ago. These trenches were deep, like the one that had swallowed Drake's original *Subdives* submarine in 1989. The deepest of these was estimated to be five-plus miles deep. Callaway rounded one of the small, unoccupied islands just outside Drake's sphere of influence and brought the outboard down to idle speed. The noise of the engine and the phosphorescence of his wake would make his presence known to Drake's outlaws if he wasn't careful. After idling in for another mile, he shut down the outboard and stepped up onto the front deck. Callaway listened in the dark silence for the sound of one of Drake's big-engine patrol boats. He heard nothing. The one advantage he had was the ability to hear the bad guys coming.

He flipped the Motorguide "Great White" electric trolling motor down on its bow mount, allowing the motor and propeller to quietly sink just below the water. The control unit, connected to two 12-volt deep-cycle batteries linked in tandem, sat on top of the electric motor. Callaway gave the tiller control handle a turn to the right, and the little electric motor began pulling the boat along at four miles per hour in almost total silence. If he could keep from being seen, he would be able to scout the island for hours. If he was discovered, he would need to pull the trolling motor up and clear out of the area, pronto. Callaway pulled a pair of huge binoculars from a case under the boat's center console. The powerful binoculars were not pretty, having served through many nights of surveillance aboard *Blue Thunder*. However, while the lenses were never that great to begin with, he could see a hell of a long way through them.

He scanned the shoreline of Drake's island, which he had done many times in the past, but usually from much farther away. Most of the time in the past, he was way out beyond the six-mile limit imposed by Mr. Drake. Now, scanning the shore from less than a quarter of a mile out, he saw some very interesting things. While still on the job, he had seen photos taken by Customs Service aircraft, and even the top-secret pictures taken by NSA satellites at the behest of the DEA. Despite the stiff competition between U.S. Customs and the Drug Enforcement Administration, and the fact that he was not supposed to see those photos, Callaway had used the law enforcement brotherhood to break down many walls. All of those pictures gave him an idea of where everything was on the island known as Golgotha, but now he was seeing it up close and personal, and in living color. He even had sound now, since Mike had drifted close enough to hear the voices of Drake's guards on the beach. Even though he could make out only a few of their words, he theorized that he'd hear it if they started shouting the alarm, allowing him time to run before Drake's private navy caught up with him. He studied the buildings along the leeward shore. Callaway saw four guards patrolling the beach, each armed with what appeared to be AK-47 rifles slung from their shoulders. *The guards must take shifts*, he thought.

Mike knew that the DEA had estimated Drake's armed work force at about forty-five men, and of course, one woman. He wondered if Carrie was on the island, and if so, what she was doing. He fought a sudden urge to sneak ashore, kill Drake, and take her from this evil place—as if it could be that simple. Just then he heard a familiar, British-accented voice, to which one of the guards clearly and loudly responded with, "Yes, Senior Drake." Mike swung his binoculars in time to see Anton Drake standing on the dock by the submarine hangar. The man he spoke with had a heavy Spanish accent that made him hard to understand. This had to be Drake's number one hit man, Martino Herrera. Herrera was a former high-ranking officer in the Cuban Intelligence Directorate, also known as the DGI, and a personal friend of Cuban President Fidel Castro. Formed in 1961, two years after Fidel's *revolución*, the agency's original mission had been to export Cuban-style communism to nearby areas in the Caribbean, as well as Central and South America. Closely tied to and trained by the Soviet KGB, their mission changed in the 1970's to foreign intelligence collection.

Herrera had personally engineered and taken part in several penetrations of Cuban exile, anti-Castro groups in Miami by DGI intelligence agents. Drake "bought" Herrera, a smart and ruthless killer, from Fidel for a nice, two-million-dollar honorarium. This purchased Herrera's services as liaison between the Cuban government and Drake's drug smuggling operation. Given that about eighty percent of the raw cocaine Drake received was funneled through Cuba with the full knowledge of that country's government, anyway, this seemed a small price to pay for this shipping arrangement.

Callaway watched the two men through his binoculars and wondered what they were talking about. He also thought about that big, sniper rifle sitting in his hidden gun cabinet aboard the *Orinoco Flow*, and how he could probably kill both men with it, even from his slightly rocking flats boat. He could see that the submarine hangar was a large concrete house that looked like it grew right out of the water. Through the large open door leading to the channel, Mike could plainly see the replacement *Subdives Submarine II* docked in the hangar building. He wondered why Drake kept the name *Subdives Submarine,* changing only the number painted on the conning tower to differentiate it from the ill-fated sunken sub lying in the trench. *That can't be good for business,* Callaway thought. It occurred to him now to wonder why Drake didn't seem to care at all how bad the tourist business was aboard this sub.

The two men on shore spoke for a while longer and then Drake walked back up the path to his residence. As he slowly cruised along, Callaway switched his attention to the video screen of a second sonar chart recorder mounted on the front deck of the flats boat. This recorder worked off the same stern-mounted transducer sending sonar beams down through the water to a depth of six hundred feet. He noted the bottom was very irregular in this part of the ocean, seeing the hills, valleys, and various coral formations of the area's topography. Every so often, though, he would run across a spot that appeared completely flat and smooth, and strangely enough, seemed to run in almost a straight line with only a few gentle curves along its path. Callaway was perplexed by what resembled a man-made expressway on the ocean floor.

The water was not very deep here, so he decided to take a chance on being discovered while he dove down to take a look at this curiously flat area. Knowing that any source of light above the water would draw immediate fire, he decided to light the bottom from under water. He pulled his trusty flashlight from under the console, the same Mag-Light that had accompanied him on hundreds of patrols as a law enforcement officer. It was the same light-source that had illuminated everything for him from several naked, drunken college coeds skinny dipping on Cape Sable beach to the flying firefight resulting in the death of the "fallen angel" cop-turned- drug-smuggler. Callaway stripped off his shirt and, after donning his dive mask and weight belt, grabbed a *Spare-Air* tank from the Hewes below-deck storage area. The tank was a one-foot long miniature aqualung with a regulator and mouthpiece attached to the top. He hoped the forty or so breaths of air in the little tank would allow him to get close enough to see if the curious paths might have any connection with Drake's drug smuggling. Callaway suddenly realized that he was excited to be back in the saddle, out snooping and investigating like a cop again. The rush felt great. He normally wasn't prone to using much air when he dove, but he knew tonight would be different. He slipped quietly into the water to avoid attracting attention with a loud splash on such a quiet night. The water was cold but clear, as there hadn't been any wind lately to stir things up. Callaway swam straight down to the smooth spot evident on the chart recorder. At about fifty feet down, Callaway pulled the Mag-Light from his belt, switched it on, and, pointing the light downward, he estimated that the bottom was about seventy-five feet down. He carefully kept the light pointed downward so Drake's goons wouldn't see it and listened carefully for the sound of boat

133

engines or propellers that might signify his discovery. Callaway stared down the narrow beam of light. He could make out corral formations and large rocks, many of which had obviously been destroyed by Drake's giant dredge. Then he saw the smooth area. It was in an almost perfectly straight line. The colors on either side were muted by the darkness surrounding the artificial light that he shined down; otherwise, the area looked the same as its surroundings. *Why are the fish only swimming over the coral on either side of the flat area?* he wondered.

Callaway couldn't make sense of this, as some of the coral in this area was fifty feet tall and all of it should have been teaming with fish. He wanted to dive down to look at the smooth area, but the small capacity of his tank prevented him from descending any deeper. He slowly rose to the surface, watching the smooth area on the bottom during his ascent. He had to know what was happening on the bottom of the ocean.

When he reached the surface, Callaway did a quick three-hundred sixty degree scan to assure he was still alone. He swam to the Hewes and pulled himself up on one side of the low-slung boat. Noiselessly, he placed his tank, flashlight, and weight belt on the cushioned seat behind the center console. Mike pulled himself around to the stern of the boat, braced his right foot on the engine, grabbed the poling platform's aluminum tubing, and hoisted himself onboard. His mind was deep in thought over the odd sea floor. *What the heck is going on down there?* he continued to wonder.

He absently watched the activity on shore. It was getting late, and the sun would be up in an hour. He shivered, chilled by the breeze beginning to blow from the west. *Probably a thunderstorm coming*, he guessed.

He pulled on a rain jacked stashed under the seat. Then he walked to the bow and started up the trolling motor. It would take a while for him to get far enough off shore to use the outboard without raising suspicions on shore, especially with the wind beginning to kick up some wave chop. He would be sailing right into it. In situations like this, it *always* seemed that the waves were running against him. He couldn't stop thinking about the smooth area on the sea bottom. He glanced at the chart recorder screen once again. There were all kinds of coral formations as usual, but then there it was still—a smooth area amidst the coral formations and rocks. He attempted to follow what appeared to be its trail. The trolling motor was having a difficult time coping with the increasing size of the waves as the wind picked up. It was getting harder to steer a straight course given the conditions. Despite this, Callaway kept watching the chart recorder. The machine was having its own difficulties maintaining a signal lock on the bottom, as the waves kicked up sand obscuring the electronic view. He kept crossing over the smooth area, even though an hour had passed, and he was now five miles away from Drake's island.

Noting that the weather and sea conditions were getting worse, Callaway decided that he was far enough off shore to crank up the Yamaha and head for the dock. He started the outboard and began the long run home. He knew the bumpy ride would be hard on his back. The Hewes was a great little boat to float across ten inches of water while poling after a bonefish, but she was hell on your spine when traversing large stretches of bumpy water. Callaway thought about Carrie again, and decided that every moment counted in getting her away from the danger that she had so willingly placed herself in. For now, he would go back to the *Orinoco Flow* and get some sleep. He glanced back at Drake's island one more time.

I will figure you out, Mr. Drake, he thought. *See you tomorrow night, jerk.* He planned his return to Golgotha for the following evening. This time, however, he would bring his dive equipment and be better prepared to see just what was happening on the sea bottom near Drake's island.

Chapter 15

Callaway awoke aboard the *Orinoco Flow* at about three in the afternoon. He had arrived at the dock at about 9:00 a.m., aching from head to toe from the bumpy ride home. A bit of whiskey helped soothe the pain and allowed him the sleep that he so desperately needed. He showered and dressed, and began loading up for another run to Golgotha that evening. He ran the Hewes over to the fuel dock and fueled up. Tonight Callaway would bring some other toys along to aid his investigation. He carried a dive tank with eighty cubic feet of compressed air, an octopus regulator and a buoyancy compensator, to the Hewes. He assembled the dive equipment and secured it to the deck. He would go fishing tonight clad in a wetsuit instead of his usual cut-off shorts and t-shirt. He placed another weight belt, with extra weights attached in case the current was strong, into the front deck storage compartment. All of this extra gear would make the Hewes heavy and slow her down a bit. Callaway figured that if he was discovered by Drake's men, he would just dump all the heavy stuff overboard, hit the nitrous "go" button, and scoot out of there before he got shot.

Back on board the *Orinoco Flow*, he decided to do one more thing while waiting for darkness to come. He placed a pad and pen near the phone so he could take notes and called Jorge Hidalgo. He had not spoken to his old partner since the bar confrontation at *Greasy Dick's*. It would be a strange conversation, since Callaway could not tell Jorge that Carrie was a "good guy" or what she was doing on that unholy island.

Jorge answered the telephone after many rings, which told Callaway that he had either been working all night, or he had a new girlfriend.

"*Hor-Hay!*" Callaway screamed into the phone, pronouncing his friend's name, as always, in exaggerated Spanish.

Jorge knew exactly who was on the other end, since Callaway was one of only a few *gringos* who addressed him that way. "Mike, what are you doing, man?" he asked in a very groggy voice. "You woke me up, you rich asshole."

"It's three in the afternoon, you lazy *Julio*, so wake up," Callaway yelled. "Did you work last night, or did you get laid?"

"No, man, we were out chasing freighters all last night," he answered. "We got a tip that some stuff was coming in. We took down two carrying coke, but the informant said there was a load more that we must have missed."

Callaway knew that this was not an unusual catch ratio, since the Port of Miami was the busiest cargo port in the country, with Port Everglades, just to the north in Fort Lauderdale, not far behind. The freighter traffic along the lower east coast of Florida was incredible. Jorge sounded pretty down about this, and Callaway understood why. The dedicated men and women of the Customs Service worked their butts off for low pay and piss-poor benefits, trying to stem the tidal wave of drugs flowing into the United States. Anytime a load made it ashore, they considered it a failure and agents did not like failure.

"Any chance it was a load of Drake's shit that came in last night?" Callaway asked.

"It probably was," Jorge answered. "The ships both came from the right direction, but as usual, they didn't get closer than twenty miles from Golgotha. We watched the radar all night, and nothing moved off that stinking island."

Again, there was nothing to link Drake with the dope that was coming in.

"So, business as usual, huh?" Callaway asked.

Jorge chuckled and asked, "Do you know something I should know, Callaway? How come you're calling me the day after a run, like you knew something was going down? You don't do this stuff anymore, Mike, remember?"

"Listen, *amigo*," Callaway answered, "I am doing a little investigating on my own down here near Nassau, and I may have a source on Drake, but I need to know everything about what you've found."

That got Jorge fired up. "*You* have a source?" he asked. "Damn it Callaway, what have you got?"

Callaway gripped the phone, and, staring in the direction of Golgatha—and Carrie—told him, "Calm down, Jorge, you can't say anything about this to anyone, or someone very dear to me will die."

"Mike, what the hell is going on?" Jorge asked sharply. "I've never heard you talk this way. You actually sound genuinely concerned about someone. What the hell is going on?" Jorge sounded wide-awake now and worried about his former partner.

"Look, the *dike-y* looking chick with Drake in the bar in Nassau, let's just say I know her," Callaway responded.

"Where would you know her from, man?" Jorge asked. "She sure isn't your type, just like Drake said."

Knowing he needed to do some serious verbal dancing, Callaway answered, "God dammit, Jorge, I'm asking you for help, man! This is your old partner, buddy, and I need you." Softening his tone, he continued, "Let's just say she approached me with some information, and I'm doing a little follow-up investigation on it. Besides, if it amounts to anything, maybe we can finally get that fucking scumbag Drake out of the way."

"Okay, Mike, I never heard you sounding . . . scared . . . before and you also sound like you're onto something, so I'm gonna trust you on this. But if you screw me, I will personally fuck up your day," he said, in a half-joking tone. "Everything was the way it always is," he continued. The containers were wrapped as usual, and some of them still had the balloons on them."

Callaway continued taking notes as he listened to more of Jorge's report. He knew he was referring to the smugglers' practice of floating containers for later pickup with big, helium-filled Mylar balloons tied to them. The aluminum in the balloon reflected well on short-range radar, making it easy for crews to find the dope and pluck it out of the sea. The agents found this strangely funny as the balloons had odd shapes and sometimes had phrases printed on them like "Happy Birthday" or "Congratulations on Your Promotion."

"The only weird thing was that one of the containers had a ragged piece of camouflage cloth stuck on it," Jorge continued.

"Camouflage cloth," Callaway repeated. "It was probably packed that way back in Colombia. What's so unusual about that?"

"Well, it wasn't your average canvas camo cloth," Jorge answered. "It was this special, radar-absorbing stuff. Kind of a stealth-type camo, I guess you could say. At least that's according to a couple of our SWAT guys who used to be special ops in the military."

Skeptical about the significance of the camo cloth, Callaway answered, "Maybe they didn't know it was this stealth cloth that you're talking about when they wrapped it on the container."

Jorge laughed. "Oh, I will bet they knew exactly what this cloth could do, since it goes for about three-hundred dollars a running foot," he answered. "You wrap up enough packages of coke with that stuff, and it's gonna cut into your profit margin, for sure. Unless you're moving extremely large amounts, that is."

"The only other weird thing was the pattern of the camouflage," Jorge continued. "It wasn't any kind of leaf or grass. It was like, I don't know, like bare trees in the winter time up north, but on a dark green and brown background. Strange, huh?"

Callaway tried to think of where he had seen something like that pattern before. He began sketching a picture of what Jorge had described.

"Other than that, there was nothing different than all the other nights of chasing down dopers," Jorge said in a somewhat depressed tone. "Oh, there is one other thing," he continued, sounding a bit more upbeat. "Supposedly Drake is in a lot of trouble with his suppliers in Colombia. He owes the cartels a pile of money that he hasn't been able to come up with. Apparently it had something to do with a big shipment that got blown to bits on a certain boat that you shot full of holes last week. Word on the street is that he needs to move a major load, like five times bigger than he ever has, and soon, or there won't be any place where he can go to keep on breathing, except Cuba, maybe. If he gets away with it, rumor has it that he will just take his money and get out of the dope business for good."

Callaway thought about the poetic justice of Drake being killed by the Colombian drug lords. The thought of Drake sitting on his beach, sipping pina coladas on an island made of drug money made him sick to his stomach. If he could stop that big shipment from getting through, it would really mess up, and maybe even end, Drake's life. But first, he would have to figure out just how the dope was being moved.

"So, Mike, what have you got going with the lesbian chick?" Jorge asked. "You trying to rescue her from her sexual preference?"

Callaway stared at the picture he had drawn on the pad. "Huh, uh yeah, that's it," he answered. "Thanks buddy, I'll talk to you later." He hung up the telephone. Jorge was still talking to him as he did, trying to find out what he knew about Drake. "You got the reason all wrong," Callaway whispered to himself, "but the rescue part right, *amigo.*"

Chapter 16

The run to Golgotha seemed shorter this time. Maybe it was because he'd started earlier in the evening. As Callaway passed the small barrier islands off the leeward side of Drake's island, he again shut down the outboard and switched to the electric trolling motor. The troller pulled hard since he'd given both deep-cycle batteries an all-day charge back at the dock. He had dialed in the way-point for the mysterious flat area on the bottom of the sea bed, and his faithful GPS led him close to the spot. Callaway again scanned the shoreline and buildings of the island, and he observed the same things from the previous night. He had managed to penetrate Drake's defenses again without being detected, but he knew it was just a matter of time before one of Drake's boats would come along and see him. He had to move fast. His attention was drawn to the guards. Tonight they stayed very close to the compound where the submarine was kept. The sub was again berthed in its little barn, obviously having a charge applied to its batteries as men scurried around on her decks. But there was something different tonight. The vessel was tied up in a way that left twenty feet of the bow protruding from the barn. It appeared that every light on the dock was trained on the submarine, making its white hull glow.

Callaway thought for a second that he didn't have to concern himself with the sub tonight, since it must be clearly visible to astronauts orbiting in the space shuttle. And since it was here, it certainly wasn't running dope. He quietly lowered the anchor off the bow of his boat. He played out about seventy-five feet of rope when the anchor hit bottom and he felt the line go slack. The bottom graph on the recorder showed the smooth area, surrounded by regular-looking coral formations. Then he noticed something different on the bottom that he hadn't seen the previous evening. Apparently, the Hewes had drifted a bit to the west before the anchor caught. From this new position, Callaway noted one of several deep trenches that seemed to be right in the path of the smooth area he was investigating on the screen. The trench was about three hundred feet wide, and according to his sea charts, around four-thousand-plus feet deep. On the bottom graph, the relationship of the smooth area on both sides, and the huge chasm in between, gave the impression of a gorge on land where a bridge had fallen down. He slid his arms into the buoyancy compensator vest with the eighty cubic-foot scuba tank attached, and reached over his shoulder to turn the regulator on. He took a few short breaths to make sure all of his equipment was working right. Years ago, his old diving instructor would yell at him for not testing the tank before strapping it on, and tonight he would have yelled even more for the more grievous offense that he was about to commit, that of diving alone.

He put on his weight belt, pulled on his fins and hung his legs over the port-side gunwale. Given the depth of the water, he figured his bottom time to be about twenty-five minutes. Staying down at that depth much longer would build up a dangerous level of nitrogen in his blood, giving him a case of the bends if he ascended to the surface too quickly. Without help and the proper equipment, that would probably kill him. He reminded himself that if he got into trouble down below, he would be totally on his own.

He looked at the island, thinking about Carrie and their future together, before pulling his dive mask over his face and sliding quietly into the water. As he began to sink, he filled his buoyancy compensator with air from the octopus regulator on his tank. He stopped filling when he reached neutral buoyancy, floating at a constant depth. He flipped over and began kicking his way straight down, stopping at about every twenty-five feet to pinch his nose and blow the pressure out of his ears. As he passed fifty feet, he turned on his diving light, which was a smaller, but more powerful, light than the Mag Light he'd used the night before. The smooth area came into view as he descended. As he got closer, Callaway made out a pattern that looked exactly like the coral formations around it. It didn't make sense. If Drake's dredge had gone through here, the coral would be ripped to shreds by the machine's cutting blades. He continued to descend until he was just above the smooth area, when he realized where he had seen this coral pattern before. It matched the sketch he'd made of the camouflage cloth as Jorge described it. He touched the smooth area, and then pulling off his right diving glove, he touched it again.

With a start, he realized it felt like cloth—not common canvas camo cloth, but some type of thick, woven plastic fiber. This was the radar-absorbing, *stealth* camo cloth that Jorge told him cost three-hundred dollars a foot. It was the same type of cloth Jorge had found on the cocaine-laden containers the previous evening. *Wait a minute,* Callaway thought. *Didn't Carrie tell me that Drake had huge rolls of camouflage cloth on the island, and that she couldn't figure out what he was doing with the stuff?*

Callaway touched the cloth again. He had to figure out why it was laid out across the bottom of the sea, apparently for many miles. The cloth was tightly staked to the coral on both sides. Callaway tried to pull one of the stakes out, but it wouldn't budge. Each metal bar had been staked deep into the coral, with about five feet left protruding above the coral. *How did they do this?* he asked himself, astonished by the efficiency of the work. *This wasn't done by a couple of guys with a sledgehammer. Drake must have some kind of big, pneumatic hammer on the dredge to do this.*

He just had to know what was under the cloth. He looked east, down the smooth area, and saw more of the same camo tightly staked to the bottom. *No joy there,* he thought. He looked to the west and saw camo, and then darkness, and then off in the distance, he could faintly make out camo again. *Of course, the trench!* he remembered. He swam down the camouflaged path to the deep trench in the sea. When he reached the end of the cloth, he grabbed the edge and flipped himself over. Hanging there, upside down, he was confronted by something he absolutely never expected—a giant tunnel carved out of the coral and covered by the camouflaged cloth.

The tunnel was huge, measuring about thirty feet across and fifty feet deep. Now he realized what Drake's dredge had done when he saw the coral on the bottom and sides of the shaft. It was utterly destroyed, having been broken into tiny pieces, which lined the bottom of this almost perfectly rectangular sub-oceanic thruway. He turned around, and shining his light on the other side of the trench, he could see that the tunnel continued under the cloth, starting on the other side.

What the hell is this all about? Callaway wondered, trying to wrap his mind around what he had discovered. He swam around the opening. It was obvious that it was carved to transport the dope with the sub off Drake's island, but how, and to where? But he and Carrie had ruled out Drake's new submarine, as it didn't have the range or speed to reach the shipping lanes, nor did it have the capacity to carry many containers full of dope. And even if the sub could get there, she would have to surface to make the delivery, and then she would be vulnerable to discovery by radar and any number of patrol aircraft from U.S. Customs, the DEA or the Coast Guard. Even his new friend,

Commander Eldridge, would have a shot at her, with *Pegasus*. He smiled when he thought of what an old Navy sea dog like Eldridge would do if he caught a sub on the surface off-loading dope. He imagined the crazy SOB trying to ram the sub, like a scene from Robert Mitchum's *The Enemy Below*.

Callaway was engrossed in examining the tunnel, running his hand along the camouflage cloth when he felt a weird vibration coming from the cloth itself. He swam up the side of the tunnel and over to the center, grabbing onto the top. He was hanging motionless down into the tunnel when he saw a blurry image coming at him from the direction of Drake's island. He stared at the object that looked small, at first. But the object grew rapidly as it advanced toward him, until it nearly filled the whole interior of the tunnel. At first, it looked like a whale. But why would a whale be swimming in a tunnel when it, like the now scared diver watching whatever this thing was, would eventually have to surface for air? Callaway instinctively swam up and over the top of the tunnel to get out of the charging object's path. What he saw pass beneath him answered some questions while raising even more about how Anton Drake was so successful in moving his product.

* * *

Both the sub's pilot and his assistant peered into the darkness, aided by night-vision goggles that were only marginally effective under water. "Jesus Christ! Was that a man floating in the tunnel?" the pilot screamed to his crewman.

* * *

Estimating that the ship was traveling at about fifteen knots, Callaway wondered if this could possibly be the same sub that had supposedly sunk near Nassau. Had they "resurrected" the first tourist submarine from a death that had never happened? Callaway stared, astonished, as the sub passed beneath him, noting that the hull seemed to be crudely covered in the same stealth material as the undersea tunnel through which it traveled. *Of course*, he thought, *it works for sonar, too. The fabric makes the sub cutting through the tunnel hard to find.* His astonishment vanished when he grasped the only way Drake could have accomplished the submarine switch. The faces of the men, women and children that died in the contrived sinking flashed through his brain, as he remembered the newscasts about the wreck. He shook his head to get his mind back to the situation at hand.

He noted that her conning tower had been removed, probably to streamline the sub, reducing hydrostatic drag and giving her more speed and range. He could also see that removing the conning tower freed more deck space for several long racks of, presumably water-tight, canisters. While the vessel moved too swiftly for Callaway to count the canisters, he could tell there were enough to hold a hefty amount of the deadly cargo.

Callaway could see the men in the submarine looking upward from the cockpit when they passed beneath him, straining for a glimpse of him scrambling over the top of the fabric tunnel.

Callaway kicked as hard as he could to avoid ending up like a love bug smashed against a car's windshield. He reached the top and quickly spun around to see the vessel traveling by. Shining his diving light through the windows on the roof of the vessel, he could plainly see the two men quickly turning their heads to avoid the light. Callaway understood why they turned when he saw the night-vision devices strapped to their heads. He knew the pain and disorientation a night-vision goggle's light amplification would cause if you looked at a bright light.

Their movements caused the pilot to veer slightly to the right. He straightened the sub's course in just enough time to avoid colliding with the coral. Then Callaway watched the sub quickly vanish into the tunnel. From behind, he noticed that some of the camouflage material was torn along the sides of the vessel and along the rack of canisters. He quickly surmised that the rack allowed the canisters to rub against the hull as they were released.

That's why Jorge and the guys found the camo cloth stuck to the canisters, he thought. Callaway slowly rose to the surface. When he broke the surface, he again scanned the shore to ensure that he was alone. He was. He wasn't sure if the submarine had any way of communicating with anyone on the surface.

No loud engines approaching, so I guess I'm okay, for now, he thought, feeling relieved. Callaway threw his fins aboard the Hewes and then pushed his tank and buoyancy vest over the gunwale. He pulled himself around to the back of the boat and climbed aboard. He couldn't believe what he'd just seen. Callaway had discovered the unknown means by which Anton Drake had been moving the drugs off his islands. He still wondered where the sub was going to release its cargo and what he could do to stop it. His first thought was to get on the radio and call for help. He turned the radio on and switched it to emergency channel sixteen.

"Mayday! Mayday! Any listening ship or station!" he yelled into the mike, forgetting the need for caution in his excitement. He feared it was a gesture in futility, as he was too far from the shipping lanes, or any land base, with the exception of Drake's island, to be heard over the tiny radio on his boat. His only hope was that a Customs or Coast Guard boat would pick him up, but, apparently, no one was around except Drake's people. *Hopefully Drake won't know where this signal is coming from*, he thought to himself. He figured the good guys were probably staying close to the Florida coast, gamely trying to intercept the *big load* that was supposed to be coming in. Callaway figured that even Navy vessels would probably be doing the same. He was very alone out on the water. By the time he got within radio range of anyone who was not picking up containers of dope, the stuff would already be dispersed to three dozen ships, and, at that point, almost impossible to stop from entering the country. It would be up to him to somehow stop the submarine, and, hopefully, put Anton Drake's business, and life, in jeopardy with the drug lords in Colombia.

Chapter 17

Callaway could probably track the direction of the submarine by simply following the smooth area on the bottom of the ocean, which he could easily read with his chart recorder. He could approximate the tunnel's location, since it appeared to follow a straight line with only a few slight bends along the way. The problem would be finding the sub, quickly, before it reached the drop point. He thought about his encounter with the vessel down below. *Thank God I was in the trench, and not the tunnel, or I would be crab food right now*, he thought. Then it hit him.

"The trench!" he said, smiling.

He pulled his area chart out of the console and laid it on the deck. Lying on his belly, using a small flashlight that he partially shielded with his hand to avoid unwanted attention, Callaway studied the underwater topography around the undersea tunnel. There were three more trenches between his position and the shipping lanes, all between three and five thousand feet deep. He could run almost three times as fast as the sub without even using the nitrous injection so he could be waiting for the sub when it appeared passing through one of them. Starting the Yamaha outboard, he turned in the estimated direction of the tunnel, which matched the direction to the shipping lanes almost exactly and pushed the throttle hard. The little boat went nose high for a brief instant and then leveled off. The goons on shore would probably hear his engine, but at this point he didn't care. If he could reach the next trench before the sub got there, and find some way of disabling it, maybe he could bring all kinds of hell down on Anton Drake.

How in God's name do I stop a submarine? he wondered. The question ran repeatedly through his mind as he sped along the surface. He reviewed everything his old man had taught him about anti-submarine warfare. He knew how the Navy would go after a hostile submarine today by just turning loose one of their trick sonar-guided homing torpedoes to hunt the bad guy down and blow a big hole in his hull. "All I have is a spear gun," he muttered as he zoomed along at forty-five miles per hour. He could see himself trying to shoot a hole in the sub with a spear as it went zipping by. What he wouldn't give for a depth charge right now.

As he raced to the windward side of the island, he could feel the sea getting a little rough. The Hewes hit a good sized swell hard. It startled Callaway, lost in thought as to how he could stop the sub. The boat slammed down on the water, bouncing equipment all over the place. The impact caused the spare fuel tank to move forward from its place under the driver's seat, hitting the back of Callaway's feet with some authority.

"Son-of-a-bitch!" he yelled in pain, trying to shove the fuel tank back. "Wait a minute, I do have a depth charge on board," he said, looking down at the ten-gallon metal tank filled with super unleaded gasoline. His mind raced as he followed the chart recorder's smooth, flat trail until he reached the next trench. According to the chart, this was the deepest of the trenches, estimated at five thousand feet. He couldn't be sure that he'd beaten the sub there, since he couldn't be sure he'd estimated its speed accurately. Callaway looked at the gas tank, wondering how to get it down to the mouth of the tunnel and make it explode on cue. He began rummaging through all the boat's compartments, looking for something to turn a gasoline tank into an underwater bomb.

First, he knew he'd need weight to sink the tank full of buoyant gasoline to the tunnel's level. According to the chart recorder, the water was sixty feet deep on either side of the trench. He needed to place his depth charge precisely at the mouth of the tunnel where the submarine would be exiting. He also needed to trigger his make-shift bomb when it was close enough to seriously damage the sub. He believed that the tank's explosion might cause enough of an underwater flash, amplified by the night-vision goggles, to temporarily blind the men on board. If so, they'd have to surface to get their bearings. At that point, he would assault the vessel, capture the crew, and sail it triumphantly to the nearest American law enforcement or military vessel he could find. "Easier said than done," he muttered to himself.

Callaway pulled both of his anchors, along with their attached ten-foot lengths of metal chain, from the locker in the front deck. He tied both his diving-weight belts and both anchors to the fuel tank's handles. He looked around for more weight and then spotted the heavy lead ball on his downrigger. Like the proverbial light bulb appearing over his head, he realized that he could attach the tank and all the weights to the downrigger and then lower it to the exact depth needed. "But how do I trigger it once I get it down there?" he asked himself. Again, one look at the downrigger gave him the answer. He opened the compartment in the rear of the center console, removed his twelve-gauge flare pistol, and loaded it with a cartridge.

Callaway unscrewed the cap from the top of the gas tank and placed the barrel of the flare gun in the opening. There was about an inch-wide gap between the barrel and the inside of the tank's opening. He took the fuel tank cap, and examining it, decided that this would be a better place to mount his detonator. He pulled the knife off his diving vest and plunged it through the center of the thin, sheet-metal cap. Twisting the knife, he made an opening that the flare gun barrel could just fit into. Knowing that a leak would kill any chance of an underwater ignition, he asked himself, "How can I waterproof this freaking thing?"

Pawing through his toolbox, he found just what he needed. Callaway pulled out a roll of duct tape and a small can of marine sealing putty. The putty would normally be used in an emergency situation, such as when you got too close to a reef while running at forty miles per hour and knocked a hole through your hull. He always kept a small can of the stuff on the little boat so he could plug a hole long enough to make it back to port. Flipping the cap upside down, he quickly pushed a large glob of the sticky substance into the opening around the gun barrel. He then sealed the contraption on both sides with the duct tape, and screwed the cap onto the tank. Next, he pulled his first aid kit out from under the seat and removed its emergency foil blanket. This would show up bigger than hell on the chart recorder to help him guide the tank as it submerged. Realizing that his "Rube Goldberg" bomb was still not watertight enough to withstand a couple of extra atmospheres of pressure, he removed everything from the kit, piece by piece, looking for a solution. He found the kit's AMBU bag, designed to manually pump air into a person's lungs. Turning it over in his hands, he had another brainstorm. He jumped to the console and opened the front panel. Inside was a circuit board providing electricity to the ignition, instruments, and livewell, and next to the circuit board was just what he was looking for: the tiny bottle of pure oxygen attached to a timer to pump pure O2 into the water of the livewell. Instead of keeping live bait fresh, the tank would now be used to pressurize the underwater bomb. He closed the valve on the tank and removed it. The small gauge at the top of the skinny cylinder showed that the tank was three-quarters full. Callaway again removed the flare gun/cap from the tank.

"Please fit," he said as he tried to insert the cylinder into the opening of the tank. The O2 bottle was a tight fit, but it made it through the

158

opening, causing some gas to overflow out of the tank and onto the deck of his boat. His thinking was part high school science class, and part high school welding class. If he just slightly opened the valve on the oxygen tank and then closed the top, the oxygen tank would give positive pressure inside the fuel tank. If it worked, the sea water would stay out, while oxygen bubbles would seep out of any leaks in the lid that held the flare gun. To one side of the tank, he attached the downrigger cable. He gently opened the valve on the oxygen tank slightly and lowered it into the gasoline. On went the cap containing the flare gun. Callaway listened for the hissing sound that would indicate that oxygen was escaping.

He heard the hissing briefly, before it was drowned out by a louder sound. He heard large and powerful engines in the distance coming from the direction of Golgotha. Drake's boats were coming for him. They were probably alerted to his presence by the sound of his outboard, or perhaps by the "Mayday" call that he put out over the radio. There was no time to worry about the approaching boats, now. He pulled his 6-0 Penn rod and reel combination from the rod rack, tied the leader to the trigger of the flare gun, then clipped it to the release clip of the downrigger. This would safely keep the gun from firing until the line was pulled free from the release clip, thus pulling the trigger on the gun. Callaway lowered the entire contraption into the water. He leaned over the gunwale and carefully cocked the hammer on the flare gun, thinking to himself that if it went off prematurely, it would explode next to the boat and surely ignite the gasoline that had overflowed from the tank and was sloshing around on the deck.

The sound of the engines grew louder. Callaway maneuvered the boat until the chart recorder told him he was right over the trench. He set the meter on the downrigger for sixty feet, the depth the recorder indicated as the bottom of the trench. Callaway put the Penn reel in free-spool, allowing the line to play out rapidly and then hit the down button on the downrigger. The tank, and all of the attached pieces, instantly disappeared beneath the surface. Callaway alternated between looking at the screen of the chart recorder and looking in the direction of the approaching boats. Holding the rod with one hand, he pressed the thumb of his other hand against the spool to control the amount of line going out and prevent a tangle that could set off the charge prematurely. At exactly sixty feet, the downrigger locked and stopped the gas tank from going any further. Callaway could see the aluminum blanket gently swaying in the current as it reflected the sonar beams back into the chart recorder. It appeared to be right at the mouth of the tunnel. If the sub was coming, it should run right into it.

Again he looked in the direction of the approaching boats. He reached into the open console compartment and pulled out the holstered Glock .40. He would have to wait until he was done handling the fishing rod to safely open the seat compartment and retrieve his shotgun. Just how long could he wait for the submarine before he ran out of time to get away from Drake's men? He was getting very nervous when his boat suddenly lurched sideways.

***

Beneath the ocean, the pilot and crewman of the cocaine-laden submarine nervously talked to each other. They traveled at their maximum speed of fifteen knots, as they were a little behind schedule. It was hard to control the vessel within the narrow confines of the man-made tunnel. Every so often, the sub would brush up against some coral still lining the trench, or up against the camouflage material above that covered its progress through the night. The captain of the submarine was the same man who had driven the vessel on the day of the contrived accident. He was very experienced, since prior to the accident he had captained this vessel for three years. The captain, who was also a hardened criminal, had endured everything from seasick passengers throwing up on him, to people experiencing panic attacks when they realized they were really going beneath the surface of the ocean.

While he guided the tourists, he pondered how much he'd make for his last night of hauling drugs for Anton Drake. Through it all, he survived without losing his temper or hitting anyone because Anton Drake had made him a promise. Drake told him his plans for the sub and that he would cut the pilot in for five percent of the money for each run of cocaine he made. He'd made more money in the past four months than he could normally make in a dozen lifetimes. This was both his *biggest* run and his last. He had already picked out the house he would buy, right outside of Kingston, where he would settle down to the life of luxury that he had previously only dreamed of. The man assisting him was new to Drake's organization, hired recently because of his ruthlessness in dealing with people who got too close to Drake's island. He'd joined Drake's private army when he was last released from a Bahamian prison; he'd been imprisoned that last time for smuggling human cargo. He made regular trips to Haiti, where for the mere sum of five thousand dollars, he would carry a Haitian refugee to the Bahamas, which would put them one step closer to their ultimate goal of reaching the United States. It was like moving heaven and earth for most Haitians to lay their hands on that kind of cash. But some did, and out of desperation, they traveled with this terrible captain who routinely raped women and killed their men on his boat. For all of his evil doings, the man had one funny quirk —he always wore a life preserver when at sea, since he could not swim.

"Why do you wear that ting, *mon*?" the captain asked. "You look so very stupid. What are you going to do if we crash, hop out of the submarine and swim to the top?" The pair still talked about the diver that they had seen earlier, wondering if he had been killed yet, when, peering through the inky darkness through their night-vision goggles, they saw something even stranger.

"What is that?" the pilot asked. He was astonished as they watched the odd-looking object ahead. His companion was just as perplexed by the strange thing fluttering in the water at the break in the tunnel. Through their night-vision goggles, the wavering object before them shone as brightly as if it were sitting under a streetlight.

"I don't know what it is," the assistant whispered, fidgeting nervously with the collar of his life preserver. "Maybe a giant squid or a huge jelly fish."

They did not slow down, believing, and for good reason, that the *creature* they were observing was alive and would scoot out of the way at their approach.

"If he don't move, we run him over, right, *mon*?" the pilot said defiantly.

The man with the life preserver was not so confident. "Slow down," he barked, "let him get out of the way! What if this ting is hungry? Maybe he takes a bite out of our boat!"

The pilot laughed, slapping the other man on the shoulder as the submarine closed on the object in the water. He stopped laughing when he saw the red object floating below the shiny silver. He couldn't see the handles, with the anchors and weight belts attached to them, but he slammed the throttle of the submarine into neutral, anyway. It was too late. The sub crashed into the object, which wrapped itself around the sub's nose. The red object bounced on and off the front window, as the sub continued to move forward from the momentum of its previous high speed. The pilot cursed as the sub began crossing the trench with the object stuck to its bow.

On the surface, Michael Callaway prepared to pull the trigger on his "Enemy Below." Search lights from two go-fast boats rapidly approached him. He snapped the lock shut on the spool and began reeling up the slack. When the line became taut, he jerked the rod upward as hard as he could, not knowing if his experimental bomb would go off.

Sixty feet below the surface, the fishing line connected to Callaway's rod pulled loose from the downrigger release clip. The pressure of the line pulled the trigger on the flare gun, firing its molten phosphorous projectile into the tank's volatile liquid. The resulting ignition caused a powerful, and shockingly bright, explosion under the water. Callaway didn't realize that by introducing pure oxygen to the mix, he enhanced the burn rate of the fuel, causing a big explosion with an even bigger flash. The pressure of the blast actually loosened the seal around the sub's front glass, allowing water to enter at a fairly slow rate, but it was the flash that would do the most damage. The bright flash of light split the darkness sixty feet down. The night-vision goggles magnified the flash a thousand times. For a second, it was as if the pilot and his assistant looked at the sun through a giant magnifying glass. The light seared the retinas of their eyes, causing temporary blindness, while the concussion of the blast knocked them from their chairs and onto the floor of the submarine that was now wet with seawater from the broken window seal.

The sub was doomed, but not from the water leaks. The two men tried to regain their feet, but the vessel was careening through the water at a strange angle. The captain tried to turn the vessel to the opposite direction. "Goddammit, I can't see a thing!" the pilot screamed in sheer terror. He could feel the submarine begin to corkscrew to the right. He grabbed at the steering wheel, trying to blindly correct the motion. He didn't realize that the vessel had swerved outside of the safety of the man-made tunnel, and was instead in the trench that was five thousand feet deep. Over-correcting the turn, he pitched the sub to the left.

His assistant was now able to stand but was also blinded. He began to cry out of fear. The pilot's vision began to clear somewhat, and he strained his eyes to see ahead, to understand why they hadn't slid into the bottom or sides of the tunnel. The answer to that question, and the end of his life came quickly after. He was able to make out something ahead. He slammed the throttle hard into reverse, stripping the gears in the transmission case. He screamed, but his scream was cut off when the submarine crashed into the huge, horizontal spire of rock and coral, which was the last thing he ever saw. The spike broke the front windows and penetrated half the length of the vessel, bringing the sub to a halt dangling above the maw of the trench. Both men were crushed to death. The reef that had been torn and broken by

Drake's machines to hide his illicit trade had now taken its revenge.

Chapter 18

Callaway watched the flash of the explosion down below from the seat of his boat. Huge bubbles of air escaped from the doomed submarine, rising to the surface so fast they almost turned his flats boat over. He held onto the wheel until the boat settled. From the sound of their engines, Callaway estimated that Drake's boats were about a mile away and closing fast. Callaway wanted to run, but he needed to know what the sub was doing. Did he damage it? Did it sink? If it did, what evidence would remain to prove that Anton Drake's "sunken" submarine had been alive and well and hauling cocaine? He pulled out his one million-candle power Q-Beam spotlight, connected directly to the boat's battery, and switched it on. Donning his dive mask, he thrust the light and his face over the side and into the water. What Callaway observed amazed him. The grim spectacle of the submarine impaled on the rocky spire was a shock. As he watched, an even more amazing thing happened. The weight of the submarine, hanging like an anvil on the end of a tree limb, broke the rock spire at its base. The sub twisted backwards and fell quickly into the trench and disappeared from view. More trapped air and some debris rose to the surface along with a body —a man wearing a life preserver. When the dead man broke the surface, Callaway grabbed the life preserver and pulled it off the mutilated corpse. The life vest slid off easily since the body was badly crushed. In the glow of the Q-Beam, he could read the stenciled writing on the vest: *Subdives Submarine 1.* "Now I have proof of how Drake was moving his dope," he said to himself.

He was about to run when he saw another strange sight. A pink, heart-shaped Mylar balloon rose eerily out of the water, just ahead of his boat, followed by a numbered canister bobbing to the surface. Under the light of the stars, he could make out the writing on the balloon.

"Get well soon."

He looked back at the dead Subdives crewman. "Must be for you," he said.

Leaning over the gunwale and grabbing the line between the balloon and the canister, Callaway slung both into his boat. Then he gunned the motor. At that moment a piercing beam of light illuminated the Hewes and its lone occupant. Callaway looked back directly into the beam and was momentarily blinded. He ducked as several gunshots from an automatic weapon splashed the water around his boat. He heard a voice come over a loud speaker on the nearest go-fast boat. The other boat was still well behind, but coming fast.

"Don't move, stay where you are!" the voice demanded with a heavy Spanish accent. The boat idled toward him, the pilot keeping his AK-47 at the ready. Callaway held his Glock out of sight, down inside the boat, and tried to think of an excuse for being here that might get him out alive.

In the next instant, any excuse he could make became irrelevant.

"Ah, Señor Callaway, we meet again!" the voice from the nearest boat declared with a laugh. Callaway realized he'd been recognized by one of Drake's goons from the confrontation in the Nassau bar. The man spoke into the headset of his radio, obviously giving his position, and probably telling whoever was listening about the important catch he just made. The second boat was approaching fast. Callaway figured he just might have time for one shot before being shot full of holes himself. Suddenly, the closest boat rolled severely to one side, apparently struck from below by another huge bubble of air from the sinking submarine. Several canisters, along with lengths of wire and large pieces of debris, struck the boat from behind, throwing the driver off balance and sending him sprawling to the deck. He struck his head on the large fire extinguisher mounted on the cockpit wall. Callaway did not wait around to see if the man would recover. He threw the throttle down hard and roared off into the night, firing his pistol at his would-be captor as he raced away.

***

The gunman stood dizzily as he fired his weapon's remaining bullets in the general direction of the screaming outboard motor. He pushed his twin throttles forward, but the boat only moved slowly ahead. He backed off the throttles and tried again. The boat moved forward, but only up to about twenty miles per hour. Cursing and shutting the engines off, he pushed the tilt button on the console, raising the two outdrives up out of the water. Still groggy from the fall, he shone his spotlight on the propellers and saw that they were hopelessly fouled with debris. He looked at the props and suddenly realized that some of the items fouling the prop were canisters of cocaine from his boss's submarine. He looked at some of the other flotsam in the water around him and saw broken fiberglass, some of which was partly covered with camouflage cloth. The other go-fast boat had finally reached him and pulled up alongside.

"What is happening?" yelled the driver of the second boat. "Where is Callaway? Mr. Drake wants to see him very badly."

The man on the first boat used a boat hook to pull one of the canisters from the water. "Look at this! Look at all of this junk in the water. Don't you see what this is?" he screamed.

The man on the second boat looked at the canister, confused. "Madre de Dios," he yelled, "this is from the submarine! He sunk the fucking submarine! Forget about Callaway, we need to go back and tell Drake what happened to the shipment!" With that, he scooped up more of the debris from the sunken submarine and hauled it aboard. After clearing the props, both men turned their boats toward Drake's island to report the unhappy news to their master.

* * *

Callaway ran the Yamaha hard. He kept the tachometer spinning just below the red line as he threaded his way among the area's many shoals

170

and reefs. He had not heard the go-fast boats' engines for about ten minutes, so he chanced turning on the GPS map plotter even though the light on the instrument might give away his position. Suddenly, he heard the big V-8's again, but now the sound seemed to be moving away from him, back toward Golgotha. He continued to run toward Nassau, while calling over the radio, trying to get help. When he reached the shipping lanes, Callaway saw many small freight ships on a course to and from Miami and Fort Lauderdale. Most of these vessels were running a straight course, but he noticed that some were slowing down and steering erratically from one side of the shipping lane to the other. He also saw the occasional searchlight shining on the surface as though someone were looking for something. Callaway reached down and touched the life preserver and container he'd retrieved from the sea. "Is this what you're looking for?" he asked out loud.

He kept broadcasting on emergency channel sixteen, getting responses from the freighters in the area that weren't smuggling narcotics or people, but he declined their help, knowing that he couldn't trust anyone out here who wasn't wearing a uniform with "United States" sewn onto it in some form. Finally he received the call back he was looking for.

"Vessel calling Mayday on channel sixteen, this is the United States Coast Guard boat *Osprey*, what is your emergency?"

Callaway took a deep breath, trying to figure out how to get the authorities in on this situation, without getting himself in trouble for the unprovoked sinking of a vessel at sea. "U.S. Coast Guard," he responded, "my name is Michael Callaway, I am a former special agent, U.S. Customs, I have information and evidence regarding means of smuggling of the contraband that you all are out looking for tonight."

There was silence on the radio for an inordinate amount of time and then Callaway heard, "Mr. Callaway, this is Lieutenant Tanner, captain of the *USCG Osprey*. What is your location, and what the hell is going on?" The Coast Guard skipper sounded upset at someone who was not connected, at least officially, with tonight's operation, having information about it.

"Skipper, I am thirteen miles from the harbor at New Providence. I need to meet with you to explain, offshore please, as I am not able to broadcast on a secure band, and this needs to be called in on secure communications, sir."

Lieutenant Neal Tanner already had his communications officer calling the U.S. Customs Service on just such a secure line to see if they even knew a Michael Callaway. The Com officer told his captain that the U.S. Customs communication unit told him that Callaway was a former boat patrol agent for the Service, and if he said he had something good, that they should most certainly believe him. *USCG Osprey* made a slow, sweeping turn, setting a course for Nassau's harbor. The one hundred ten foot patrol craft went

172

to her best speed, as her captain advised Callaway that they would be waiting just outside the harbor entrance. Callaway acknowledged and backed the throttle off a bit on the Hewes. He didn't want to arrive earlier then the Coasties, as anyone, including Anton Drake, might have monitored his broadcast. He did not want to arrive and find the wrong party waiting for him.

As he approached the harbor twenty minutes later, Callaway made out the distinct white and orange paint scheme of a U.S. Coast Guard vessel outside the harbor. The patrol craft had just stopped, and Callaway could see men manning the two fifty-caliber machine guns on either side of the bridge. Callaway flashed on his bow and stern lights a couple of times to let them know he was approaching. He pulled alongside the patrol craft and was thrown a rope with which he secured his boat to the larger vessel. After climbing on board, Callaway was taken to the small dining area on the vessel where Lieutenant Tanner was waiting.

"Mr. Callaway, I presume," Tanner said as he rose from his chair.

He was a small man, about five-feet-three in height, and very wiry in build.

"You want a cup of coffee?"

Given the fact that it was approaching 4:00 a.m., Callaway nodded. He sat down at the small dining table. "Lieutenant, I figured out how Anton Drake has been smuggling his dope," he blurted out.

A crewman put a Styrofoam cup full of hot coffee down on the table in front of him.

Lieutenant Tanner advised the crewman to leave the room. He sat back in his chair and looked at Callaway with eyes narrowed to little slits. "Mr. Callaway," he began, "you've pulled my boat off its station in the middle of a night interdiction patrol because you say you have information on contraband smuggling that we are out here trying to stop. Just how does a *former* agent of the Customs Service know anything about a very secure op that is taking place as we speak?"

Noting that the Lieutenant appeared a little perturbed, Callaway answered, "I know you are not gonna want to hear this, but I can't tell you how I know about the operation." Callaway knew that this would not sit well with this obviously impatient man. He didn't want to get Carrie or Jorge in trouble for giving him information about Drake and the big run that was supposed to be happening tonight.

Tanner put his hand to his face and rubbed his tired eyes. "Look, you better stop playing games, and give me something real good, or I'm going to throw you over the side and drag your narrow ass behind my boat all the way back to Miami Beach!" the commander answered, confirming Callaway's assessment.

Knowing full well how difficult it was going to be, Callaway knew he had to convince him of what he had found. "All right, skipper, here it is," Callaway answered. "Drake's been using his submarine to haul the dope out to the shipping lanes."

Tanner's slight, painful grin reverted quickly to an angry frown. "Mr. Callaway," Tanner said, getting up from his chair, "we have had the man's island under close surveillance for a long, long time, and I can say emphatically that he is not using his sub. As a matter of fact, I just received a call from the DEA about two hours ago, and they were looking at a satellite photo that showed the sub in its pen on Drake's island, all lit up for everyone to see. And you have the balls to come out here and pull me off of *my* post for this kind of bullshit?"

Callaway rubbed his face with his hands. Then he looked up at Tanner and told him, "The sub the DEA was looking at on the satellite pictures is his second sub. He's using the one that sank to move the dope. It didn't really sink after all."

Tanner's look changed from disbelief to utter scorn. "I was on patrol on the day when the call went out about the first sub going down!" the lieutenant sputtered. "What do you think, that they faked the sinking, and killed all those people, just so he would have another submarine to smuggle dope with..." The lieutenant suddenly stopped talking, looking as if he just got the joke. Tanner thought for a second about all of the briefings he had gone to with the DEA, FBI, Customs Service, and the Navy. He remembered overhearing two DEA guys talking, in very descriptive terms, about what a cruel bastard Anton Drake was. One of the men he was listening to was Alberto Cruz, the DEA Special Agent supervisor who was shot aboard *Blue Thunder* the night Callaway

175

"accidentally" blew up Drake's go-fast yacht. Tanner instantly realized the brilliance of such a scheme. But even if it were true, he was puzzled as to how Drake could pull it off, even if he had the sub. "You have some kind of proof about this?" Tanner asked as he sat back down.

Callaway went into the whole story of what had transpired over the past two nights, stopping abruptly before the part of the story where he sank the submarine.

"So where is this submarine? If we have an idea where that undersea tunnel ends, we can post boats all around it and pick up the drugs before the ships can get to them," Tanner said, smiling somewhat.

"Well..." Callaway began to answer, looking at his feet. "The sub's gone."

Tanner got on the ship's phone, telling his communications man to make secure contact with all parties involved in the interdiction operation. "What do you mean, gone?" he asked. "Gone where? Did it already drop off its load?"

Afraid to make eye contact, Callaway continued staring at his feet as he answered, "No, I mean gone as in gone, to the bottom of one of the trenches between Golgotha and the shipping lanes. Gone as in sunk."

Callaway noted that Tanner was sitting, holding the telephone away from his ear, and staring at him with his mouth open. "And just how in hell did it sink?" the Lieutenant asked loudly.

"Uh, it must have been a mechanical failure," Callaway replied. "I mean these big air bubbles and debris and junk

came to the surface, and when I looked at it under water with a spotlight, it was sinking like a rock."

Tanner looked at Callaway for a while before speaking. "So you really don't have any proof, do you?" the lieutenant said abruptly.

"Well, actually I do," Callaway said as he bounded to his feet. "Come with me," he said, as he walked out of the cabin, and up the narrow stairs to the deck.

Tanner rolled his eyes as he followed, looking at Callaway like he was crazy as hell. Callaway hopped into his boat and pulled up the bloody life preserver he removed from the crew member of the stricken submarine. He asked one of Tanner's crew to shine a flashlight on the vest. At Callaway's insistence, the captain leaned over and read the writing stenciled on the back. When he did, his eyes opened considerably. "What's with all the blood, Callaway?" he asked, gritting his teeth.

"Oh, well, the guy who was wearing this was pretty busted up when he came to the surface." Callaway improvised, trying to sound as if he knew what he was talking about, "It must have been the rapid depressurization of the sub that did it." He avoided Tanner's suspicious eyes. "Oh, and I have this," Callaway said as he picked up the long container with the now deflated pink balloon attached.

177

"I've been out here two years," Tanner said, sounding more interested and less skeptical now, "and we've found three of these canisters. Every one of them was loaded with cocaine." As he spoke, he pointed at one of his crewmen, who knew exactly what to do. Per their usual procedure, the crewman brought a cordless drill on deck and cleaned the drill bit with denatured alcohol. He drilled a hole through the side of the tank and slowly pulled the bit out. Under the glow of a work light, Callaway could see white powder on the bit. The crewman dipped the bit into a solution-filled vial that immediately turned blue, confirming that it was cocaine.

Grinning from ear to ear, Tanner told Callaway, "Come on," as he climbed the short stairs and entered the bridge. Callaway sat on the floor of the cramped bridge trying to fight off sleep, as Tanner relayed his findings to the rest of the task force. As he started to doze, Callaway thought of Carrie and wondered what was happening on that evil little island called Golgotha.

Chapter 19

After that, it didn't take long for things to start happening. The Navy diverted the crew of its destroyer *Calvin* from their well-earned liberty call in Fort Lauderdale to make best speed to the area of the alleged submarine sinking. At this point in the game, the uncorrupted members of the government of the many islands of the Bahamas chain, tired of protecting Mr. Drake's ass, finally gave in to the State Department's pressure and granted permission for the ship to nose around in Bahamian waters and the private waters around Drake's island. Now it looked as though the invincible Anton Drake was finally going down in flames, contingent on the destroyer finding more evidence to back up Callaway's claim.

The Navy sent a second vessel, the underwater research ship M.V. *March*, to assist in the hunt. The *March*, on loan to the Rosenstiel Marine Institute at the University Of Miami School Of Oceanic Studies, was equipped to explore, photograph and videotape the bottom of the sea down to seven thousand feet. The *Calvin*'s captain and crew, knowing that a good liberty awaited them in "Ft. Liquerdale" upon completing this assignment, used the vessel's high-speed capability to arrive at the scene by noon. Upon arrival, the crew signaled *USCG Osprey*, on stand by, and began pinging away with her high definition sonar looking for the sub. It didn't take long for the destroyer to find a large metallic object near the bottom of a trench, at an approximate depth of forty-seven hundred feet. The crew marked the spot with the ship's GPS and anxiously awaited the arrival of the *March*. When the research ship appeared at a little after 4:00 pm, the Navy crew directed her to the place where the target was resting. Normally, they would wait until the next morning to put their gear in the water, but this was different. Upon receiving notification of Callaway's information about the sub, his old Customs Service partner Jorge Hidalgo and DEA Supervisory Agent Alberto Cruz had both flown to Nassau aboard the Customs Service Falcon jet to add their personal appeal to their agencies' pressure that the *March* crew make an immediate attempt to identify the object below.

Hildago and Cruz cruised out to the site with Inspector Rupert Winston of the Bahamian Police, aboard a Bahamian Defense Force boat. Callaway and Lieutenant Tanner joined them aboard the research ship.

Winston was in an uncharacteristically good mood, apparently savoring the possibility that he would be ending the reign of terror and corruption that had been rampant in his island nation for so long.

Hidalgo, Winston, Lieutenant Tanner, Cruz and Callaway crowded around the console that operated by Dr. Felicia Sanchez of the Rosenstiel Marine Institute.

"We've got something!" she said, her eyes opening wide. Forty-seven hundred feet below, a camera equipped, remote-controlled submersible vehicle prowled around the object in question. With a small joystick, Dr. Sanchez deftly steered the vehicle tethered to the ship with a steel umbilical cord. The lights on the submersible were not overly powerful, so she had to steer it close to the object to get a good look. All could clearly see the shape of a tourist-type submarine, sans conning tower, on the screen. Most of the camouflage cloth had been ripped from the hull by the sub's protracted tumble down the rocky trench walls.

Winston gave out a big laugh, something Callaway and Hidalgo had never heard this ultra-serious man do, when the submersible illuminated the name *Subdives 1* on the side of the broken submarine. The submersible moved up and over the back of the submarine, showing them the deck of the vessel. There they observed, and videotaped, thanks to the *March's* sophisticated equipment, the deck's racks, most of which were full of containers with only a few missing. There it was. This was pretty conclusive proof many people, and agencies, had been searching for, showing them the unknown means by which Anton Drake smuggled his dope, unmolested, for so long. It also came to the minds of the men staring at the video that Anton Drake had the blood of the passengers killed in the bogus sinking on his hands, and that he needed to pay for his evil deed. All that was needed now was to bring the containers to the surface to test the contents.

Dr. Sanchez steered the submersible around to the front of the submarine, illuminating the broken front glass, with a large piece of coral rock protruding from it. Callaway looked at the screen and suddenly felt a cold chill. There, for all involved to see, was a large portion of his silver emergency blanket, along with the two anchors, the weight belts, and what was left of the fuel tank, tangled in the wreckage at the front of the sub. Callaway didn't say anything, praying and hoping that nobody would notice, or that if they did, they would assume that all of this paraphernalia came from the submarine.

"What the hell is that stuff on the bow?" Lieutenant Tanner shouted in his own subtle way.

Dr. Sanchez played around with the camera's zoom and focus, enlarging and clarifying the items on the bow. Tanner, Hidalgo and Rupert all peered at the screen and then at Callaway. They all seemed to be wondering just what had happened during the previous evening. Just then, the door to the control room opened, and in walked Callaway's new friend, Commander David Eldridge. The skipper of the *USS Pegasus* had been advised to come to this meeting in case the information gained from the submersible resulted in a warrant for Anton Drake's arrest. The powers in Washington and Miami wanted some serious firepower available, if it became necessary to storm Drake's island. Callaway turned and gave Commander Eldridge a worried smile, as the big man squeezed his shoulder with one of his huge hands. Dr. Sanchez continued to fiddle with the

182

knobs, adjusting the picture on the monitor. She zoomed in on one of the weight belts dangling from the twisted wreckage that used to be the bow of the submarine. Something caught her eye. She zoomed in on one of the weights, to what appeared to be some kind of writing on the object. When she further adjusted the focus, it was obvious that the writing spelled a name: "CALLAWAY."

There was silence for about three seconds.

"God dammit," Lieutenant Tanner yelled, looking at Callaway. "You did sink that friggin' sub, you lying son-of-a-bitch!"

Eldridge, Hidalgo and Cruz gave a quick, worried look at each other, and instantly decided to try and save Michael Callaway's hide.

Giving him one of his sternest looks, Commander Eldridge insisted, "Can I speak to you out on deck, Lieutenant Tanner?" He held the door to the outer deck open. "*Now!*" he barked. Tanner swallowed hard and walked out. Hidalgo and Cruz began speaking to Dr. Sanchez in Spanish, while Winston staring intently at the monitor, looked as if he was trying to make some kind of decision.

Outside in the cool night breeze, Commander Eldridge zipped up his windbreaker and made his pitch, with "Look Tanner, I know you're pissed off about Callaway lying to you about sinking the submarine..."

"He committed a crime!" Tanner yelled, interrupting him.

"Yeah, yeah, okay," Eldridge replied. "But he also kept a couple of thousand pounds of cocaine from hitting the streets in *our* country, right?"

Tanner mumbled something as he turned away to look at the water, and Eldridge could swear he heard the word *pirate* mentioned in the middle of the sentence.

"Hey Tanner, I've been out here trying to bust that bastard Drake for almost a year," Eldridge said. "How long have you been out here?"

Tanner began rubbing his eyes again, looking out at the ocean. "Two years," he replied.

"I don't know about you, man, but I don't give a rat's ass about that sub, or the scumbags that were aboard her," Eldridge said. "I'm sure that they were fine, upstanding citizens, right?"

Tanner answered with a little laugh.

"Don't you get it?" Eldridge continued. "This happened in Bahamian waters. We can't do anything about it. But if we make a big deal over it, old Inspector Winston may just be getting two arrest warrants—one for Drake and one for Callaway."

Tanner looked up at the sky and slowly shook his head before he spoke. "Humph," he replied. "Sure is a shame that submarine hit that coral head and sank."

Eldridge looked at the man and smiled, slapping him on the back.

Tanner suddenly gave Eldridge a concerned look and said, "Okay, Eldridge, you sold me, but what about Winston and the good doctor? They saw that stuff on the monitor, too. And I think she was taping it." Now Eldridge looked concerned.

The two men opened the door and walked into the control room. Hidalgo and Cruz were still standing by Dr. Sanchez as she continued to play with the video equipment. Agent Cruz looked at Eldridge and Tanner and asked if they would like to see the videotape of what the submersible found below. Eldridge joined Callaway in front of the monitor. Callaway was sweating as the images flickered on the screen. They watched again as the submersible's camera recorded the name on the submarine and the rack full of canisters, but then the tape came to an abrupt end.

"There was obviously a technical malfunction with the camera," Dr. Sanchez said, as she retrieved the videocassette from the recorder and held it out to anyone who wanted it. "I trust this will be enough evidence to do whatever you must to arrest Mr. Drake," she stated.

It appeared that most everyone in the room was on board with the *accident* scenario regarding the demise of Drake's submarine. They still couldn't be sure of Inspector Winston, however. Callaway, Hidalgo, Eldridge, Tanner, Cruz and Dr. Sanchez all watched the big Bahamian as he reached out and took the tape. He looked at all of them and then he looked hard into Callaway's eyes and smiled. "Shame about dat submarine crashing into the reef, huh, *mon*?" he said, shaking his head.

Callaway began breathing freely again. He had forgotten about Winston's hatred for Drake over the loss of his son. As Winston turned toward the door, he told them, "I have a little warrant I have to write for Mr. Drake's arrest. I am sure the Bahamian government could use some help serving it," he said looking at the men from the

Navy, Coast Guard and U.S. Federal Law Enforcement. They all started walking toward the door.

"Mr. Callaway!" Winston's voice boomed. "As much as I am sure you would like to come along, I think you had better sit this one out. I will have enough of a problem explaining your involvement as it is. Why don't you go fishing . . . somewhere away from Drake's island. I hear there are lots of bonefish down near Andros Island."

Callaway nodded and stepped back, turning toward the rest of the group. "Hey Cruz, can I talk to you a minute?" Callaway asked, and Cruz and Callaway walked out on deck.

"Two things," Callaway began. First, how did you get the doctor lady to get on board with the accident scenario?"

Cruz smiled and answered, "Well, Jorge and I started telling her what an evil shit 'ole Drake is, killing those people in the sub and importing all that cocaine and everything, and how we've been trying to bust him all of these years, and she up and starts crying," he replied. "Turns out she just got back from her nephew's funeral in Miami. The kid was twenty years old, and he was selling, big time. A real freaking' gangster. She said he started out the way most of 'em do, a little pot now and then, but then he graduated to nose candy and that was all she wrote. He started selling to support his own habit. When he hoovered up a bunch of the junk he was supposed to sell, he got shot, several times, by the owner of the dope. We told her there was a good chance that our friend Drake supplied

186

the coke that got her nephew killed. Which really is a possibility if you think about it."

"That's great," Callaway answered, but then asked, "Where's Carrie, Cruz?" He decided it was time to let the cat out of the bag in a big way.

Cruz's smile faded instantly. "What are you talking about, man?" he asked. "Who the hell is Carrie?"

"You know who I'm talking about," Callaway answered. "The agent you've had undercover on Drake for the past year."

Squinting, Cruz shouted, "How the fuck did you know about that, man?

Callaway didn't want to stir up any more problems, but he just had to know. "Just tell me where she is and I'll be good," he said. "Otherwise I'll storm Drake's island myself to find her, and you don't want me doing that, do you?"

"What's your connection with her, Callaway?" Cruz asked. "I need to know what's happening here."

Looking down at the deck, Callaway answered, "Let's just say we're kind of in love, okay?"

Cruz took a deep breath, shook his head and told him, "I don't know what her status is. She was supposed to report in last night, but we didn't hear from her. I think your little escapade may have messed up her scheduled trip to New Providence, so she couldn't call in. I'll tell you what man, as soon as I find out where she is I'll call you. Just stay the fuck away from Drake's place, you hear me?"

The two men shook hands and walked back into the control room. Winston, Hidalgo, Tanner and Eldridge were hunched over a map, looking at a chart with Drake's island right in the middle of it.

Dr. Sanchez walked up to Callaway, and gave him a long hug and a kiss on the cheek. "Thank you," she whispered as she walked out on the deck, starting to cry.

It was the first sense of vindication that Callaway felt for what he did the previous evening, and it felt damned good.

Chapter 20

The raid went off like clockwork. The Bahamian government, now under intense pressure from Inspector Winston and the U.S. State Department, conceded that it was time for Mr. Drake to go away.

The good inspector had written a search warrant for the two Drake-owned islands and an arrest warrant for Anton Drake himself that would have gotten Perry Mason's shorts in a knot. By mid-morning, the windward side of Golgotha looked like a miniature version of the 1944 Normandy invasion.

The destroyer *USS Calvin*, hydrofoil *USS Pegasus*, and Coast Guard patrol craft *USCG Osprey* sat off shore with cannons and machine guns aimed at the shoreline. The Customs Service Falcon jet aircraft, along with a U.S. Coast Guard Dauphine helicopter, orbited the island. From three thousand feet up, the jet monitored everything going on in the area, while the helicopter came in low, looking for Drake and his men. Since, with the exception of the narrow channel dredged for the submarine, waters on this side of the island were too shallow for the big surface vessels, the invasion had to take place on the opposite side of the island from Drake's facilities. The house and the submarine pen were all on the leeward side of the island. Curiously enough, while the cocaine lab was on another island a mere seventy-five feet away, Drake had never connected the two islands with a bridge, which meant they needed a small boat to move from one island to the other.

Regardless of this fact, a small flotilla of shallow-draft boats from the Bahamian Defense Force patrolled the shoreline around both islands. The plan was for the Bahamian Police and Bahamian Defense Force, accompanied by armed US Navy sailors, Coast Guard personnel, and US Federal Agents to storm the island from the deepwater side. If anyone on shore got froggy, the rapid-fire cannons on the three United States ships would speak and silence them forever.

The armed assault team would then traverse the islands, beginning with the smaller one containing the lab, cross to the residential island and then cover the mile or so to the buildings, taking them by force, if necessary. Sixty armed men slogged ashore from the small boat, armed mostly with small arms, pistols, M-16 rifles, and the *Osprey*'s old M-79 grenade launcher, passed from one Coast Guard vessel to another since the Vietnam War. The landing went off unopposed and the men began their walk across the first sandy island. They reached the first building, which appeared to be the lab, without seeing anyone. Commander Eldridge was about two hundred paces behind a Bahamian soldier who looked as though he was about to enter the building.

"Hey pal, why don't you wait a minute before you go in there," the commander shouted.

The soldier gave Eldridge a cocky look and stepped through the door. Immediately, there was a loud explosion that knocked Eldridge and several others to the ground, hard, and the laboratory building appeared to sink into the earth. A booby trap, made from a large amount of high explosives was located just inside the door. The blast instantly killed the impatient Bahamian soldier and wounded two others. It was also powerful enough to level every palm tree within fifty feet. Eldridge stood up, bruised from his unexpected fall, and wiped sand from his face as his portable radio crackled. It was Lieutenant Tanner, who had stayed aboard his patrol craft to coordinate the air, sea, and ground effort.

"Eldridge! Are you okay?" he yelled over the radio. "What was that explosion?"

Eldridge was having a tough time understanding the man since the concussion of the blast affected his hearing. The low flying helicopter made hearing even harder. The French-made Dauphine rescue helicopter made a very unique sound. The turbine engine almost sounded as if it was grinding itself up as it flew. At the moment, that's all Eldridge could hear.

"Tanner! We have wounded!" he replied. "Send the chopper in now!"

Upon hearing of the situation, the USCG pilot maneuvered the orange and white helicopter to a clearing behind the assault force and touched down. The medic the Bahamians had sent along for the operation tended to the two wounded men. Both had suffered lacerations to their legs from the bomb. Reacting immediately to the new threat, Tanner called his Miami base on the secure line. In what had to be some of the best inter-agency cooperation ever, it only took thirty minutes for bomb squad specialists from Miami and Miami-Dade Police Departments to be airborne on the U.S. Customs Service Blackhawk helicopter, and heading for Drake's islands at one hundred forty miles per hour. While they were waiting for the explosives experts to arrive, Eldridge and the inspector called all of the assault force together and set up a perimeter around the part of the island they'd already secured. After the bomb guys from the two police agencies arrived, the force moved out again, albeit much more carefully.

Poking around, Eldridge found a cave entrance and sent the bomb squad cops in first, who carefully cleared every step they took. Eldridge followed at a safe distance to avoid being knocked on his rear end for the second time in one day by another surprise explosion. He heard one of the bomb guys let out a loud yell, and the commander broke into a run, pistol in hand, to help the man. When he reached him, he saw the officer staring down the beam of light from his flashlight and breathing very heavily. Eldridge looked down and gasped. There he saw bones and sculls, and more bones and sculls, littering the floor of the cave for fifty yards.

"Holy Mother of Christ!" he yelled, horrified by the sight of the mass grave. Looking around, Eldridge went from horrified to furious in one quick second seeing the remains of so many people, some adults, and some obviously children. He noticed one of them wearing a rotted *Subtdives* t-shirt. Realizing again that this was how Drake faked the first sub's sinking, the commander was angry as hell about it. When they crossed to the larger island and reached Drake's residence, they were greeted by a large hastily written sign that said, "Welcome!" It was attached to the open, heavy steel-barred inner front door. The bomb squad officers went in first and cleared another booby trap just past the doorway. One of them came back out and motioned to Eldridge.

"It was a pretty sophisticated device, Commander. C-4 wired to a detonator and triggered by an infrared beam aimed across the doorway."

Eldridge shook his head as he looked at the triggering device. It was made from two infrared emitters of the type used to keep electric garage doors from closing on anyone or anything in their way. "Sophisticated and simple," he muttered.

The Bahamian soldiers and police cleared the rest of the house.

"Nobody home?" Eldridge asked Winston as he entered the living room.

Winston was reading a letter left in a very obvious place on a table in the middle of the room for the police to find.

"Come look at this, *mon*," he said, motioning to the commander.

Eldridge looked at the paper and read, his anger growing with each word.

Dear Bahamian Police and American Police,

I hope you understand why I decided not to stay around to greet you when you arrived on <u>my</u> island. I realize that you probably have some silly warrant for my arrest by now, so I have decided to take an extended vacation on the island of Cuba.

Yes, I have gone to visit my dear friend Fidel and you can't do a bloody thing about it. My closest people are going on vacation with me. The rest of them have gone on their way to wherever they want to go, on my credit card, of course.

My son Derrick will assume control of my island after you vacate it, since he is not involved in my business, and you haven't any evidence to prove that statement incorrect.

Help yourself to wine and food while you are there, and do enjoy your stay.

Your Devoted Servant,

Anton Drake

"Son-of-a-bitch," Eldridge whispered. Then he heard a crash behind him. Spinning around, he saw Inspector Winston standing next to a broken glass photograph frame, his right hand bleeding, apparently, from punching the glass. The emotion was just too much for him. He had struck at a picture of Anton Drake standing on the bow of one of his go-fast boats. Another officer calmly pulled gauze from a first aid kit and bandaged his hand.

"All of this, and he runs to Cuba," Winston hissed. "I cannot touch him there unless Castro gives him up, and I don't have the kind of money to make that happen."

Eldridge saw the inspector was almost in tears. He realized that no amount of pressure exerted by the Bahamian or United States governments would make Cuba's *presidente forever* give up Anton Drake.

"All of his speedboats are gone," Eldridge said, trying to get the inspector's mind off Drake. "If his guys took the boats, they may still be in the area, and we can hunt them down..."

Winston nodded, still staring at the broken picture of Drake. "I have him, but I cannot get to him," he said sadly.

"What pisses me off the most is that we will probably have to turn this whole place over to his idiot son when this is over with," Eldridge added, sounding almost as sad as the inspector.

"Unless of course, your government sees fit to seize the island, since it was used in a continuing criminal enterprise."

"My government is not as up to date as yours, when it comes to fighting this war," the inspector sighed. "It will be tough to take away his land. And besides that, the corrupt ones in my government will probably side with his son, for the right price."

Just then, one of the Defense Force soldiers called Winston and Eldridge out to the dock. On arrival, they learned that bomb squad cops had searched and cleared the area. All marveled at the huge structure Drake had built for his tourist submarine. *Subdives II* was berthed in a huge

195

concrete structure that almost replicated the submarine pens used by the German Navy during the Second World War. Every part of the building was extremely robust.

But the really interesting part of the structure appeared to be below the water. By standing next to the dock and looking straight down in the now noonday sunlight, Eldridge could see that the resident submarine was sitting in water just a few feet deeper than her keel. Below that was a concrete floor joined to the walls of the structure. He saw a large square hatch where the submarine house met the island sand. Eldridge was standing next to the hatch when the bomb squad tech from the Miami P.D. exited through the open door.

"She's all clear downstairs," the officer said.

"Downstairs?" Eldridge asked, looking at the man.

"Yeah, and you won't believe what's down there," the officer replied. Eldridge walked down the wide stairs, half expecting to find a torture chamber with more human remains strewn about the floor. Instead, he found a large room with a painted steel dock, complete with cleats to tie up a vessel, but minus one important item, as there was no water. The floor under the dock was covered with several one-foot thick rubber blocks that were roughly cut in the shape of the submarine. *But how would you get a vessel to the dock*, Eldridge wondered, since this *harbor* was forty feet below the surface of the water? One of the Bahamian soldiers found an electrical breaker switch in a watertight box on one of the walls. Throwing the switch lit the entire chamber under dazzling light, revealing a large watertight door twenty feet past the end of the dock. The commander had seen some incredible construction projects built by the military, but this one topped them all. Somehow, Mr. Drake had built an underwater submarine base, apparently to house his *sunken* submarine, while keeping it totally concealed from the outside world. Eldridge surmised that there must be switchgear somewhere up on the dock used to flood the chamber. This would equalize the water pressure from the outside and allow the doors to be opened. The sub could then cruise into the chamber, where the pilot could then bottom the vessel on the rubber bed, saving the hull from damage. The doors would then be closed, and the water pumped from the chamber, leaving the deck of the submarine even with the dock. It could then have its batteries charged and its deck rack loaded with canisters of cocaine for shipment.

Exiting the underwater chamber, Eldridge walked to the nearest building, a small, block structure with a metal roof about fifty feet from the dock. This building had already been cleared of explosives and searched, but no one had found anything remarkable, mainly because they didn't know what to look for. Upon entering the building, Eldridge immediately noticed a metal panel on the wall with a very expensive padlock. After a short discussion with Inspector Winston, it was decided that the panel should be opened. Given the fact that the invaders of Drake's island didn't have much in the way of power tools, they decided to use the most expedient method available to remove the lock. After putting a warning out by radio, one of the Bahamian soldiers placed the muzzle of his ancient British .303 caliber SMLE rifle next to the lock, while another soldier held a piece of plywood to shield him when he pulled the trigger. The bullet shattered the lock into pieces that bounced across the concrete floor. Eldridge opened the panel revealing switches simply labeled "water in" and "water out" along with another set that simply said "doors." This was all that Drake needed to move his covert submarine to and from the shipping lanes, as the undersea tunnel that Callaway discovered began a short fifty yards from the dock.

"This is slicker than eel shit," Eldridge said, looking at Winston. "He spent a bunch of money building this."

The inspector, still rather despondent over not catching Drake, just shook his head in disgust.

DEA Supervisory Special Agent Cruz landed on the island. He came in after the assault force, as he was still recovering and moving slowly from the bullet wound he'd received aboard *Blue Thunder III*. He was looking for some kind of a clue as to the location of his missing undercover operative. He had not heard from Carrie Marvin since before the operation shifted into its assault phase. He had no way of advising her of Callaway's discovery of the submarine drug boat, or the impending invasion of Golgotha. He'd hoped that someone would find her hunkered down somewhere on the island, but so far there was no sign of her.

Callaway was back in New Providence, chomping at the bit in anticipation of finding his lover. Cruz went back aboard the Coast Guard patrol craft and made two calls: one to his superiors at the Miami office of the DEA and the other, which was against all regulations, to Michael Callaway. In both calls, he reported the same thing, that there were no clues as to the whereabouts of Special Agent Carrie Marvin.

Callaway tried to remain calm. He walked around the interior of the shrimper, trying to busy himself to take his mind off Carrie. It wasn't working. He sat and took another sip from his glass of whiskey, in which the ice had melted hours before. His hands shook. "Boy, you got it bad, this time," he worried aloud. "Why did I let her go back there, dammit! I should have busted a bottle over her head and dragged her away from here." He laughed, knowing that as tough as she was, it probably wouldn't have dissuaded Carrie from going back. Dusk arrived and with it, his worry increased. He thought that there must be something he could do. *But what?* he wondered. *If she was not on Golgotha, than she must have gone to Havana with that scumbag Drake. What else could she do? It wasn't a matter of keeping her cover anymore, it would be survival. If she tried to deviate from Drake's plans, it would expose the fact that something wasn't quite right with Shae, the lesbian bodyguard, and Drake's men would kill her in a heartbeat.*

The more Callaway thought of it, the more complex the problem seemed. If she did end up in Cuba, it would be very difficult for her to leave or even communicate with anyone in the United States, since, as she was well aware, all communications to and from that island were monitored by the government. Fidel wouldn't look too kindly on a U.S. Government agent in his midst. Callaway momentarily considered single-handedly infiltrating Cuba to find his girl, when he heard the rumble of large engines idling up alongside his boat. He immediately went into a defensive mode, just as he had the night Carrie had paid him a visit after the almost barroom brawl with Drake. He quietly opened the gun cabinet, this time selecting his Remington 870 pump shotgun. His was in ultra-cautious mode and he thought that, perhaps, since he had been seen and identified by Drake's man after sinking the submarine, that Anton might have sent a crew to kill him out of revenge for screwing up his drug operation. Callaway figured that if the visitors were bad guys, they would come in through the large rear entrance to the cabin. He turned the lights off, quietly creeping to the front of the cabin, while slowly racking the action of the shotgun. Callaway shimmied up the ladder to a small front-deck hatch. He pushed the hatch open and poked his head and the shotgun out. Looking through the sights, he examined the deck in a 360-degree circle. *Nothing*, he thought.

He stepped out onto the deck and glanced down the starboard side of the shrimper. In the darkness, he could make out the unmistakable shape of a Midnight Express speedboat. The bow of the boat was tied to the corner of his boat's stern, but there appeared to be no one aboard. He crept back toward the Midnight, constantly looking up at the bridge of his own boat in case a would-be assassin was hiding up there.

Again, nothing. Callaway reached the rear of his boat and still could see no one in the cockpit of the Midnight. He stepped onto the bow of the flat-black-painted boat, shotgun mounted on his shoulder, and walked back toward the cockpit. When he reached it, he pointed the weapon down, and saw a man lying on the deck. His hands and feet were bound, and there was a piece of duct tape across his mouth. He wasn't moving at all.

Calloway was now officially weirded out. He turned and looked around the topside of his boat, and again saw no one. *Okay, this Midnight didn't cruise up here and tie itself to my boat, so the driver or drivers must be below decks,* he surmised. Sweat rolled down his face and into his eyes. It was fight or flight time. He could easily jump to the dock and go to a telephone to call for help, but once a cop always a cop. He advanced toward the large rear door of the cabin, seeing a small silver of light glowing under the door. He began turning the doorknob with his left hand, while keeping the scattergun mounted to his shoulder with his right. Throwing the door open, he saw a lone figure near the liquor cabinet with their back toward him. He was holding just a bit of pressure on the trigger when the person spun

201

around pointing a pistol at him. For a split second their love story almost came to an end, as Michael Callaway and Carrie Marvin stood poised to shoot each other. All of the training the federal government gave them kicked in, as they both hesitated just long enough to recognize each other. Callaway pushed the safety on and threw the Remington on the couch. He and Carrie met in the middle of the room in a hug and a long passionate kiss.

"Thank God you're here," Callaway whispered, as both of them lost control and began to cry. Callaway again hugged her tightly for a long time and then led her to the couch. Moving the shotgun out of the way so they could sit, Callaway had about a hundred questions to ask her. Before he could say anything, she put the tip of her index finger to his lips.

"You are all I have thought about for the last two days," she said. "I was there when the boat driver who saw you near Golgotha reported to Drake. He said you *sank* his submarine? How the hell did you do that, Callaway?" She shook her head.

He smiled at her, stroking her hair, which was all matted down with salt from what had obviously been a long ride in a fast boat.

"It was an old trick that my daddy taught me, but that's not important," he answered. "The sub that I sank was carrying cocaine, and lots of it . . . ."

She interrupted him to ask, "How can that be? I saw the submarine docked at the island when I left."

"What you saw was his new sub. The one I sank was the one that supposedly sank on the tour, which didn't really sink..." he answered, lowering his face and looking up at her.

She looked confused for a second, until it all clicked in her mind. "Son-of-a-bitch," Carrie yelled, slamming her fist on the counter next to her.

Callaway went on to reveal what Special Agent Cruz had told him about the island, including the cave full of bones and the underwater submarine pen.

"That's why he wouldn't let me near the dock where the sub was," she said. Now it was Callaway's turn to be curious.

"So how did you get away, and who's your unconscious buddy in the boat outside?" he asked.

"Oh, him?" she answered smiling. "Yeah, well Drake told us he was heading to Havana so he could camp out with Fidel until the heat died down. He figured that with what you saw, the Bahamians would certainly have enough to put him away, so he made good his getaway. I guess he's had this planned for a while because he was gone within an hour of getting the word that you sank the sub. How did you do that, again?"

Callaway just gave her a wink and asked, "So what happened then? He didn't want his ace bodyguard to go with him?"

Carrie stood up and grabbed the bottle of whiskey on the counter. "We were told to leave in a staggered formation, two boats full of his boys, then Drake in another boat with Martino Herrera and a couple of his Cuban confidants," she said. "And then the rest of us were to leave at half-hour intervals. He wanted people out there to protect his ass if the cops or the Defense Force came after him."

Callaway pulled her back down to the couch and held two glasses out for her to fill. "So why didn't he just take the plane?" he asked as he sipped his drink.

"Well, timing is everything, you know," she answered. "As luck would have it, the plane was in Fort Lauderdale with sonny-boy Derrick. The old man doesn't want him getting into any trouble. Of course, that isn't out of any kind of paternal love or crap like that. He just wants Derrick available to take back the island after the Bahamians get through with it."

"Okay, go on," Callaway said, sliding a little closer and taking her hand.

She responded by giving him a long kiss and then suddenly pulling away, yelling, "I've got to call in. The agency must be going nuts trying to find me." She started to grab for the telephone, but Callaway pulled it away from her hand.

"Finish the story, dammit!" he demanded impatiently.

"Okay, my boat left after Drake and five others took off," she continued. "They told me that my driver, you know, the unconscious guy outside, would take me to Havana, where I would meet up with Drake. We were running along, and I knew I would have to make a break for it or end up in a Cuban jail or dead. I figured I would take the driver out and run, but I knew the others would chase me. I don't know much about driving fast boats, but I got real lucky because we ran right into a strong squall, and everyone lost sight of each other. I neutralized the driver, and hauled ass out of there."

"*Neutralized*?" Callaway said with a funny look.

"Yeah, neutralized," she said, smirking. "You know, like the way you *neutralized* Drake's submarine. Only he'll live to tell about it."

He laughed and then began kissing her neck.

"I need to call in, Callaway," she said laughing, as she stood up and grabbed the cell phone off his belt. She dialed the number and gave the operator a code. Carrie was immediately connected with her supervisor, Special Agent-in-Charge Alberto Cruz. Callaway listened while gently rubbing Carrie's back. She explained that she was in a secure place in Nassau without mentioning Callaway's name. She then told Cruz about her abrupt exit from the island when Drake heard about Callaway and his submarine. She also advised him that Drake was probably already in Cuba, unless his boat broke down, crashed into a reef, or was eaten by a sea monster or something.

When the debriefing was over, Cruz told Carrie to stay on the line while he arranged her passage back to Miami. He put her on hold while he called

Washington to report in. When he came back on, Cruz changed the conversation completely.

"Carrie, I know about you and Callaway," he said in a soft voice. "How the hell did that happen?"

"It just happened, Al. It's just as simple as that," she answered, as Callaway held her from behind.

"I guess I should call the lucky bastard and tell him you're okay," Cruz replied.

Callaway was close enough to hear the conversation.

"Hey, it's cool man, I know she's all right," Callaway said with a laugh. Cruz laughed, too. But, it was a cautious laugh. Carrie told Cruz that she wanted to stay in Nassau for a couple of days to chill out, and that she would be well protected with Callaway. Cruz argued that Nassau was not a safe enough place for her, in case Drake was wise to her status, or if he just wanted to take revenge on Callaway for messing up his operation. Callaway advised Cruz that he would bring Carrie to Miami aboard the *Orinoco Flow*, and that they would leave immediately.

"Umm, I guess I'm going to need a little house keeping done at the marina where Callaway's boat is docked," she advised. "There's a Midnight parked next to it with one of Drake's men on the cockpit floor. He should probably be interrogated." Cruz advised that he would contact a couple of his guys stationed in Nassau and have them make the pickup. He was certain that Inspector Winston would want to have a chat with the man, as well.

"Oh and there's one other thing, Al." She gritted her teeth in anticipation, knowing her next statement would make Cruz very angry. "When I get to Miami, I'm turning in my resignation from the agency," she told him, smiling at Callaway.

"You're quitting! Why in hell are you doing that? How can I lose one of my best undercover people?"

"I've had enough of living two lives, Al," she answered. "I'm thirty-three years old and I've been undercover in one hellhole or another for the last eleven of them. I've had enough."

"So take a friggin' vacation," he said, trying to salvage what he could.

"Oh, I plan to. Like a forever vacation," she said as she looked deep into Callaway's eyes. "We'll be in Miami on Friday, right Callaway?" she said to both men.

Callaway smiled and looked at her lovingly. "How about Saturday? I think we need to go fishing," he said with a pleading look.

"Saturday," she said, with a degree of finality.

Cruz grumbled something in Spanish then conceded with, "All right, all right, Saturday. But if anyone comes after you on that big, slow boat, you will be on your own, unless you're lucky enough to be near one of the Coast Guard boats or some of our other assets out there."

"Drake's in Cuba, Al," she said. "The last thing he will do is show his face anywhere where Castro can't protect him."

"The guy has people all over the place, and besides, do we have absolute proof that he's in Cuba?" Cruz asked. "Hell no, we don't."

"Well, for once I'm gonna take a chance, Al. Besides, I have Callaway to protect me," she said as Callaway ran his hands up under her shirt.

"Um, Al, I have to go, now. I'll see you on Saturday."

Chapter 21

It was the kind of morning that fishing guides exalt over. The sky was clear, except for a few fluffy, white clouds, the ocean was calm, and there was just a slight breeze blowing from the east. Carrie was sleeping soundly when Callaway threw open the drapes allowing the bright morning sun to blast the room with light. It had been a night of drinking and wild sex, starting even before the DEA guys came and removed the Midnight Express and its occupant from the birth next to Callaway's shrimp boat. After all that, Carrie was looking forward to sleeping in. She thought about how late she would sleep as she and Callaway finished their lovemaking, and realized that this would be the first morning in over two years that she would sleep past six o'clock in the morning. She drifted off with a grin remembering all the lovemaking and anticipating sleeping in, which would almost be as good as the sex itself.

However, Callaway had determined that this wasn't to be the morning that she would find that out. "Come on baby, the fish are waiting for us," Callaway said loudly.

As groggy as Carrie was, she suddenly realized that the boat was moving, and the noise from the shrimper's diesel engine was the reason Callaway was raising his voice. "Are we moving?" she asked. "How did I manage to sleep through the sounds of you starting the engine, untying from the dock, and heading out to sea, and all the other noises bouncing around inside this boat?"

"We are moving and we are hell and gone from Nassau," Callaway said with a grin. "We should be at our fishing spot in about a half an hour, and I should have you hooked into a bonefish fifteen minutes after that."

Seeing that he was wearing shorts and a button-down short-sleeve shirt with a half-dozen pockets, Carrie knew he was serious. She gave him a kind of half pissed-off, half desperate look. It was true confession time. "Uh, Mike," she began, looking sheepishly up at him, "did I ever mention that I have never been fishing before?"

Callaway's expression instantly changed from a happy smile to total confusion. "You are kidding, right?" he asked, looking very serious. "I mean everybody has been fishing at least once! I mean it's the world's biggest goddamn participant sport!"

"I'm sorry, but I grew up in Indiana, far, far away from the ocean," she answered. "The closest big river was near Gary and the only things they pulled out of that water were dead gangbangers and stolen cars."

Callaway stared at the floor, and sadly intoned, "I cannot marry you."

For an instant Carrie thought he was serious, as she thought back to their first encounter at FLETC, and how all he talked about when they weren't in bed, was fishing. Callaway threw a pillow at her and began laughing.

"I'll teach you how to fish. You're gonna love it," he said.

"Asshole!" She threw the pillow back. "By the way, who's steering this tub if you're down here?" she asked.

"I have her on autopilot," he replied. "An alarm will go off when we reach the spot."

"And that spot is, where?" she asked in a very sexy tone. She rolled out of bed and stood naked before him. She really didn't want to learn to fish, at least not today, and she thought she might be able to entice him back into bed. Callaway looked her up and down. *My plan is working*, she thought, but only for a second.

"You'd better put on some sunscreen until we can get you tanned up a little bit," he said as he grabbed a large, plastic shopping bag off the floor and tossed it to her. "We'll be fishing near a little island that's one of my secret spots," he said proudly.

She clenched her teeth and fished around inside the bag finding shorts, a couple of t-shirts, and a fairly skimpy, but very cute, blue, palm-tree-print bikini. "Where did you get this stuff? Or did you already have it on board for all of your *other* women?" she asked snidely.

Grinning, Callaway shook his head. "I called the guy who owns the dock store back in Nassau, and asked him to hustle this stuff over this morning," he replied. "I hope they fit you."

Examining the labels, she answered, "Yeah, they should be perfect. But when did you call the guy?"

"I called him at home right after you went to sleep," he answered. "He bitched a bit, cause it was like 3:00 a.m., but he calmed down when I told him there would be a hundred dollar tip waiting for him. He got them here promptly this morning."

Carrie finally realized just how wealthy Callaway was. She knew how tight money was for federal agents and was amazed at how easy it had become for Callaway to dole out money for whatever he wanted. However, Carrie was still not in the mood to try fishing for the first time. She'd envisioned a relaxing ride to Miami while sunbathing nude on the front deck and drinking pina coladas. All she could imagine now as she donned the bikini was salt water and cut bait. Callaway saw the concern in her eyes.

"I'm telling you, you're going to love where we're going," he said reassuringly. "It's a beautiful place, this little island." Hearing the GPS alarm, Callaway announced, "Ah, we have arrived," and led her up to the cockpit and went to the front deck to anchor the boat. Immediately thereafter, he walked to the back of the boat to lower the Hewes into the water from the stern-mounted davits.

Carrie could see that Mike had loaded the flats skiff with all kinds of stuff, such as eight fishing rods in all shapes and sizes, while she was still sleeping. There were wispy long rods with tiny reels mounted on them, medium-sized rod-and-reel setups, and one big and bad looking black and gold rod. On the end of that rod's line was a long, cigar shaped lure with two sets of huge hooks. The two sets of three hooks were shiny like chrome, with points that looked as if they had been ground sharp with diamond dust. The lure was hooked to a small wire ring at the base of the rod, right in front of the reel. Callaway could see that Carrie was interested in the big setup.

"That one's for tarpon, if we see any," he said.

She looked confused.

"Tarpon are huge silver fish that can go two hundred pounds," he continued. "They put up a hell of a fight."

"Are they dangerous?" she asked appearing mesmerized by the nasty looking lure.

"No, they are absolutely harmless, unless one jumps out of the water and bumps into you," he answered. "That's been known to happen now and then."

"So, do I get to use that one?" she asked with a devious smile.

Callaway laughed. "Uh, no, we'll start you off with something a little smaller, so I can teach you how to cast," he answered, happy that she finally seemed interested.

"What does that matter, Callaway?" she asked. "I think I can hit the ocean with the bait."

Callaway shook his head. "Baby, fishing is a little different here," he said grinning. "This isn't some little pond, where the fish are a captive audience. Look around. That's a big ocean out there. You have to find the fish and then cast to them. You have to be accurate. It's kind of like hunting with a rod and reel."

Looking around and seeing nothing but water, Carrie asked, "Callaway? Where the hell is this island that we're going to?"

"Look off the left side of the bow, at about eleven o'clock," he said, pointing at what appeared to be nothing but more ocean. "That's where we're going."

Carrie looked and looked, squinting like a little kid. "All I can see is a little speck, way out on the horizon," she said.

"Yeah, that's the one," he replied without hesitation.

She looked even more confused. "Why are we stopped…"

"Anchored," he interrupted.

"Okay, why are we anchored, all the way out here? We must be a good ten miles away from that little spec out there," she said, again looking worried.

"Actually, it's more like fifteen," he replied. "We can't get any closer because the water is very shallow from here on in. There are a couple of fairly deep channels on the other side of the island, but they're not deep enough for the big boat to get into. I had to time this out perfectly so we go in at high tide, and leave at high tide, or even the flats boat won't get over the sand bar. The upside of this is that the island is naturally well protected, so nobody goes there. That means we have all the fish for ourselves, and," he continued with a leer, "total privacy on the island."

Carrie was still not on board with fishing, but warmed up to the idea of being alone with her man on a deserted island. Before they climbed into the boat, Callaway threw a small one-man raft into the water on the starboard side of the *Orinoco Flow* and tied it to the rail in the middle of the boat.

"I've got a little repair work to do on the hull when we get back, so I'll need the raft to sit in," he said. Carrie gave him a concerned look, but he assured her the shrimp boat wouldn't sink while they were gone.

As they climbed into the flats boat, Carrie pointed to a large cooler latched to the floor in front of the console and asked, "What's in here, bait?"

"No, it's just food and stuff," Callaway said as he fired up the Yamaha outboard.

She opened the lid and found plastic bags, all neatly packed with sandwiches and fruit. There were also bottles of water, and one large bottle of Dom Perignon champagne. "What's this for?" she asked, rubbing the cold bottle with her fingers.

"That is for celebrating your first fish, after you catch it, of course," he replied.

What Callaway didn't tell her was that hidden in the ice below the bottle were two gold chains in a gift box, hidden in a Tupperware container. Each of the chains had half of a world medallion attached. When you put them together, they formed the whole world. His game plan was to give Carrie one of the chains after he asked her to marry him. He thought it was a bit hokey, but it was the best thing he could get his hands on in such a short time. He figured that when they reached Miami they would go ring shopping. He had a friend who made custom jewelry at the Seabold building downtown. After that, he thought, the two of them would travel the planet together.

Michael Callaway was totally involved, as his fire fighter-friends used to describe a hopelessly burning house, in love with this girl. So much so that he wanted to spend the rest of his life with her. "Have a seat," he said, patting the padded bench seat beside him. He did not want her digging around in the cooler and finding his surprise. She sat down and he pushed the throttle forward. The little skiff aimed her bow at the sky before settling down to a nice smooth plane on top of the emerald green water. They raced toward the little island in the distance at about forty miles per hour. Carrie got comfortable as they zipped over the smooth water. She reached into the cooler, much to Callaway's concern, and pulled two bottles of water from the ice. He tried to watch her while keeping a straight course for the island.

Carrie had seen that guilty look before, mostly on criminals. "What's wrong, Callaway?" she asked with her hand still in the cooler. Callaway was at a loss to change the subject, but the ocean did it for him. The little boat began bumping around as they hit choppy water in a trough that bordered a twenty-mile long sandbar hidden by the water at high tide. Carrie yanked her hand out of the cooler and began looking for something to grab on to. She found out quickly that while the driver of a flats boat had the steering wheel to hold on to, the passenger had little or nothing to grip. She ended up reaching under the gunwale to grab the edge of the fiberglass, hanging on as tightly as she possibly could. Callaway grinned when he saw this — his surprise would be safe.

He slowed the boat as they drew closer to the island, enough for Carrie to see detail. She was immediately impressed. With a length of about one mile, and a width about half as wide, this small piece of land was covered with coconut palms and lush foliage, and one of the most beautiful natural beaches she had ever seen. She kept thinking about how she would love to do nothing today except lay naked on the beach with the man she loves. That thought ended with the sound of the outboard slowing down to idle, as Callaway slowed the boat to a crawl about a half a mile from that beautiful beach. He pulled out one of the lighter rod and reel combos and handed it to Carrie. She took it and looked at him with a, *'and what do I do with this?'* look on her face.

Callaway explained, "I'm gonna teach you how to cast. By the time I'm through you'll be an expert," he said convincingly. As patient as he was, it took a little longer than he'd thought it would, but he eventually succeeded. Along the way, there was a lot of tangled fishing line, some slightly hurt feelings, and at least one case of Carrie accidentally hooking Callaway in the rear end. But after a while, she got the technique down. Spot the fish, aim, and smoothly cast the lure about five feet in front of it, and then flip it back so it looked like a scared baitfish.

"The guides in the Keys call that the 'Callaway flip,'" he said proudly, as he continued to explain how all of the parts of the reel worked. He showed her how to use the drag adjustment, to slow the fish down, and then set it somewhat loose. Callaway climbed onto the platform over the outboard at the rear of the boat and silently pushed the craft along through the foot deep water with an eighteen foot graphite push pole. He pointed out a couple of fish swimming on the flat, a large shallow area near the island, but she couldn't see them. He realized that her sunglasses weren't polarized; hence they wouldn't allow her to see through the glare on the surface. He took an old, nasty looking pair of fishing glasses out of the console and gave them to her.

She took them with an inquisitive look. "What am I supposed to do with these?" she asked. "These are disgusting."

"I know they're not the designer glasses you're used to. Just put 'em on, and then look into the water," he said.

She did as he asked, and immediately could see all kinds of things on the bottom. Pieces of coral, rocks, and even a lobster were now visible. "Oh cool," was her instant reaction.

Callaway figured that as long as he kept her away from a mirror so she couldn't see how clunky the glasses looked on her, she would be fine with them.

The first two bonefish she tried for spooked from her errant casting. But on the third try — magic. The fish pounced on the small shrimp jig like it hadn't eaten in days. At first, there was only a slight tug, but then the ten-pound "ghost of the flats" kicked it into high gear. The fish began a run that peeled the line off the reel at an extremely fast rate. Carrie screamed, not something she was used to doing, and looked a Callaway. He realized that he'd spent hours teaching her how to cast, but had not told her anything about what to do when she hooked up. He tried to keep her calm.

"Don't reel against the fish. Just hold on and let him run," he said soothingly over the high pitched sound of the reel's drag system fighting the fish. The finned bullet finally stopped after scorching about two-hundred fifty yards of line off the reel. The bare spool was beginning to show through the remnants of fishing line.

"Okay. Now, start reeling him in," he said softly.

She reeled and the fish slowly came her way. Smiling up at Callaway, she said, "That wasn't so hard." She continued working the line as she spoke. "Fish are like men in bed — they go like hell for a while, then they up and quit."

Callaway just smiled at her. Having caught thousands of bonefish, he knew what would happen next.

"Shit!" she yelled, as the fish turned suddenly and began to run again, ripping off almost as much line as it had the first time. Again the fish stopped, and at Callaway's urging, Carrie reeled in again.

This time the fish came all the way to the boat, and again she thought the fight was over. Callaway stood on the platform shaking his head at her obvious overconfidence as the fish turned and poured on the coal again. This run was much shorter, and this time she was able to work the bonefish to the boat. Callaway stood beside her with a short-handled net in his hand. He scooped the fish head first into the net and brought the twenty-six incher aboard. Carrie was spent. She was sweating like mad and her face was beet red from the fight. She sat down, and her mouth dropped open when Callaway pulled the fish from the net.

"All that work for that little fish?" she yelled. "I thought I was fighting something big."

"That's the amazing thing about these guys," Callaway said as he carefully wrapped the fish in a wet towel. He held it out to her, and Carrie smiled.

"Hold him so I can take your picture," he said.

All jazzed up over winning the fight, she immediately took the fish from him. Callaway retrieved his old Pentax 35 mm camera from the waterproof storage bin, made sure there was film in it, and then took several shots of Carrie with her first bonefish. He then gently laid the fish in the water, pulling it around by its lower jaw to aerate it and give it some strength before he set it free. He did not want such a magnificent fish devoured by some lucky reef shark that happened upon it when it was too weak to swim away.

"Well, what do you think?" he asked, half fearing that she thought the whole experience was a stupid waste of time.

She stood up and hugged him. "Let's go find another one," was all she said. She noticed though, that Callaway wasn't looking at her, as he was fixated on something in the water midway between them and the island. "What are you looking at, Callaway?" she asked as she glanced toward the island, but then realized his eyes were trained on the water, not land.

"I think it's time for me to fish a little," he said as he spun the throttle on the electric trolling motor and turned the boat toward the island. He grabbed the big bruiser rod, the one that Carrie had shown so much interest in while back on the *Orinoco Flow*—the rod that was baited with the big lure with the shiny treble hooks.

"Look about one hundred feet in front of us," he whispered. She could see that he was fired up, peering intently into the sea. She looked out ahead of the boat and saw something break the surface. Whatever it was, it appeared to be huge, as the part that was visible *above* the water was at least six feet long. The creature's sleek back was black, with shiny silver showing underneath. "Tarpon," he whispered, as he maneuvered a course to intercept the giant fish. Carrie watched the master guide at work, moving the boat deftly and silently nearer and nearer to his prey. She was amazed at Callaway's intensity in this situation. He suddenly crouched down, as if hiding from the fish, and shut off the trolling motor.

The Silver King broke the surface one more time and Callaway instantly reacted. He stood up and fired the lure out as if it was shot from a gun. The lure hit the water about seven feet in front of the fish. He gave it a "Callaway Flip," snapping it back so it dropped into the water near the tarpon's nose. She finally saw just how big the fish was when it rolled its eight feet of length over the submerged lure and ate it in one big gulp. She could hear Callaway softly counting down. "Five, four, three, two, one," he whispered, and then he struck the fish hard. He yanked the rod up, three times, digging the hook deep into the tarpon's boney jaw. The fish ran as Callaway held tight to the rod, which was now severely bent. As he strained against the fish, the line suddenly went slack.

"Oh no!" Carrie yelled. "Did you lose him?"

The words had barely left her lips when the silver giant leapt from the water. For a brief instant, the fish appeared suspended in the air, six feet above the surface. Callaway bowed the rod to the fish to keep the tension on the line. The fish began a run, stripping line off the reel at an alarming rate. Callaway kept his thumb on the spool, gently exerting pressure on the giant. "Gotta make him work!" he grunted, as the fish slowed, and then came to a stop. It now seemed as if Callaway was trying to pull a one hundred fifty pound log off the bottom of the ocean with thirty pound-test line. "Come on, give it up!" he yelled as the tarpon rose. He worked the fish slowly to the boat.

Carrie was amazed at both the size and the beauty of the fish. Its shiny scales looked like silver dollars. The fish had its huge mouth open, and Carrie almost screamed when Callaway reached down and grabbed the monster by the lower jaw. She thought the tarpon would bite his hand off. Callaway took in her shocked look as he wrestled with the fish that was still trying to get away.

"Relax!" he said. "They have teeth like sandpaper." He then gave out a bloodcurdling yell just to freak her out. It worked, as she jumped from the floor to the front deck in one quick leap. She was less than pleased when she saw him laughing.

"I will kick your ugly ass, Callaway!" she said, only half joking.

This time it was Carrie who would take the pictures. Callaway dragged the big fish aboard and gingerly pulled it up to the front platform. "When I lift him up, you take the picture," he said, straining to lift the behemoth.

Carrie sat on the small seat at the front of the console and focused the camera. Callaway pulled the head of the huge fish up to the level of his chest, which was as high as he could possibly lift it.

"Smile you two," she said as she pushed the shutter button. At that very moment the tarpon decided to use its last line of defense to shake the grasp of its captor and emptied its bowels all over the deck. Carrie screamed as about four gallons of liquid tarpon poop rolled down the deck toward her. She ran around the console cursing the fish as she slipped and fell, jumping back up to avoid the stinking mess coming her way. Callaway laughed hysterically as he lifted the fish over the gunwale and back into the water. He jumped in next to it, and pulled the fish around until it could regain its strength. Then he let it swim slowly away.

He looked up to see Carrie standing on the seat frowning down at him. He just smiled up at her. "Hi, honey," he said sheepishly as he hoisted himself up into the boat. He pulled a hose and nozzle out of a storage bin, hooked it up to the raw water outlet on the transom and hosed all the fish excrement out through the scuppers at the rear of the boat.

"I promise you'll enjoy the rest of the day more than you did the fishing," he said softly.

She smiled and pulled him to her, giving him a sloppy kiss. "It made me so hot!" She laughed as she said the words in jest. He laughed at the joke realizing that she was actually having a good time. It was good to see that she was starting to loosen up and relax. They fished for another two hours until the tide changed. Callaway then ran the boat toward the island.

"Where are we going, now?" Carrie asked as they neared the shore. Callaway slowed the boat down, and gently bumped the bow up on to the sandy beach.

"The tide changed, so the fishing won't be good for a while," he said, half-lying. Even though the fish would be biting for at least another hour, he wanted to be alone with her on the beach. He did have his priorities.

Carrie was amazed at the beauty of the little island. The sand along the beach was a beautiful shade of light tan, and it was so smooth that it almost seemed a sin to make footprints in it. Callaway grabbed the cooler and jumped into the surf. He held out his hand and helped Carrie off the boat. The water, a mixture of the Atlantic Ocean and the Caribbean Sea, was refreshingly cool. It was a nice change from the heat of the day. They walked down the beach until they found a spot where the water had cut a miniature inlet into the island. They put down a big towel and sat down to eat lunch. They ate sandwiches and drank beer and laughed about people and things that they had encountered in their past. Then it happened. They looked at each other silently and realized that they were happy and relaxed for the first time in many, many years. It was a strange and pleasant feeling that they both attributed to each other without saying a word. It was as if each of them was finally exhaling a great breath of air they'd been holding in their straining lungs for way too long.

They kissed and within minutes were making love on the beach towel, not caring who, if anybody was watching. Not that they had to worry, since the only creatures that might see them were dolphins surfacing off the beach. When they finished, they held each other for a long time, dozing, as they listened to the waves making love to the beach. It was in this beautiful solitude that they knew they wanted to be with each other forever. Callaway reached into the cooler and produced the slightly wet gift-wrapped box containing the pendant and chain. He handed it to her with a boyish grin. She grinned back, while tearing the box open like a kid with a box of Crackerjacks. She held the pendent up and looked at the small, gold half-world.

"Pretty corny, huh?" Callaway asked, softly.

"Where's the other half?" she asked.

Reaching back into the cooler, he retrieved the small plastic bag containing the other half of the globe. He took it out and then removed the chain from around his neck. He threaded the chain through the loop on the end of his side of the pendent and put the chain back on. Now he had a cross, his Saint Michael medal, and the pendent on the same chain.

"How does it look?" he asked.

She stared at the combination for a minute. "If you added a golden horn, you'd look like a real guinea Italian," she said with a laugh. She saw the hurt look on his face and stopped laughing. "I'm joking with you, Callaway!" she said. "It looks good, honest. And I love mine."

He hooked the chain around her neck and held her tight.

"I want to be with you forever, Callaway," she whispered. She didn't realize just how close they were to losing that dream.

Chapter 22

"I told you to use my sun block," Callaway scolded as he put his hand on Carrie's darkening shoulder. She winced from the painful contact. They gathered all of their stuff, being careful not to leave anything that would spoil this beautiful place. They vowed to come here again, and, then, with an engagement ring in hand, Callaway would propose to her once more on this incredible beach where their souls finally met.

Callaway grabbed the cooler and Carrie grabbed the beach bag, and the two of them strolled naked down the beach holding hands. When they reached the boat, they dressed, and it was then that she realized how burned she was. While Callaway was stowing all the gear away, Carrie sat sleepy-eyed on the front console seat. He thought she looked like a tired little girl. "Why don't you curl up on the deck under a towel, and go to sleep for a while?" he suggested.

She smiled, rolled herself up in the soft terrycloth, and dozed right off. Callaway pushed the Hewes off the beach when he heard the sound of large engines, a lot of large engines, coming from a distance on the other side of the island. He didn't think there was a boat race scheduled in the area, so the sound seemed odd. *Maybe it's just some rich guys in one of the Miami "go-fast boat" clubs, doing a flotilla run to the Bahamas*, he thought. He knew these wealthy folks would go from island to island, stopping only at night to party and act stupid. He laughed to himself, remembering, *Wait a minute, dumb-ass; you're one of those rich guys now, too.*

The thought of having millions of dollars at his fingertips had faded away while he was with Carrie. He thought for a second of how she was really all he needed in life, but he was practical enough to know the money was nice to have, too. He started the outboard and began idling away from the island, when he noticed an airplane approaching from the east. The sound of the large boat engines suddenly quadrupled in magnitude, roaring toward them. Looking up, he noticed the airplane was now circling at high altitude. He stared up at the plane as the flats boat cleared the north tip of the island. It appeared to be a Beach King Air. He suddenly remembered who owned this type of airplane. He turned and saw seven rooster-tale wakes coming toward him at very high speed.

"Drake!" he hissed, as he turned the Hewes away from the approaching boats and slammed the throttle down. The bow of the little boat reached toward the sky and then settled into a dead run, flat out at fifty miles per hour.

Hearing the name and feeling the boat's increased speed, Carrie woke up, and asked, "What the hell's going on?" She tried to extricate herself from the cocoon she had created in the towel.

"Stay down and covered!" Callaway commanded, trying to watch both the aircraft and the boats. "Obviously our friend Drake has sent his boys to take their revenge on me. Stay down, dammit!" he yelled. "He probably still doesn't know who you really are, or that you're with me. Let's keep it that way for now. Just stay under that towel and hang on, cause we're gonna go fast."

Carrie, feeling the boat bucking along harder than she had experienced all day, thought they were going fast already.

The seven boats were gaining on them, quickly. Callaway could make out the heads of the men running the boats as they approached. He searched the waters around them looking for a place where his boat could go, but theirs couldn't follow. He realized he had only one option to keep them both alive. He would run his boat as fast as he could at the shallow sandbar extending twenty miles in either direction. If they could clear the bar, they just might have a chance. The big boats would have to run, either way, up or down the bar to find water deep enough to traverse the shallow bar, and then come back and try to pick up his trail. He again told Carrie to hold on, as he aimed the Hewes at the area of the flat with the smoothest water, indicating that it was the deepest area. He knew it would be risky. If he misjudged the capability of his boat and his ability to negotiate the sand, they would grind to a halt, stranded, with nothing to do but wait to be killed.

Callaway set the trim tabs on the back of the boat for maximum lift to get the hull out of the water as much as possible. He then grabbed the handrail on the dash and put his finger on the button marked "NoX." Taking a quick, deep breath, he flipped the switch. After a slight delay, just long enough for the gas to reach the carburetors, the reaction was *quite* noticeable. The little boat rose up as the outboard screamed like the engine on a jet fighter.

Carrie cursed, as she felt herself driven into the front of the center console, pushing as hard as she could against the front of the console with her feet to stay flat on the deck.

From the feel of the hull rocking from side to side as the bottom edges of the hull alternately touched the water, Callaway could tell that the only part of the boat in the water was the bottom of the motor's lower unit and the prop. The g-force produced by the sudden velocity increase almost pulled Callaway off the back of the boat. He held on, praying that they had enough speed to clear the flat. He noticed splashes around them and turned his head to see muzzle flashes coming from the lead boat following them. The AK-47's the bad guys were firing were not very accurate, but they were reaching them, sending plumes of water six feet into the air.

They reached the sandbar and Callaway held his breath, expecting to be slammed forward by a sudden stop. Instead, the Hewes flew over the bar, with the bottom of the motor bumping the sand just a couple of times. Glancing at the digital speedometer, Callaway grinned at the ninety-eight mile per hour read-out. He didn't know how long the outboard could take this kind of strain before it came apart, but they had to keep going. They continued racing from their pursuers, who could travel at about that same speed all day, by virtue of their more powerful engines.

Callaway looked back just in time to see the lead boat, a forty-three foot Formula, reach the bar. The boat would draw at least a foot and a half of water, but he feared the big boat would have enough momentum to carry it over the bar and continue the pursuit. The boat was running bow high when she ground her keel into the sand. Its stern pitched forward so hard that the boat almost flipped, throwing its two-man crew violently a good seventy-five feet from the boat.

The men had to be dead on impact—both bodies floating face down in the water. The other boats slowed abruptly, the men on board firing a few more shots at the fleeing flats boat. Callaway was well out of range by this time and he was still flying along fast on nitrous. Now it was his turn to slow down, as the last of the laughing gas ran into the engine. The Hewes slowed down, as if on cue, and settled to her former top speed of fifty.

"Are you all right?" he yelled, as Carrie poked her head out from under the towel.

"Yeah, I'm fine," she answered, emerging from under the towel.

"Stay under there. That jerk in the plane is still dogging us. Let him think that I'm alone down here," he told her. He would protect her in any way he could.

Carrie tried to peek over the gunwale. "Where did they go," she asked, "the guys in the boats, where are they?"

Callaway looked back toward the rapidly disappearing island. He could see the rooster-tail wakes heading due north.

"It appears they're heading north, trying to find a way across the flat. It will take them at least a half an hour before they find any deep water to cross, and then at least that much time to get back here. That should give us an hour to get out of here. We'll get back to the *Orinoco Flow* and put as much distance between us and them as we can."

The little boat was faster, but it didn't have enough fuel to reach a safe harbor. The shrimper was slow, but it had a powerful radio on board that would allow them to call for help. They would also be much safer defending themselves from that big, floating pile of lumber with all those weapons on board.

Things were going well, since even the airplane following them was turning toward Andros Island. The small thunderstorm they were heading into was probably the reason why the aerial pain-in-the-ass was leaving, but Callaway knew he would be back. Callaway told Carrie to come out from under the towel, as he could just barely make out the shape of the *Orinoco Flow* in the distance and through the light rain. It was then that the high pitched squeal of his motor alarm sounded from the rear of the boat.

Callaway shut the motor down, trying to figure out why the warning had sounded. The alarm meant one of two things—the motor was not getting enough water circulating through it, causing it to overheat, or it was not getting enough oil. He hit the electric tilt motor, raising the rear of the motor up, but this revealed nothing obviously wrong. Next, he opened a hatch cover in the rear casting deck and immediately saw the problem. The small hold, where the oil reserve tank was located, was full of a grimy mixture of oil and seawater. Two bullets had blown through the transom at the rear of the hull, making short work of the plastic oil tank. The outboard would only run for another minute or so, without any oil, before it blew up.

"So what do we do now, row?" Carrie asked, trying to lighten the moment and erase the pained look on her lover's face.

"No, we keep going, only slower," Callaway said as he moved to the bow and dropped the electric trolling motor back into the water. The flats boat could make about five miles per hour at full speed running on electricity. "It'll take us a while longer to get there, but we will get there. We're gonna have to move fast when we do. As soon as we get to the *Orinoco Flow*, I'll go on board and call for help. You tie the little boat to the stern of the shrimper, and I'll get us moving. I've got oil on the big boat that we can throw right into the fuel tank, so we'll have this boat to use if we need it."

"Do you have anything bigger than a shotgun on board?" she asked, looking up at him on the bow.

"Yeah, I have a few pieces for us to use. Don't worry baby, we'll get out of this, somehow," he said, sounding more confident than he felt.

It took a half hour to reach the *Orinoco Flow*. When they pulled up to the stern, Callaway glanced around the big boat to see if anything looked out of place. All appeared as they had left it, with the boat riding quietly at anchor. Callaway made a mental note to cut loose the one-man raft he had tied to the starboard side of the shrimp boat to do some hull repairs. He didn't need it slowing the already slow boat down once they got underway.

The two of them went to work without saying a word. The thunderstorm had moved off toward Andros Island, and Callaway was already figuring on catching up with it and using it for cover from the approaching boats. He bounded on board, while Carrie tied the bow of the flats boat to the rear cleat of the shrimp boat.

Callaway went right for the radio, figuring that if he could raise a Coast Guard, Navy or even a Bahamian Defense Force boat, their chances of survival would rise considerably. He flipped the power switch on and grabbed for the microphone.

It wasn't there.

All that remained was a wire that had obviously been cut. The wire to the remote speaker was mostly gone, appearing to have been ripped out. Before he could say a word, Callaway felt the unmistakable shape of a gun barrel being shoved hard against his back.

"Mr. Callaway!" the voice behind him said in a strong British accent. "It's so nice to see you again."

Callaway turned slowly around as he backed away, knowing exactly who was talking to him. "I thought you would be drinking rum and smoking cigars with your pal Castro, Drake," he said loudly so Carrie would know just what was happening.

Anton Drake came out of the cabin with a 9mm Beretta pistol and aimed at Callaway's face. "I'm sorry to disappoint you old boy, but I just had to see you one more time," Drake said with a sneer. "You really messed up my operation this time. As a matter of fact, you have put me completely out of business. Now, I just had to find you so I could put *you* out of business, permanently."

Callaway didn't see a lot of options open to him at the moment, but he hoped Carrie was coming up with a plan to stop this maniac before he killed them both. She had the element of surprise on her side, as Drake obviously didn't know she was in the flats boat.

"I warned you, *Saint Michael,* that this would happen. You see, the good guys actually don't do too well in situations like this." Drake motioned to Callaway with the barrel of the gun to trade places with him. Callaway stood in front of the cabin door, while Drake sat leisurely on the deck railing, keeping the Beretta leveled at him. He reached in his pants pocket and pulled out a hand grenade. "I've been waiting for you here for hours," he told him, "ever since we found this tub of yours. My airplane and my boats have been searching for you all morning. I told my men they were looking for a needle in a hay stack, and that the smart money was on you coming back here. I guess I was right."

Drake flipped the grenade up and down as he continued: "I just spoke to my men by radio, and they are all on their way here. They're probably about fifteen to twenty minutes out." He poked the middle finger of his gun hand through the grenade's pin loop and slowly pulled it out. "I know what a bloody dangerous bastard you can be, so I'll just make this ready," he continued. "That should deter you from trying any heroics. You and I can sit and catch up on old times while we wait for my men to arrive. I want them to enjoy the sight of me killing you and blowing up your miserable boat."

As long as Drake held the handle, known as the "spoon," on the grenade, it would not explode. Callaway knew that if he tried to jump Drake, the grenade would fall to the floor and explode in a few seconds, certain to kill them both, leaving Carrie to fend for herself against the men on the approaching boats.

Crouching silently in the stern, Carrie heard everything and tried to assess the situation without giving herself away. She peeked above the transom and saw Drake standing sideways to her, pointing the pistol at Callaway. She could take Drake out, but the distance between them was too great for her to reach him and disable him, without him getting off a shot. She looked around the flats boat for anything she could turn into a weapon. Her gaze was again drawn to the big fishing rod that Callaway had used to catch the tarpon. She crept silently forward and then removed the rig from the rod holder. She crouched and duck-walked up onto the front casting platform, staying as low behind the big boat's transom as she could.

Callaway saw her and what she was holding, and believed he knew what she was planning to do. He swallowed hard, trying to think of a way to distract his adversary. He was concerned that Drake would hear her unhooking the lure from the rod, or opening the bail on the reel, and it would be all over for him and Carrie. He wasn't sure if she had seen the now live grenade Drake held. The distraction Callaway needed came from above. As the King Air came in low over the bow of the shrimp boat, Drake looked up and smiled at his crew in the cockpit. Seeing her chance, Carrie unhooked the long lure with its two sets of razor-sharp treble hooks and let it swing in the air. She held the fishing line fast against the bottom of the pole with the index finger of her right hand.

Suddenly Drake's radio beeped. He precariously shoved the grenade between his thigh and the railing, and plugged an earphone into his left ear. "Uh, I'm kind of busy right now, what's the matter?" he demanded.

What Callaway and Carrie couldn't hear was the excited voice of Derrick Drake, screaming at his father from the right seat of the airplane above.

"She's on board, father! She's on board!"

"What are you saying?" the elder Drake asked skeptically.

"Shea! Shea's at the back of the boat!" screamed Derrick.

At that second Carrie flipped the lure up and over Drake's right shoulder with such force that it swung around his face and imbedded its hooks in his chest above his left shoulder. Drake turned and saw Carrie. He began to turn the gun toward her when she snapped the stiff rod back with all of her strength executing a perfect Callaway Flip. The hooks ripped out of his chest and tore into the left side of Drake's face. She pulled so hard that two of the points dug deep into Drake's jawbone. He screamed in excruciating pain. She pulled even harder, snapping his head around to the right, causing him to lose his balance. He flipped over the rail and fell seven feet, only to land in the rubber raft below.

He began to stand up in the raft, when he noticed that the hand grenade had accompanied him on his fall and was now rolling between his feet. He could see the spoon lying on the floor of the raft separate from the grenade, and he knew the bomb was counting down to explode. He reached for it in an attempt to throw it into the water, but he was too late. The sharp explosion seemed to shake the world. It caused Drake to disappear from view in a cloud of smoke and bloody mist. The concussion knocked Carrie off the front deck of the flats boat and onto the lower deck in front of the console.

Callaway had been thrown backwards, but managed to keep his balance while covering his face. He ran to the stern of the boat, worried more about Carrie than the threat from Drake. He saw her lying on the deck of the flats boat with her eyes closed. He jumped over the transom and put his arm under her head. She opened her eyes and instinctively grabbed him by the throat.

"Carrie, it's me!" he yelled, knowing she had gone into defensive mode from the shock of the blast. She relaxed her grip as her eyes focused on his. "Drake?" she murmured, as he helped her to her feet.

"I don't know," he said, as they climbed over the transom into the shrimp boat.

Callaway pulled her into the cabin and ran to the hidden gun cabinet. He opened it and let out a sigh of relief when he found all of his guns still there. He grabbed his shotgun and ran out to the deck. He racked a shell into the chamber, shouldered the weapon, and advanced on the rail, half expecting Drake to pop up like a jack-in-the-box. He reached the rail and swung the 12-gauge "thunder stick" over the side, pointing it at the water.

Nothing.

No sign of Drake, just the shredded remains of the one-man raft and . . . bubbles, lots of big bubbles coming up the side of the hull from below. "Oh shit, that's not good!" he yelled, as he ran through the cabin and down into the engine room. Carrie followed, not knowing what the concern was. She figured it out as soon as she entered the engine room. There was six inches of water on the engine room floor, and more was pouring in from between the joints of the wooden planks making up the starboard hull.

Callaway put the shotgun down and feverishly tried to start the bilge pump. It wouldn't work. He tried to start the diesel engine, figuring that they could get moving away from Drake's men and force the water to the back of the boat so he could evacuate some of it with a hand pump. The engine wouldn't start, either. He looked around, cursing, when he saw that the engine battery wires had been cut in several places. This machinery was not about to start any time soon, but he had to stop the water from coming in somehow. He pulled open a cabinet and began flinging cans of varnish, paint, and other boat repair stuff on the floor.

"There it is," he said, grabbing a white, half-gallon can. "Come on!" he yelled as he ran up the stairs. When she reached the deck, Carrie saw him pulling a dive mask and a Spare Air tank from another cabinet. "I'm going over the side to try and patch the leaks from the outside. You go down in the engine room and watch. If the water stops coming in, bang on something metal so I know it worked."

She watched him jump over the side and disappear under the water. She ran into the cabin and down to the engine room again where the water was still pouring in.

Callaway swam down and grabbed the bottom edge of the hull to keep him from floating up. He could see just where the leaks were from all of the air bubbles pouring out of the cracks. He braced his feet under the bottom, teeth clenched on the mouthpiece of the little aqua lung, and pried the lid from the top of the can with the fishing knife from his belt. Both the knife and the lid sank to the bottom. He grabbed large globs of the marine joint compound from the can and pushed them into the cracks. Since the compound was meant to seal small leaks, Callaway was not at all sure that it would work on leaks this large. He pushed the white putty into the cracks with all his strength, and, slowly, saw the number of bubbles decline at each leak point and then disappear.

Callaway was working hard and using a lot of air in the process. Knowing the miniature tank would run out soon, he prayed he would hear Carrie banging on the pipes in the engine room soon. His arms were about out of strength when he heard the sound of Carrie beating on one of the water intake pipes. Carrie dropped the large wrench she'd used and ran up onto the deck to see if Callaway was all right.

Finding it hard to take a breath, Callaway knew the little tank was just about empty. He floated back away from the hull, dropping the can of compound, as his arms hung tired. He was admiring his work when he noticed something in his peripheral vision, partially blocked by his dive mask. At first he thought it was a curious fish, attracted by all of the commotion and the bubbles. But then he saw a bloody human hand, coming around his face from behind. And another coming from the other side of his head.

Taking a deep breath, he quickly spun around and saw something that scared him so badly that he spit out his mouthpiece and screamed all of the remaining air out of his lungs. There before him, he saw the lifeless and totally mutilated corpse of Anton Drake. The blast from the Vietnam-era fragmentation grenade had split him open from his waist to his throat. His face, which showed several shrapnel wounds, was locked in an agonized contortion, with the big fishing lure still imbedded in the left side of his jaw.

Callaway clawed for the surface to keep from swallowing seawater. He broke the surface, desperately gulping for air. Carrie yelled down to ask if he was OK. When he didn't answer, she threw a life jacket into the water next to him. After grabbing the vest and pulling it to his chest, Callaway poked his face back down under water to see where his dead enemy was. He could see Drake's body sinking toward the bottom. Small reef fish were already picking at his intestines and his face. Callaway knew that it wouldn't be long before the sharks would come calling, with all of that blood in the water. He swam to the rear of the boat and climbed up the ladder on the transom.

Carrie was waiting and hugged him hard. She could feel him shaking. "What's wrong, Callaway?" she asked. "You look like you've seen a friggin' ghost!"

He hugged back, taking a deep breath. "I think I did," he answered. "The good news is if it was a ghost, then he was really, really dead."

She had no idea what he was talking about, but she went to the rail to look down into the water. There was nothing. Callaway sighed. Finally, he could stop worrying about Mr. Anton Drake, who was, hopefully, introducing himself to the devil in hell right about now. He didn't have a chance to relax as he heard the droning engines of the Super King Air still circling over them. He had no idea who was in the plane, other than the fact it was someone who worked for Drake, but he hoped that whoever it was had seen Drake's demise and would call it quits and run.

* * *

Five hundred feet above, Derrick Drake was thrashing about in the cabin of the plane, screaming hysterically. He'd just seen the only person on this planet able to control him blown to bits by an old foe and a woman who he now considered a turncoat. He called the boats that had now cleared the miles-long sandbar and were heading toward the *Orinoco Flow* at high speed. "My father disabled their boat and their radio," he yelled, his voice filled with rage. "When you get to them, I want him killed very slowly, and I want the girl brought to me!" He was already planning his revenge. He believed, based on what he had seen, that "Shea" had sold his father out. He would make her pay over a long, long time, during which she would suffer torture and rape, until she reached the point where she begged him to kill her. From his vantage point, he could just see the white wakes of the approaching boats, still fifteen minutes away from Callaway's boat.

* * *

Aboard the *Orinoco Flow*, Michael Callaway was below deck trying to figure a way to make the diesel engine run so they at least wouldn't be a stationary target. "It ain't happening," he muttered aloud.

Carrie saw his obvious frustration. "Can't you rig something to make it run?" she asked.

"If I had a day to work on it," he said shaking his head. "We don't have a day. We've got to get help, now."

They went back to the helm station and he played around with the radio. The microphone and speaker were nowhere to be found. He surmised that Drake had thrown them over the side with the engine wiring. Turning the radio knob, he was surprised to see that it still powered up. The problem was that they couldn't send a message without a microphone. Callaway stared at the microphone wire for a long time, wondering if that were true. Suddenly, he grabbed the frayed end of the wire and pulled the two leads apart. He touched the two bare wires together and saw the transmit light glow on the front of the set, indicating that he was transmitting something. The question was, just what was he was sending? Was it anything anyone could receive? He started touching the two wires together, rhythmically.

Sounding perplexed, Carrie asked, "What are you doing?"

"Adam-12," was all he replied, obviously concentrating on what he was doing. "Adam-12. You know, the police TV show back in the sixties. Oh yeah, I'm ten years older than you, so you would have missed it. Anyway, it was about these two L.A. cops, I think Martin Milner played one of them and the other was Kent McCord. One night,

Milner is alone in the police car and he gets in a chase. He crashes and rolls his patrol car down the side of a mountain and ends up pinned in the car, upside down, and son-of-a-gun, the microphone was torn off the radio in the crash. He starts touching the mike wires together, like this, and he sends a call for help in Morse code."

She gave him a skeptical look. "You're sending a message in Morse code, now? Do you even know Morse code?" she asked.

"Yeah, it was something my dad taught me when I was a kid. The problem is, it's been a long time since I've done this, so I don't know if I'm saying what I want to say, and hell, I don't even know if the damned thing is really transmitting! Let's just hope that someone hears it, and understands that we're in deep trouble."

* * *

"Bridge, this is radio," Seaman Robert Myers called up from his tight cubbyhole aboard *USS Pegasus*.

"This is the captain, go ahead Myers," answered Captain David Eldridge. He was on his third cup of coffee on this last day of the last patrol of his fast little boat. He was a bit bruised from his involvement in the invasion of Drake's island. Not happy about being at sea, Eldridge had been grousing to his officers about how sick it was for a grand U.S. Navy vessel like the *Pegasus*, and her sister ships, to be out flying around the Caribbean, with their crews fighting nothing but boredom. "I thought maybe, just maybe we'd get to mix it up with somebody on our last day out here."

245

The hydrofoil was zooming along at thirty-five knots while her lookouts scanned the water for any suspicious looking activity. Nothing looked even remotely suspicious today.

"Skipper, I'm getting what sounds like it may be a distress call, but it's coming in by Morse."

Eldridge walked back to the radio operator's desk at the rear of the wheel house.

"He's transmitting erratically," Myers said as he wrote down what he could translate from the code. Eldridge read the message over the young sailor's shoulder: "SOS SOS SOS Any listening station Motor Vessel Orinoco Flow 20 miles east of Andros Island Chased by drug runners Vessel broken and we cannot run Send help ASAP Expect attack very soon Please relay to US and Bahamian authorities M Callaway SOS SOS SOS KN"

"Son-of-a bitch!" Eldridge yelled, then turned and ran to the chart table, quickly studying the waters around Andros. "Helm! Turn to 210 degrees and go to all-ahead full!" He turned to his executive officer, who seemed shocked at his reinvigorated captain. Eldridge had a great grin on his face. "Tell the men to go to battle stations, ship, Mr. Parks!" His pensive exec stood, staring. He seemed to be wondering what kind of trouble this throwback to the old Navy was about to get him into as his captain glared at him. "Now, mister!" Eldridge snapped at him.

Pegasus turned to her new course and its sixteen-thousand-horsepower General Electric turbine engine pushed her to fifty knots. After numerous drills and exercises, the crew had become accustomed to hearing the "All crew, man your battle stations" announcement over the loud speaker and the klaxon horn sounding along with it. This time, however, they were surprised to hear their executive officer's quivering voice yelling, "This is *not* a drill!"

The radio operator sent a distress call by voice to all U.S. Navy, Coast Guard, and Bahamian Defense Force vessels or aircraft in the area. Ships and aircraft from all of those services responded and gave their estimated time of arrival. But the closest vessel was the one doing the calling. It was up to Eldridge, his crew, and *Pegasus* to be the cavalry, charging to the rescue. The question on Eldridge's mind was whether they would make it to the fight in time.

Chapter 23

Callaway had the gun locker open and was creating a quick battle plan in his head. He pulled his Savage 110P bolt-action and Colt AR-15 HBAR rifles from their racks and handed the AR to Carrie, asking her, "Do you remember how to use this?"

She responded by pulling the pin that held the upper and lower sections of the rifle together. Cracking it open, she checked the barrel, slapped the two sections back together with authority, and racked the bolt back, as if waiting for inspection.

"Never mind," was all that Callaway could get out.

She had taken a keen interest in the "black rifle" at the Quantico DEA academy. Her Marine Corps firearms instructors stood and shook their heads when she "cleaned" the target out to six hundred yards, from the prone position, with this type of rifle.

Callaway handed her three, thirty-round magazines, loaded with .223 caliber full-metal-jacket rounds. She already had her DEA issued Sig Saur, 9 millimeter pistol, too, in a shoulder holster slung over her back. Callaway slung the Savage over his shoulder and then buckled a gun belt rig around his waist. In the holster was his trusty

Smith & Wesson Model 686, .357 Magnum. He jammed two speed-loaders, carrying twelve extra rounds, into their pouches on the opposite side of his body. He also grabbed his pump shotgun and a bandoleer holding an additional twenty rounds of double-ought buckshot. In the meantime, Carrie had picked up a metal ammo can containing ammunition for all of the weapons and carried it out to the deck.

Callaway's battle plan was simple. He would engage their enemy as far out as he could, shooting at them with the long range Savage, and, hopefully, taking out a few of the bad guys before he and Carrie were in range of their guns. He figured, with the steady mount afforded him by the shrimp boat, he might be able to hit some of them out to one thousand yards. If nothing else, hitting their boats could dissuade them from coming too close. If this didn't work, Carrie would begin working on them when they were within six hundred yards, with the AR-15. They would both continue shooting the rifles until the threat was gone, or the druggies got real close. Then, it would be a battle up close and personal, with the shotgun, handguns, knives, oars, and whatever else they could get their hands on. Out on the back of the boat's cockpit, Callaway laid his arsenal down on the deck, with the exception of the Savage, which he placed on a fish cleaning bench built into the inside of the gunwale.

He extended the legs of the Harris bi-pod, at the front of the stock, and set it firmly on the bench. He looked through the Leopold telescopic sight, turning the magnification ring to its maximum power of twenty-four. Squinting through the scope, he turned the parallax adjustment until the boats came into crystal clear focus. He could see the lead boat, followed by five others, racing toward them. Each boat appeared to have two or three men aboard. Most of those not driving appeared to be armed with AK-47 rifles. Callaway smiled, knowing the AK wasn't very accurate outside of two hundred yards. But one look at the boat farthest away sent a chill up his back.

The gunner on that boat had what appeared to be some type of rocket launcher on his shoulder. Callaway could not make out what type it was, but he could see it was a lot longer than a standard rocket-propelled-grenade launcher. Even if he could keep them out farther than a thousand yards, they could probably blow him and Carrie to bits with a rocket. Still, he had to try.

He watched the boats weaving in and out of the rocky, ten-foot-high spires protruding from the water, the tops of underwater islands that didn't completely breach the surface. Callaway flipped open the top on an ammo can Carrie had carried out of the cabin and picked up a white ammunition box with the words "Artillery Rounds" and the number ".300 Win."

Carrie watched as he loaded one round into the chamber and four more into the internal magazine. He held down the top round and closed the bolt.

"A friend of mine hand-loaded these for me. He says they hit like a cannon," Callaway told her.

He turned and looked nervously through the scope again. "I guess we'll find out soon enough," he continued, as he settled into a comfortable shooting position. "I'm sorry," he said, without raising his head from the scope, "for getting you into this fix. If I had just stayed out of it, you'd probably be arresting Drake, right now, and you wouldn't be out here fighting for your life." He was concentrating so much on the crosshairs in the scope, that he didn't notice her next to him, until she kissed him on the cheek.

"I'm good," was all that she said, as she knelt down and laid the fore end of the AR-15 over the gunwale rail.

Callaway placed the crosshairs as best as he could on one of the bobbing targets. He was aiming at the cockpit of the lead boat when he squeezed the trigger. The boom of the .300 Magnum round going off was deafening to their unprotected ears. It seemed like a second later though, that a thirty-foot geyser of water erupted about one hundred yards in front of the drug boat, accompanied by the deep thud of an explosion.

Callaway was shocked. He grabbed the box of bullets and stared at them for a second. He then looked at Carrie, who stared, dumbfounded, back at him. "Jesus!" he yelled, "the guy who loaded these wasn't kidding."

It was then that they heard something whistling over their heads, coming from behind the *Orinoco Flow* and heading toward the drug boats. Another geyser of water shot up from the sea between them and Drake's men, only this one a little closer to the bad guys. Then they heard a booming sound behind them. Callaway turned to see a vessel approaching. He looked through his binoculars and yelled, "Yes!" as he glimpsed the beautiful sight of the U.S. Navy hydrofoil *Pegasus* flying toward them at a high rate of speed. She was still a ways off, but he figured the bad guys would be running like hell to get away from her by this time. He turned and was shocked to see the boats hiding behind the rock formations that were protruding from the water.

"Why aren't they running away?" he asked Carrie. His answer came when he looked again through the rifle scope and saw the man on the boat with the shoulder-fired rocket launcher aiming it not at them, but at the approaching warship. The pilot of the boat pulled out from behind the rocks just far enough for the rocket man to get his sights on the hydrofoil.

* * *

Aboard the boat, Commander Eldridge was also amazed that the attackers weren't running. "What the hell's going on here?" he asked. "Do they think we can't see them by the rocks or something? Helm, swing a little to port so we can keep an eye on them."

His executive officer, Lieutenant Brian Parks, being his usual cautious self, asked, "Skipper, are you sure we were right to fire on those boats? I mean the Posse Commutates Act clearly states the rules of engagement..."

"Fuck Posse Commutates, Parks, and fuck you, too!" Eldridge screamed. "They were attacking

252

that boat, a U.S. registered boat. We have every right to stop them. And besides, those were just warning shots."

About to argue the point further, Parks was interrupted by the screaming voice of a sailor in the Combat Information Center.

"Vampire, inbound! Vampire, inbound! We have a missile coming from one of the boats, starboard side!"

"Hard a-port! Counter measures starboard, now!" Eldridge boomed instantly.

The little boat heeled over on her left side, the helmsman straining to turn two-hundred sixty-five tons as quickly as possible. On the right side of the ship, two canisters "borrowed" from the remains of a wrecked F-18 trainer fired projectiles into the air producing bright white magnesium flares flying in a high arc away from *Pegasus*.

The system that the bad guys had used to fire the rocket was a French-made Mistral anti-aircraft missile. Similar in design to the American-made Stinger, it launched a twenty-two pound missile with a three-pound, high-explosive warhead at three thousand feet per second, with a range of almost four miles when fired horizontally. The missile tracked its prey by locking onto the heat of its engines and following until the missile connected. In this case, the missile was locked onto the heat coming from the jet engine of a different type of craft—a U.S. Navy hydrofoil.

Pegasus lurched sideways as all eyes watched the smoke from the approaching missile. The missile appeared to be coming right at them, but suddenly veered to the right, flying through the smoke of one of the flares. The missile continued on until it smashed into a rocky protrusion and exploded, blowing away a large chunk of the spire.

Fuming with anger, Eldrige screamed over the headset, "Fire Control! Lock on to whoever fired on us and take 'em out!"

Below deck, four sailors pushed the buttons to aim the remote-controlled 76 mm forward gun. The Italian-designed weapon could fire a continuous stream of fourteen-pound projectiles at eighty rounds per minute. The Mk-92 Track-While-Scan fire control system directed the weapon at the tall stack of rocks hiding the missile-firing boat. "Fire control, Captain. We have a lock on where he's hiding."

Smiling at his executive officer, Eldridge declared, "I think we've satisfied the rules of engagement, Mr. Parks. Fire!"

The ship rocked as the cannon went to work. The gunner fired four rounds and then scanned for effect, grinning at what he saw. The first two rounds had hit the rocks midway between the waterline and the peak. The high explosive shells shattered the spires, blowing the tops half off and obliterating the boat's cover. The men on the boat were helping the missile shooter aim a second Mistral at the hydrofoil. Hearing the approaching shells, they ducked as the spires they were hiding behind exploded and disappeared, showering them with rocks. Hearing more shells coming in, they looked up to see there was nothing left to protect them. The next shell crashed through the bow of

254

the boat, penetrating all the way through, and exiting at a downward angle on the starboard side. The fiberglass hull did not provide enough resistance to trigger the fuse in the nose of the projectile and explode the round. It hit the water fifteen feet from the boat and exploded under the surface, showering them with water and shrapnel.

The last round was a bit more effective. It hit the rear of the boat, penetrating the deck and striking the port engine. That large hunk of cast iron stopped the shell and exploded the warhead. The boat practically disintegrated from the explosive shell combined with the gasoline on board. A large ball of fire reached for the sky as the explosion reduced the boat, and its occupants, to tiny pieces and a fine mist. Upon seeing this, the men in the other boats immediately shut off their engines and raised their hands in surrender.

High above, Derrick Drake sat in stunned silence for a moment and then directed his pilot to head for Fort Lauderdale. He knew that the police would be looking for the plane, but he had a plan to sneak by them. Drake looked down one last time at Callaway's boat. He could see the man and woman standing on the rear deck. He swore that someday he would make them pay for killing his father and ruining the Drake empire.

Chapter 24

Pegasus slowed to where she was no longer riding high on her foils. Cruising slowly toward the drug-runner boats, her crew kept them covered with her menacing deck gun. Several sailors armed with M-14 rifles walked out on the front deck to take charge of the prisoners.

It wasn't long before a U.S. Coast Guard patrol craft and two Bahamian Defense Force boats arrived to take the men into custody. *Pegasus* then idled over to the *Orinoco Flow*. Commander Eldridge was beside himself with glee, since he had, at last, taken his ship into "Harm's Way" as John Paul Jones referred to it. He walked out onto the front deck of the hydrofoil, and when they were close enough, he jumped down onto the deck of the shrimp boat. "Mr. Callaway, you are a severe pain-in-the-ass!" he said, smirking, as he gave his friend a strong hand shake. Carrie came out of the cabin just as he completed his words.

"Oh, sorry miss," he said, somewhat embarrassed.

"Don't be, Commander. I absolutely agree with you," she said, grinning.

Eldridge looked at Carrie, and asked, "Have we met before, miss?"

"Yes, we did, in the bar in Nassau when you and your men almost got in a fight to save his ass," she said, nodding at Callaway, who just stood there smiling. "I was with Anton Drake and his men that night." Carrie kissed Callaway on the cheek, giving him a devious smile and walked to the stern of the boat.

Eldridge leaned in close to Callaway and asked, "Is she okay?"

Callaway smiled, realizing that, as far as the good commander was concerned, Carrie was Drake's bodyguard. "Relax, skipper," Callaway told him, "she's DEA. She was working Drake when you saw her at the bar that night. You don't have to worry about her."

Eldridge looked at Carrie as she bent over to pick up the ammo can that she had brought on deck. "Yeah, okay, I understand that," he answered, "but she looked like a total dike that night. Does she go both ways?" he whispered with a funny grin on his face.

"I'll take that as a compliment, Commander. I guess my acting was pretty good."

"I guess she heard you," Callaway said as Eldridge turned red with embarrassment.

The machinist from *Pegasus* came on board, and he and Callaway jerry-rigged the electrical system that Anton Drake had taken such pains to destroy. After three solid hours of work, the big diesel coughed to life. The remaining go-fast boats from Drake's fleet would make a fine prize for the Bahamian government. Callaway was to follow them to New Providence to make a formal report about the attack.

Commander Eldridge came back aboard to say farewell to Callaway and Carrie. Eldridge went to shake Callaway's hand.

"That won't do," Callaway said as he gave the big man a hug. "Thanks for saving us, skipper."

Eldridge was taken aback, but immediately understood that a bond of friendship between the two of them had been secured. It was the type of bond that only cops and soldiers who had been in the stress of battle together, understood. "Any time, my friend, any time."

Carrie gave Eldridge a kiss and a hug, and her sweet, sweet smile.

Eldridge went back aboard his boat and prepared to leave for Key West. He knew there would be hell to pay for firing on Drake's boats before they fired on him, but he didn't care about that at the moment. Since this was her last mission, his little boat was to be taken from him, anyway, as soon as they reached port. He knew her fate would not be pretty. He also knew that his chances of getting another vessel, especially after this incident, were pretty slim. He would probably end up in some boring, administrative shore job until it made him crazy enough to retire. He feared the possibility that he would end up as a coffee boy for some fat-assed administrative admiral, instead of lord and master of a fighting ship at sea.

Pegasus circled the *Orinoco Flow* as she turned toward Key West. Callaway could see Eldridge through the port-side bridge window, just as he had when he returned from his last mission as a U.S. Customs Special Agent aboard *Blue*

Thunder III at the Port of Miami. Again, he threw the Navy man a salute, and Eldridge promptly stood at attention and saluted back. Eldridge then turned to his helmsman and gave an order that he knew would be given for the last time. "Helm, get *Pegasus* in the air! It's time for her last, fast ride." The turbine spun up once more, raising the ship up over the waves, flying her way up to cruising speed.

Callaway watched the little, but mighty ship get smaller as it headed away. He wondered if he would see his new friend again anytime soon. He made a mental note to invite the good commander to the wedding, whenever he and Carrie figured out when that would be. Callaway set the map plotter for Nassau, but before he moved the throttle, he did one last thing. He dialed the coordinates for this spot on the ocean into his GPS. *This is a special place for us*, he thought to himself as he looked at Carrie. *This is where we found love and beat the devil. We'll come back here again some time*. He threw the throttle forward, and the big boat lurched into a slow troll toward their destination.

* * *

Operation Blue Lightning was on the aircraft like a drunk on a bottle of Chablis. The two-story tall, helium-filled balloon floated serenely above Kudjoe Key, tethered to the ground by a two inch thick steel cable. The *Look-Down* radar on the balloon was lighting up everything that moved across the water, and every aircraft that might find it advantageous to try to sneak in under the ground-based radars.

For years, the drug runner pilots had entered United States airspace, and the State of Florida, undetected, by merely dropping below five hundred feet in altitude and "wave-hopping" their way in. They were a brazen lot, too. On the sometimes occasion when a Customs or DEA aircraft got on their tail, these smuggler pilots would do some rather unorthodox, and extremely dangerous, things to elude capture and deliver their load.

Blue Lightning had eliminated much of the tracking guesswork. Tonight the people in the control center, five thousand feet below the balloon, were looking for, and tracking one particular aircraft—a Beechcraft Super King Air —the same King Air that had been following Michael Callaway and Carrie as they made their escape from Anton Drake's killers—the same King Air that was the vantage point from which Derrick Drake saw his father meet his death. And it was the same King Air that spirited the younger Drake toward Florida when, what became *his* henchmen, failed to follow his orders to kill Callaway and the traitor that he knew as Shea.

Drake knew that the police would be after him, and he'd already formulated a plan for his escape. His late father had the King Air customized after it was built. The pilot had the ability to turn off the aircraft's transponder, which he did by flipping a switch hidden under his instrument panel. Now the plane could not be readily identified. He ordered the pilot, a seasoned smuggler, to fly south and enter U.S. airspace in the traffic pattern for Miami International Airport. He hoped this would interrupt the traffic pattern and cause air traffic controllers to order airliners on approach to change course, making a mess of the airport's and federal law enforcement's radar screens. He was trying to buy time.

Just prior to reaching the coast, the pilot put the plane into a sharp dive, going below the ground-based radar's tracking capability. The aircraft then turned north and headed along the edge of the Everglades, following the road known as Krome Avenue.

* * *

They escaped detection by ground-based radar and aircraft, but they could not get away from the people manning the consoles at Blue Lightning headquarters. The radar operators there had seen this tactic before. They shook their heads as they watched the aircraft maneuvering its way north.

"This guy's good," one operator commented to another. "But he ain't getting away tonight."

The radar operators directed aircraft and ground units from several agencies toward the aircraft as it transitioned from following Krome Avenue north bound until it exited on to U.S. 27, which, like Krome, was still on the eastern edge of the Florida Everglades.

The controllers had an idea of where he was going. There was a practice airfield, nothing more than a wide asphalt strip on the east side of U.S. 27, just over the Broward/Miami-Dade County line, in the city of Miramar. The strip was miles away from the nearest house in the city, since development had not yet reached that far west. The closest living people were some hermit cattle ranchers living in trailers, and one house, a ways up the road.

During the day, the strip was used by pilots practicing landings and "touch-and-goes" as they called the maneuver of approaching the strip, getting wheels on the ground, powering up the engine, and taking off, in one shot. The remote strip was affectionately known as Opa Locka West by pilots, cops, and smugglers, as it came under air traffic control of Opa Locka Airport in Miami-Dade County. Pilots that were legitimately using the field to practice would call that airport tower to get clearance to use it.

Of course, smugglers would not. They would land there and off load, mostly at night, although some had the balls to do so in broad daylight, and then fly out of there like a bat out of hell to avoid capture.

Derrick Drake knew he was probably being tracked by Blue Lightning as he flew through the night. He was actually counting on it for his escape plan to be successful. His late father had spent large amounts of money developing a mole in the DEA, who had been feeding him all kinds of secret information about government defenses and tactics used against the drug smugglers. The mole was slowly rising up through the ranks of the agency and gaining access to more and more information with every promotion he received.

The younger Drake planned to utilize this informant even more than his father had when he returned to Golgotha and resumed his daddy's illicit trade.

The Customs Service and DEA were alerted about the inbound suspicious aircraft and its suspected destination. They had everything that could fly and drive heading for U.S. 27 and the Miami-Dade/Broward County line. They even invited the local cops to the party by notifying the City of Miramar Police Department, Broward County Sheriff's Office and Florida Highway Patrol about the priority of capturing the passengers on this particular airplane.

Drake's pilot continued to fly north until he was even with the airstrip. He suddenly flipped the aircraft on its side in a hard right turn, leveled out toward the strip, and dropped his landing gear and flaps in almost one fluid movement.

He feathered the props, lifted the nose and touched the rear wheels down pretty hard, bouncing the seat-belted Drake around in the back seat.

The pilot reversed pitch on the props even before the front wheel touched down, causing the nose wheel to slam down with a sharp, screeching noise. He stood on the brakes, bringing the plane to a halt using only half the length of the field. He stopped the big turbo-prop almost dead even with a Lincoln Town Car waiting with the motor running and lights off.

The driver's door was opened and the driver stepped out. Another very tall man with an H&K

MP-5 sub-machinegun slung over his shoulder, exited on the passenger side. The passenger door at the rear of the fuselage was opened, and Drake began climbing out. The pilot was expecting Drake to tell him to take off and do what he could to elude the police, but the message he received was totally different.

"You did well, tonight. Wait here a minute, would you, I have something for you," Drake yelled as he exited and then walked to the Town Car. He conversed with the driver and the man with the MP-5 for a minute and then walked back toward the plane. The pilot grew concerned. His chances of getting away were growing fainter with every second Drake kept him on the ground. He changed the pitch of the props and held the brakes for a quick, short-field take-off, while opening the window on his side of the cockpit of the custom-built plane.

"Mr. Drake, I've got to get going if you want me to draw the cops away from you," he shouted out the window over the din of the idling engines.

Drake leaned into the airplane through the open passenger door and yelled to the pilot, "No one can know I was aboard this plane, no one!"

The pilot turned his head to see Drake at the rear of the plane. He was nodding his head to signify that he understood when he felt something bump against the left side of the aircraft. He turned to see the tall man with the MP-5 standing on the wing next to his open cockpit window. The pilot struggled as he was grabbed through his open side window by his jacket collar and jerked sideways to the window. Drake's henchman stuck a seven-inch blade into the pilot's neck at an upward angle so the tip pierced the man's brain stem, killing him instantly. He pushed the pilot back into his seat as Drake continued to speak.

"No one can know. And for the record, old boy, I *want* the cops to come here!"

He jumped back out of the plane and walked to the car, where the driver was waiting with the rear door open. The man with the MP-5 pulled the weapon off his shoulder, removed the magazine, and shoved the gun through the window. Using the muzzle of the machinegun, he pushed both throttles forward to maximum power. The propellers bit into the thick night air, as the two eight-hundred fifty horsepower Pratt & Whitney engines screamed. The plane's bulk began to lurch forward as the henchman leaped to the runway from the rear of the wing. He rolled on the ground, jumped up, and sprinted to the car as the plane picked up speed heading quickly down the runway. Drake and his men were in the Lincoln as they sped in the opposite direction from the plane, and on to U.S. 27, heading south toward Miami Beach, and home.

The King Air had accelerated to 72 miles per hour when it veered off the airstrip and crashed into some coral boulders off to the side of the runway and exploded. The fuel on board ignited into a super-hot fire. Drake smiled as he looked out the window of his getaway vehicle and saw a bright, fiery, flash coming from where they had just been. The fire quickly burned the aircraft, and burned the pilot's flesh to the point that no medical examiner would ever notice the knife wound. When the first law enforcement units arrived, two patrol cars from the Charlie shift of the Miramar Police Department, the officers were astonished to see the burning hulk of a plane explode. The officers who worked this zone had routinely been dispatched over the years to reports of planes off-loading dope at the airstrip, and occasionally even caught the smugglers red-handed, but they had never seen anything like this.

One of the officers radioed in that a plane had crashed at Opa Locka West and was on fire. The dispatcher sent fire units to the scene. By the time they arrived and extinguished the fire, two things had already occurred. One was the assumption, backed up by the DEA and later by National Transportation Safety Bureau investigators that the plane had landed on the runway going way too fast, causing the pilot to lose control and crash into the rocks, was confirmed. The "accident" would be attributed to the pilot-smuggler's screw-up that cost him both his aircraft and his life. The aircraft would be traced to the late Anton Drake, and another assumption would be made that this pilot had been assigned, by the elder Drake, to search for Callaway and Carrie at sea, and had made a run for it after the attempt on their lives failed.

Just as the NTSB was wrapping up their initial investigation of the crash site, Derrick Drake was sitting down with a glass of wine in the living room of his luxury condominium in Miami Beach without the slightest care in the world about the police crashing through his door. He knew there was no way for law enforcement to place him on that plane. He stared out at the ocean, thinking of the two people who had, at least temporarily, messed up his way of life and his anger seethed.

He'd planned his escape well, and now he would plan his revenge.

* * *

Callaway felt sad walking Carrie through Nassau's airport terminal. After arranging to have the *Orinoco Flow* repaired and made seaworthy for the cruise back to Fort Lauderdale, Callaway and Carrie had mutually decided, with the strong urging of the DEA, that she take a commercial jet to Washington, guarded by two DEA agents, so she could be properly debriefed by her superiors at headquarters. She also intended to officially tender her resignation. Carrie also wanted to go home to see her family and sit down with her mom to tell her that she would need to do something the older woman never thought she would get the chance to do—plan a wedding.

Carrie called her mom from the airport to tell her what had happened in the last two weeks, and that she was quitting the agency to get married. Her mother did not respond, and at first Carrie thought she had passed out from hearing her news. When her mom began crying, she knew the message was received. It was a happy cry. Her daughter was getting married and leaving the ultra-dangerous life she had led for so many years. There was not much time on the phone to fill her mom in on the groom to be, or his recent good fortune. But she would have plenty of time to do that later. She ended the call and turned to Callaway.

"I will miss you like crazy," he whispered in her ear as he held her tight. He was amazed that Carrie, the hard-ass undercover ace, was crying all over his shoulder. "When will I see you?" he asked.

She raised her head, showing him her red, puffy eyes and her sweet grin, and answered, "It should take a couple of days to settle everything up with the agency, and then it's off to mom's for at least a week…"

Callaway groaned at hearing this.

"I owe it to her, Callaway. I haven't seen her for a while, and we have things to do. You know, like picking out a dress for the wedding and all that girlie crap. You don't want to be involved with that now, do you?"

He looked at the floor and shook his head no. "I'll join you up there later so I can meet your Mom," he finally said.

She gave him a stern look, and told him, "Small doses for now. She's been through a lot. Go get Jorge and go fishing or go buy something, like a house, or a nice car, or whatever." She laughed.

"Well, I was thinking about buying a Wave Runner. I know someone in Eleuthera who puts superchargers on them so that they can hit one hundred miles an hour."

She laughed again, mainly because he sounded like a little boy describing the hot, new bicycle he wanted to buy. "So buy it," she whispered in his ear, in her deep, sexy voice, right before she kissed him on the neck. "While you're in a spending mood, go find us a real strong bed, too. We're going to need it."

He laughed and gave her a long kiss goodbye. He would go back to Florida and wait for her call, and he would have that bed ready to rock and roll when she returned. Carrie waved to him as she walked into the airport with her two bodyguards. He walked to his car, a little choked up. It would be too long until he saw her again, no matter how little time it was. He promised himself they would spend the rest of their lives together and that nothing would ever change that.

* * *

At that very moment, however, a furious young man paced his luxurious Miami Beach living room devising a plan to ruin their happily-ever-after ending.

The End

About the Author

Doug Giacobbe is a retired law enforcement officer, having served twenty four years working the mean streets of South Florida. He retired at the rank of Major and Commander of the Criminal Investigations Division of the Miramar Police Department in 2001. During his service with the department, he was assigned as a narcotics investigator, detective, and internal affairs investigator.

Giacobbe is currently a Professor and the Lead Instructor of History at Daytona State College, in Florida, teaching courses in American, American Maritime, and American Military History. He has earned two Bachelors Degrees, and a Masters Degree from Florida Atlantic University.

He enjoys going on trips with his family (wherever there is something historical to see), as well as golfing and fishing.

Giacobbe is a member of Mystery Writers of America and the Phi Alpha Theta National History Honors Society.

Please enjoy the first page of my second Michael Callaway book,

A Fierce Vengeance

Chapter 1

"I can't get your bra undone!" John Hessler laughed through his anger at himself for drinking as much champagne as he had in the last four hours. What a damn lousy time to lose motor skills, he thought, lying at the ocean's edge about fifty yards behind a fancy hotel on Miami Beach trying his best to undress one of the bridesmaids from his friend's wedding. Time for some wild beach sex was all that ran through his alcohol-laden head. Things were not going his way. The young lady, who he had met just one hour prior, was extremely willing to take part in his coital plans; however she was as drunk and as clumsy as he. "Roll over on your side a second," he said trying to accomplish his task.

Earlier in the evening, she boasted about how much she had paid a plastic surgeon to create those huge boobs, and that they were absolutely perfect. Hessler was desperate to get his hands around them. She laughed, closed her eyes and rolled onto her left side, facing away from him. He resumed fiddling with the hooks on the bra, fumble-fingered from his consumption of so much of Moet's finest. Finally, he managed to unhook her bra and felt the weight of her massive breasts pull the bra straps from his hands.

"Okay! Now we're in business. Roll back over, sweetheart," he said. Suddenly he felt her body shiver and shake as her breathing came in quick, breathy pants. *Wow! She's ready to go!* he thought, but only for a second. She let out a horrific scream, and then slammed him in the face with the back of her head as she came up off of the sand like a coiled spring. He tried to hold on to her as she continued to scream. "What the hell is a matter with you? What's wrong?" he yelled as she ran up the beach, her bare breasts—Hessler only dimly registering that they were indeed quite perfect-- bouncing in the night air. He tasted blood from his now smashed nose. The beach lights from the hotel winked on, signaling that the wedding party would be moving outside.

Hessler rolled over to see what had freaked her out and froze. His eyes locked on the cold dead stare of a naked woman, her body partially submerged. He saw two things that stunned his mind and reactions with fear. The woman's throat was slit open from ear to ear, her tongue pulled out through the incision, and straining his eyes, he could read the word "PAYBACK" written on her chest, right above her breasts.

CPSIA information can be obtained
at www.ICGtesting.com
Printed in the USA
FFOW02n1121031217
43810230-42761FF